TWICE WRITTEN

K. Sridhar

Popular Prakashan
www.popularprakashan.com

Popular Prakashan Pvt. Ltd.
301, Mahalaxmi Chambers
22, Bhulabhai Desai Road
Mumbai 400 026

(4409)
ISBN 978-81-7991-661-2

Cover Image: Baiju Parthan
Typesetting and Design: Mahendra Ghanekar

Printed in India by Sai Print O Pack Pvt. Ltd.

Published by:
Harsha Bhatkal for
Popular Prakashan Pvt. Ltd.
301, Mahalaxmi Chambers
22, Bhulabhai Desai Road
Mumbai 400 026

All characters in this book are real and, therefore, bear no resemblance to any person living or dead.

Acknowledgements

The journey with *Twice Written* (which in its unpublished form was called *Palimpsest*) has been as demanding as it has been fruitful and rewarding and this journey would not have been completed without the support of several friends.

While the idea of a novel had been brewing in my head for a long time, it was a conversation with Meenakshi Mukherjee that gave me the much-needed impetus to start writing. I am also grateful to her for reading my manuscript and sharing her insights and comments with me. It saddens me that she is not alive to see this book finally in print.

Dilip Chitre, another person whose presence I miss, encouraged me in the early stages of this work.

Amiya Dev and Jerry Sokol are people I am specially indebted to. I will always treasure their responses to my novel. I would also like to thank Kiran Nagarkar for reading the initial chapters and responding with insightful comments. Early conversations with Giacomo Polesello were also very valuable.

I am also deeply indebted to Baiju Parthan for not only reading the book and responding to it with his comments, but also for designing the cover of this book.

I would also like to thank the others who read the book and responded both positively and critically, and put up with me, the writer, who could not stop talking about his novel: Mitra Mukherjee Parikh and Prabodh Parikh, Reshmi Mitra, Arundhathi Subramaniam, Jerry Pinto, Mallika Sekhar and Sushruth Jadhav, Vidita Vaidya and Ajit Mahadevan, Leena Abraham and Ravi Subramaniam, Sourendu Gupta and Radiya Pacha, Uma Mahadevan, Ipsita Chanda, Sumi Krishna, Mandira Sen, Chayanika Shah, Frank Rodrigues, Elliot Leader and Boika Sokolova, Mary Sokol, B. Ananthanarayan, Sudhir Vempati, Diptiman Sen, Ben Allanach, Fawzi Boudjema, Soumya Bhattacharya, Naushil Mehta, Girish Shahane, Shanta Gokhale, Sanjukta Wagh, Markar Melkonian, Sumati Surya, Vasantha Surya, Uma Alladi, Mukund Lath, Virendra Singh, Rama Ragunathan,

Sukant Saran, A.R. Rao and Manjula Rao, Emma Sanders, Vinay Sitapati, V. Ravindran and Bhuvana, Bala Rajagopal, Akila Narasimhan and Arjun Rajagopal.

Heartfelt thanks are also due to:

My band of young loyalists who will stand by me no matter what (and even if they have no intention of reading this book!): Beena and Shyam, Yogesh and Neha, Pranav, Ananya, Indus and Sameer, Leher, Drishti, Chaitanya, Mugdha, Leela and Alina.

To Preeti Singh, Jayanthi Mahalingam, Harsha Bhatkal, Manish Purohit and Swapna Shinde of Popular Prakashan. I am particularly indebted to Preeti for being the support that she has been.

To family, for being family: Mummy, Dharen, Reshma, Girish, Sangeeta, Shashi, K.K. and, most of all, Sudha (who is the only one I know who actually read this book in a day!)

This book is a humble offering to:

The people who would have been the happiest to see this book: Amma, Chittappa and Daddy.

To Gitu and Iru, who have been the harshest critics and, yet, the greatest inspiration for this book. The quiet expression of joy I see in their eyes on seeing this book published is worth every bit of the effort I put into it.

Prologue

Legend has it that Vyasa, the author of the Mahabharata, chose Ganesha as his amanuensis to put down his epic in a written form. Ganesha agreed but laid down the condition that Vyasa would not pause in the course of his dictation. Vyasa, in turn, demanded that Ganesha grasp the meaning of each stanza before writing it down. It is through this collaboration that the text of the epic came to be.

Tradition also holds that the Mahabharata, when completed, was orally transmitted down the generations: from Vyasa through Vaisampayana to Suta. It was apparently Suta's public recital of the epic that made it known to a larger number of sages. If the epic was transmitted orally, then what does one make of the legend of Ganesha as the amanuensis of the epic?

As an allegory, the transcription of the spoken word of Vyasa, the Wise One, as the written word is mediated by Ganesha, the Lord of Categories. It is through the active agency of categories of reason that the oral appears as textual. It appears that speech stakes its claim over truth by its proximity to truth, whereas writing lacks that immediacy and can, at best, be only a derivative representation of truth. While the categories of reason seek continuity in their representation of truth, speech suspects writing of non-comprehension of truth. Yet, paradoxically, it is through writing that the text of the epic is created.

The epic did not exist before the Lord of Categories had put it down in a written form: the edifice of the typographical layout in terms of words, sentences and paragraphs, the silences of the punctuation, the nuances of the diacritical marks and the whispers of the marginal notes.

Writing cannot be wished away; it becomes a necessity. The Mahabharata is as much Ganesha's as Vyasa's.

1

Prahlad was lost to the world around him engrossed as he was in his thoughts.

'Is there a truth that is independent of the way we write about it? Or talk about it? Would we have an idea of truth if there were no language? '

The only space available in Bus No.84 every morning was for such meditations. This morning was no different from any other. Prahlad had to squeeze himself in, contorting his lean frame in a dozen different directions, before he could actually satisfy himself that he inhabited the bus's interior. In Bombay buses, it was a thin line that divided people who were in and who were out. The few lucky ones who managed seats usually slept all the way to work. For Prahlad, the time in the bus could hardly be wasted in sleep. He had to read and think and create and he had to make time for it outside work. And home was not the place for it because, in a strict sense, the 10 ft. x 8 ft. room that he inhabited inside Johnson House could hardly be called a home.

Johnson House was a dilapidated structure which had clearly seen better times. Mr. Johnson, who lived there with his niece, had to make ends meet with the rent that he got from his three paying-guests. The house was not in the upmarket part of the locality; not on the sea-facing Cadell Road side but on the Agar Bazaar side. Even then the three rents fetched Mr. Johnson quite a bit. But after his hunger was taken care of, a man needed something to quench his thirst with. Mr. Johnson took good care of that need of his, consequently paying very little attention to anything else. Prahlad did not mind that; in fact, he liked the fact that Mr. Johnson left him alone. He did not even mind the fact that his room was so small. What made him uneasy in Johnson House was the deep sense of defeat and gloom that seemed to permeate it.

Prahlad had discovered this to be true of all the houses he had visited when he had gone in search of paying-guest accommodation.

The Kantharias of Kemp's Corner would remain vivid in his memory, though his visit to their house had lasted hardly ten minutes. He would not forget the dirty cup they served him tea in – tea made with a bag dipped in lukewarm water. The two Kantharia daughters, about five and three years old, looked frail and unhealthy. The son cried incessantly, craving for his mother's breast. The poor mother looked exhausted even at that early hour and went through the motions of showing Prahlad his room in a listless manner. The room was, in fact, much cleaner than the rest of the house. Yet Prahlad came out of the Kantharia home gasping for fresh air. Even Rakesh Damecha could see that it had not worked.

Prahlad had approached Damecha when his attempts at finding accommodation through newspaper advertisements had failed. Damecha was representative of a significant slice of Bombay in the eighties: street-smart, capable of delivering but often promising more than he could deliver. He fancied that he was gauging his customer by showing him flats like that of the Kantharias. He felt that he now knew what Prahlad was looking for. When he called up the next morning with a new offer, Prahlad was surprised. This was a room on Colaba Causeway: an independent room with an attached shower and toilet and even a sea view. Prahlad couldn't believe his luck. He was too excited to wait for Damecha so he took a break from work as soon as he could and set off on his own to see the room. The owner was a tall Pathan who had a shop in the same building. The room, he told Prahlad, was on the fifth floor and the lift in the building never worked. It turned out that the Pathan did not have the key to the room but he agreed to show Prahlad the neighbouring room which was identical. The room was small with only enough space for a bed and a shelf. The toilet was not exactly 'independent' but had to be shared by the three paying-guests who lived on the same floor. This room had a tiny window opening on to Colaba Causeway, so there was no sea view. But the Pathan assured him that the other room was similar but opened out on the sea-facing side. Prahlad felt that the rent was very reasonable, especially for Colaba Causeway. He paid the Pathan a month's rent in advance and planned to move in later that day.

As he climbed up the narrow staircase with the Pathan that evening, Prahlad had his first doubts. More doubts crept into his mind at the sight of a woman on the second floor landing, wearing gaudy lipstick and a vulgar smile on her lips

The room was similar to what Prahlad had seen earlier in the day. It was bare except for a bed and a shelf. But the sea view was something Prahlad was not prepared for. There it was: the view of this tip of South Bombay in all its glory. The red dome of the magnificent Taj Mahal Hotel was on the left and past the roofs of the other buildings was a spectacular view of the sea. The dramatic view was thanks to the lack of a wall on the sea-facing side! It was as if the room had started growing out into space and suddenly decided to stop growing.

The Pathan launched into a description of the repairs being carried out in the building. He argued that the bed and the shelf were at least five feet away from the edge. He conceded that it would be somewhat difficult to live there when the monsoons arrived but he was confident that the repairs would be completed much before that. Even in his perturbed state, Prahlad noticed the Pathan's refusal to be dragged into a metaphysical discussion about the non-existent wall. Remarkable for someone who had probably never heard of the Vienna Circle...

The argument that followed had a theatrical quality to it. It was quite possible that they had an audience – the people sitting along the sea-front near the Gateway – to watch the performance. Damecha arrived on the stage and tried to handle the situation. Finally, it was agreed that Prahlad would not be obliged to rent the place for a month. He would live there for a week. In the meantime, Damecha would find Prahlad another place to move into.

That week Prahlad experienced high-rise living as never before. It was surreal being suspended in space, something which one never experiences when one is protected by a wall. In the dark, fears of going over the edge terrorised Prahlad and when the room was flooded with light he felt naked and exposed to the world. In the morning, he would be up early and out before 7 a.m. He would return late at night and crawl into bed without as much as switching the lights on.

But sleep completely deserted him the first couple of nights – that was how terrified he was. If he slept the third night, it was simply out of sheer exhaustion. He was woken up from deep slumber by a noise from the floor below. When he was fully awake, the night was silent again. He sat on his bed and looked at the city that was spread out in front of him. How composed the city looked at that time of the night! It was probably the only time Bombay had to sit back and look at herself. If, like in so many other cities, there was a river running through Bombay she would probably have, following Heraclitus and the Mahayana Buddhists, used the river as a metaphor for time. Bombay had only the sea.

The picture of time she had was Nietzschean: chaotic, Dionysian and eternally recurrent like the waves of the sea which kept lashing her. The sea of time brought with it festivities and mournings, arrivals and departures, births and deaths, successes and failures and Bombay was there in all of it – celebrating, lamenting, crying, singing, humming, howling or silently accepting – and she was at it all day and all night. But it was between 3:55 a.m. and 4:10 a.m. that she had the time to look back at the experiences of the day gone by from a different perspective – not from the perspective of the actress, the director, the producer, the critic or even of the viewer but from that of one who sees these experiences as fleeting, transient images on a screen. She had the luxury of that point of view for just fifteen minutes. Just fifteen minutes before she had to start moving again: someone pushed a hand-cart, another started the engine of a car and Bombay prepared herself for another long day.

The week was drawing to an end and Damecha had not done anything to find Prahlad a new place. On the last morning of the week, Prahlad had tried desperately and unsuccessfully to get in touch with Damecha. When he finally got through to him, it was well past noon. Prahlad was furious with his casual attitude but Damecha was a Bombay broker: cool and unruffled. He assured Prahlad that he would find him something by the evening. That night Prahlad was back again in his small room in Johnson House.

Prahlad's mornings, like those of Bombay's millions, were characterised by a sameness. The bus ride to Fountain, the brisk walk from Fountain to Kala Ghoda, the detour down Ropewalk lane to Madras Cafe and the *wada sambar-sada dosa*-coffee breakfast that would add up to Rs. 2.60/- were all essential and invariable elements of his morning. He was usually the cafe's first customer, early enough for the waiters to be still setting the tables in place and mopping the floor. The kitchen would be at it busiest and the aroma of cooking and frying would fill the entire cafe. The owner would be performing his worship of the photograph of Lakshmi behind his cash desk and then of the cash box. Having pleased the goddess and the cash box, he would pick up a glass of freshly-made coffee and throw it out onto Ropewalk Lane as a sacrificial offering to nature. Having thus established the equation of his enterprise with the forces of the cosmos, he would return to the mundane with a smile on his face.

Often, at that early hour, the only other customer in the restaurant was Ashok Bhende, the well-known poet. Prahlad would watch Bhende eat his *sada dosa,* slicing it carefully, balancing it on the fork and dousing it with *sambar*. Prahlad noticed how Bhende's stick-like arms jutted out awkwardly as he ate. After watching Bhende over many days, Prahlad knew every detail of the way he ate. He once wrote down a description of Bhende eating his *dosa,* mocking the poet's style. He knew Bhende's work well enough for him to parody it. In truth, he admired Bhende's poetry and secretly wished that Bhende would acknowledge his presence in the cafe. He had met Bhende and had been introduced to him. Bhende freelanced as a copywriter and had on a few occasions used Prahlad's office to work in. But Bhende had never acknowledged Prahlad's existence, then or now.

Over breakfast, Prahlad would read the newspaper. By the time he made it to coffee, he would be staring intently at the cryptic crossword. He would not leave the cafe till he had worked out at least a few clues but he would try to remember them all so that during the day, a part of his mind would still be working on some of them. Prahlad's passion for crosswords and his passion for theoretical physics were not unrelated. He remembered a teacher in college who disapproved of Prahlad spending time on solving crosswords.

'You will never be able to pursue physics if you waste your time on such idle pastimes,' he remembered this teacher saying.

'But, Sir,' he had said, 'crossword clues are so like the experimental data that a physicist works with. There are some set procedures he follows, but he also needs considerable ingenuity to crack a clue. In physics as in a crossword, a solution does not makes sense if it does not fit in with existing solutions to other clues.'

'How can you even compare physics to something as trivial as a crossword?' said his teacher, irritated.

'Physics may be more complicated and there is one profound difference.'

'Which is?'

'The issue of the compiler. Physics is agnostic. It tells you that just because there is a crossword it does not mean that there is a compiler who put it together. Don't you agree?'

He had seen a faint light of understanding dawn in his teacher's eyes.

'Very often,' Prahlad had continued, 'a physicist gets so carried away at cracking a few difficult clues that he becomes atheistic and claims that there is no compiler.'

It was only over breakfast that Prahlad had time for crosswords or physics. As he walked from Madras Cafe to his office at Omega Phototypesetters, he had to start thinking about work. It was a fortuitous co-incidence that Omega had been set up a few months ago, just when Prahlad, fresh out of college, was looking for a job. He wasn't formally trained to work in a typesetting unit, but then most people working in the printing industry weren't. Prahlad, in fact, had an advantage over his colleagues because he was a graduate in physics. How this helped him in typesetting was not clear but he liked others at work to believe it did. His colleagues were also impressed with Prahlad because he could speak with authority about typography and impress even the art directors of advertising agencies which, by the city's standards, was a mark of intellectual prowess.

The secret of Prahlad's knowledge of printing and typography lay elsewhere. His grandfather, his father, his uncle and several cousins were all printers. Prahlad's associations with the world of printing were as complex as they were ancient. The first time he had visited a press was roughly twenty years ago. His mother had gone looking for his father at his press with Prahlad in her womb and a worried look on her face. Prahlad's sister, Prabha, had come back home from school with tears running down her cheeks and a note from the principal. Fr. Diaz was not pleased that Prabha's parents had not paid the examination fees even a week after the due date.

'Please make sure that the payment is made at the school office by noon tomorrow,' he had written, saying that Prabha would otherwise not be allowed to appear for her exams.

This was Prabha's final year at school and Kamala did not want anything to come in the way of her daughter's education. She had herself not been able to complete school so she very much wanted her daughter to have a decent education. But there was no money at home and Krishnan hadn't come home for three days. He was very busy with the printing of a bank's annual report or so he told her. Kamala tried to call him a few times from the telephone at the grocer's shop down the road but did not find him in the office. The grocer did not make any attempt to hide his displeasure when she turned up at his shop for the fourth time asking to make a call. That was when Kamala decided to go to the press looking for Krishnan.

The press was in Mahalaxmi which was a long way off and the bus ride was not exactly pleasant. Kamala was exhausted by the time she reached there. As she entered the press, she could feel Prahlad stirring inside her. She was in the final stages of her pregnancy. And, now, as she stepped into the press she could feel Prahlad moving inside her – twisting, turning and dancing to the rhythmic beat of the Heidelberg machines.

Meheru, who worked in the press as a telephone operator, came rushing to meet Kamala. She had not met her in ages and was thrilled to see her so obviously pregnant. In her joy, she did not notice the anxiety on her face. Kamala wanted to waste no time and was keen to meet Krishnan right away. When she was told that Krishnan was not in the office, she simply collapsed into a chair that stood behind her. Meheru's shrill voice receded into a distance and so did the sound of the Heidelbergs.

A hundred confusing thoughts rushed through Kamala's mind. Where was Krishnan? And where was she to get the money for Prabha's fees? Was there anything at home she could pawn? The regularity with which her jewellery had made it to the pawnbroker's made her wonder whether the jewellery she had got as dowry at the time of her marriage was for Krishnan or for Chelliah, the pawnbroker. Her gold chain, the last ornament which she had set aside for Prabha, had been pawned last month and she had only managed to save the pendant of Tirupati Balaji from a similar fate.

Kamala's mind was in a whirl; she tried to calm herself down. But just then, the baby's desire for self-hood overwhelmed the moment. He demanded that he be delivered into the world then and there. There was no confusion in his mind: he was pushing with all his might to leave the dark, solipsistic space of his mother's womb and inhabit the world of light and being.

Meheru's voice became shriller as she panicked. The men gathered and, as men do on such occasions, stood around helplessly. One of them (after all, his wife had delivered seven children) volunteered a helpful suggestion. 'Let's call a doctor,' he said. Savitribai, who worked in the binding section, pushed him aside and took charge of the proceedings. Her experience told her that the baby was coming any moment and it was time for action and not for idle suggestions. She sent for Rukmini, bidding her to get a pan of warm water and napkins.

For Rukmini, who had spent twenty years or more cleaning, sweeping and mopping the press, this was the work of a moment. Behind the guillotine in the binding section was the only empty space in the press; empty except for the reams of paper that were stored there. The men were finally made to feel useful. The reams were moved out. Sheets of paper were laid out and Savitribai and Rukmini helped Kamala lie on them. A ream of paper was tucked beneath her neck for support. Sweat mingled with tears and flowed freely over the ream as Kamala lay with her head on it. A linotype machine, a Heidelberg printing machine and the guillotine shielded the west, east and south-east respectively. The northern borders were taken care of by a wall and Meheru moved her corpulent self to defend the south.

In this sacred space and at the auspicious hour of 6:35 p.m., on Thursday, 25th January 1962, was born to Krishnan and Kamala, a male child weighing all of 3.09 kg.

Though it didn't occur to anyone, Prahlad's birth in the printing press was a synthesis of sexual and textual reproduction. When Francis Crick and James Watson unravelled the structure of the DNA molecule, it underlined the dramatic similarity between a printed book and life. The assembly of the four nitrogenous bases along the DNA molecule represented by various combinations of the alphabets A, G, C, T (typesetting); the replication of the DNA (page printing) and the synthesizing of the DNA in the new cellular organism (binding). It was only fitting that this new understanding of life and heredity was acknowledged the year Prahlad was born, by the awarding of the Nobel Prize to Watson and Crick. In Prahlad's birth it had already been celebrated, albeit in an unwitting manner.

The products of a printing press inevitably make it to a bookshop and Prahlad's life was no exception to this rule. It was inside Thacker's bookshop that Omega Phototypesetters was located. Thacker's was a comfortable, old-fashioned bookshop and one of the important landmarks in Kala Ghoda. One part of the mezzanine floor of the bookshop had been used as a dumping ground for old, unwanted files and papers. This was where Omega was now, with an office on one side of a long corridor and the work area on the other.

Visitors and clients would meet Prahlad in the office with their layouts and text while he patiently reiterated the impossibility of their delivery schedules. He would be less patient if he had to argue with a customer about the aesthetics of page-design. He had trained himself by reading old books on typography from his grandfather's library and these books demanded a rigorous adherence to the principles of design. When it came to discussing rates, Prahlad would let his boss, Nadkarni, take over.

Nadkarni had made his fortune in the packaging industry and was beginning to make inroads into the printing industry. He had to spend the better part of his time setting up the printing press and at his packaging firm. He would come down to Kala Ghoda only late in the evening to take stock. He considered himself fortunate that he had a technically competent person like Prahlad taking care of his typesetting business by day.

Prahlad liked to spend time in the work area which was partitioned into three: a small ante-room, a machine room and a dark room. The dark room opened into a corridor through a back door and a visitor who saw it had once asked, 'Is it an entrance to the outside?'

'No, it's an exit,' Prahlad had said exasperatedly.

Prahlad had not forgotten the excitement of the early weeks when he experimented with the machine, creating pages with complex typesetting formats as exercises, printing these pages on photo-sensitive paper and then developing the paper in the dark room. He could feel his blood surging when he saw the patterns of typeset material appear faintly at first and then get bolder as he gently rubbed the paper with his rubber-gloved hands. In the dim red light of the dark room, it was fascinating to see the creations of master designers like Hermann Zapf and Eric Gill appearing magically on, what was to begin with, a blank sheet of paper.

Prahlad spent hours in the intimate company of typefaces, the Bembo and the Garamond being amongst his favourites because their elegance, in his subjective appreciation, found no equal. Eric Gill's Perpetua with its synthesis of neo-classical and modern sensibilities was another of Prahlad's favourites. Zapf's masterly twin creations, Aldus and Palatino, he genuinely admired and Baskerville's italics were, in Prahlad's opinion, the creation of genius.

This morning Prahlad was in the dark room when he was told by Chetan, his colleague, that there was a Mr. Borges waiting for him in the office. Borges was the publicity director of a pharmaceutical company and he had come with the art director of a small advertising firm.

'We are bringing out a supplement about our company in Thursday's papers. We need some urgent typesetting work done,' said Borges.

'It's one of those I-want-it-yesterday jobs,' thought Prahlad to himself.

'There is quite a lot of material to be typeset.' said Borges. 'Do you think you would be able to give it to me early tomorrow? '

He had come to Omega on a friend's recommendation and he was not impressed to see that the work here was handled by a twenty-year-old.

Prahlad liked these challenges. 'You can collect it tonight if you like,' he said in a somewhat conceited tone.

It was plain text with no fancy formatting so Prahlad knew it wouldn't take much time. He got the two data-entry operators to work on Borges' job right away and felt content that everything was under control. That sense of control lasted only a moment for when he came out of the machine-room, he saw pandemonium in the book-shop below. He rushed down.

'There's a fire in the auditorium upstairs,' said Melissa the girl who managed the bookshop, her voice quaking.

Prahlad ran back to the machine-room. 'Quick, we have to switch off the machines,' he shouted.

The auditorium on the top floor of the building was not used much. Prahlad realised it would be empty but he had no idea how big the fire was. Was it descending to the lower floors?

An hour later, they still did not have an answer. Nadkarni had rushed to Kala Ghoda and they were now standing on the road outside the building, watching the fire rapidly engulf the top floor. The fire engines had arrived but they had not managed to control the fire yet. Nadkarni was shaken.

A drunk, who slept on the pavement opposite Omega, was amused with all the goings-on. People had invaded his space – they were standing where he slept every night – but he did not mind. This morning's entertainment was worth it all – *paisa vasool*. With everyone worried about the fire spreading, the drunk also decided that it was time to speculate about the issue.

'In another half an hour, it will come down to the third floor,' he said little realizing that he was saying this to the man who owned the typesetting unit on the first floor.

'Go away, you filthy drunk,' shouted Nadkarni. And for good measure he added, 'Bastard!'

Prahlad walked up to Nadkarni in an effort to comfort him. Nadkarni tried to calm himself but his voice was trembling

'I have not insured the machines. Damn! The insurance agent didn't come when I called him and I did not find the time later.'

It took two hours to completely douse the fire, and to Nadkarni's relief, before it could reach the lower floors. When it was all over, Prahlad's throat felt completely parched. The dry sensation in his throat brought back memories of another fire which he had lit a few months earlier. He had experienced a similar sensation when standing next to his mother's pyre three months before, hardly a couple of months after he had joined Omega. The immediate cause of death at the young age of 53 was a massive heart attack, but she had been dying a slow death for years. Years of grinding uncertainty, poverty and humiliation that had left her battered. If she willed herself to live, it was for her children for whom she wanted an existence less wretched than her own.

Prabha had called Prahlad that evening. 'Amma is in hospital,' she had said.

Fighting his way through rush-hour traffic, Prahlad had reached Sion hospital after three hours. All through the journey, he had been full of remorse at not having spent time with her on Sunday when he had gone home to see her. She had wanted to spend the afternoon talking to him. She was unhappy that Prahlad had given up his education. She had seen how passionate he was about physics and mathematics and she dreamed that he would study and get a Ph.D. in physics some day. She realised, of course, that Prahlad had taken up the job to support the family. He was living on his own because he did not get along with his father, but he was contributing to the household expenses. Kamala knew that Prahlad had no option but to work but she wanted him to dream no matter how brutal the reality was. Kamala did not plead with Prahlad neither did she pressurise him to stay. Prahlad just wanted to leave before Krishnan arrived; he had no desire to meet his father.

'Why couldn't I have put up with him and spent more time with her?' Prahlad had chided himself.

Prabha had been waiting for him outside the ICU. She had looked exhausted. Prahlad had suggested that she return home and have dinner. He had then gone to Kamala's bedside and stood watching her frail body stretched out across the white sheet. After what seemed an eternity she had opened her eyes and asked for a drink of water.

As he had raised her head and put the glass to her lips, she had asked,'Is the movie over?'

Prahlad had looked at her puzzled, and then he felt the tears flowing down his cheeks as she slumped back onto the pillow. The form disappeared and what had remained was only the whiteness of the sheet. It was as though the prismatic colours of the experience of the physical had merged into that one whiteness. When he looked again, even the sheet had disappeared; there was nothing. In those few moments, Prahlad experienced not only the death of his mother but death itself; death as void, death as nothingness.

Those were the only moments that Prahlad had to himself. The next twelve hours had been a blur. Family and friends had taken over. There had been documents to sign and hospital staff to bribe before the body ('No, that's not a body. That's my mother!') was released.

A sleepless night had given way to a dreary, grey morning. The priest, a small man with a high-pitched voice, had come with two of his assistants to conduct the rituals. The next few hours had been a confusion of fire and smoke, rice and sesame seeds, the chanting of the *mantras* and the wailing of the relatives. He had lit the pyre and as the flames leaped up, Prahlad had finally broken down and sobbed. He had felt the same sensation of dryness in his throat.

2

Ananya was waiting anxiously for the Thane-bound local at Bombay's magnificent Victoria Terminus. Such a long name for a railway station was too much for Bombay's busy millions to handle so Victoria Terminus had become V.T. In doing so, the significance of the 'V' of V.T. was erased from the collective memory of the city. What better subversive strategy could a modern city on the move adopt to break free from the shackles of colonialism! Neither did the millions associate V.T. with the magnificent gothic building that housed the station. The dome and the doorways, the arches and the gargoyles were of no concern to the crowds alighting or boarding at V.T. every day.

Ananya was late. On any other day, she would have reached home by this time but today she had not even started her journey back home to Mulund. She looked up at the newly-installed electronic indicator to make sure that the train was on time. It was the 18:53 local from Bombay V.T. to Thane. Instantly, Ananya's anxiety gave way to a smile when she realised that the time on the indicator coincided with an important historical event in the life of the city: the first train in India had made the journey from Bombay to Thane in 1853.

When she had boarded the train a few minutes later and settled into the comfort of a seat by the window in the ladies' compartment, she cast another glance in the direction of the indicator and wondered what the first train journey in 1853 had been like. It seemed like the train was traversing a time-line, moving not only from one station to another but from one age to another, mapping the history of Bombay. Each stop was a significant marker in this history allowing, as it did, so many to come in or go out. But this one great history was also composed of the several little histories of passengers in the train. While the grand history did not recount each one of these stories, it owed its very existence to these little stories. Every passenger on the train was moving to her own destination, but even as she boarded the train she knew where the train was headed and how far she could go in it – how far her history would mesh with the grand history – and where her own little story would diverge.

18:53: The train leaves Bombay V.T.

16th April, 1853

To:
Mrs. Christine Fowler,
46, Gower Street,
London.

My dear Christine,
Even when I have finished this account of my little, but nevertheless charming, adventure you will scarce believe it for, I must confess, that I too was greatly surprised when, a week ago, I received a card from the General Manager of the Great Indian Peninsular Railway with an invitation to join him on a journey on the first train in India from Bombay to a small town called Thana some 20 miles away. While the G.I.P. Railway did avail of the services of a small group of men from the Queen's Royal Lancers, who are directly under my charge, I did not imagine that I would figure on the list of invitees for the inauguration ceremony alongside many distinguished guests which included statesmen, military officers, civil servants and men of letters.

The afternoon began with a ceremony in a tent erected outside the terminus at Bori Bunder. Several officials and invitees made speeches some of which turned out to be tryingly long and it was only the excited anticipation of the train journey to follow that helped us sit through the ceremony. The terminus at Bori Bunder is still a temporary wooden structure but, from the reports that we received from several officials of the G.I.P. Railways, plans are underway to build a magnificent station which will be a fitting monument to the civilizing presence of the British in this land. For all of us who undertook this historic journey, which lasted over a hour and a quarter, it was clear that the railways will be a more lasting and enduring a monument to British rule in India than any other: its impact on the life of this ancient land will be enormous and fully comprehensible only to future generations of students of history.

It was amusing to note the reactions of the natives to the railways. There is a general sense of bewilderment amongst them and, barring a few who have had the benefit of Western education, non-comprehension about the science of modern locomotion. Before the train moved out of Bori Bunder, quite a few of them had gathered around the locomotive to figure out how it could effect motion and having convinced themselves that there were no cattle inside the engine, which could be used to drag the train, concluded that the English were using a form of wizardry or witchcraft that would bring no peace to their land. Some others, convinced that the locomotive was a demonstration of the power of the gods, came with offerings of flowers and coconuts. But, even among the English-educated Indians, there is scepticism about how effectively the railways would replace other modes of transport in India for they cannot envisage a day where the high- and low-castes would journey together in the same compartment.

The events of the day have left me not a little exhausted, a good part of it due to the early summer heat, but my excitement has been great enough for me to want to write you this letter before I retire tonight.

With love to my little sister,
John Higgins

Ananya remembered when her mother Deepa had finally managed to get a gallery to agree to exhibit some of her paintings and the day her show had opened – a very special day for her. She had wanted Ananya to be with her for the opening of her show but had to co-ordinate picking her up from home. Deepa worked in an advertising agency in the city so this meant she had to go home to Mulund and come back with Ananya for the exhibition. When they were on the train to V.T., Ananya stood by the window while Deepa was lulled, by the chaos of the day and the rhythm of the moving train, to sleep. It was only when the train reached V.T. that Deepa's eyes opened. She got off with Ananya in a hurry even as she tried to protect her daughter from the fury of the incoming crowd. When she was on the platform with her daughter, she realised that she had left her handbag in the train. She ordered Ananya to stay where she was and sprinted back to the compartment they had alighted from. Deepa had asked her not to move but it was unnecessary for her to do so, for fear had frozen the little girl. The minute or so that elapsed seemed like an eternity to her. As the enormity of the station and the crowd impressed upon her seven-year old mind, she realised that she could be helplessly lost. She felt a chill run through her heart when she saw the train move – she thought she had seen the last of her mother.

The next instant she saw Deepa jump out of the running train, bag in hand and a triumphant look on her face. It was only later when her mother held her in her arms that Ananya started crying. It took another five minutes of Deepa's time to talk to Ananya gently and make her stop crying. Then she glanced at her watch, realised how late she was and headed out, putting the incident behind her. As Ananya walked out holding her mother's hand, she turned around once to look at the station again. She would not forget this incident easily; she had for a moment, lost her mother.

18:56: Unscheduled halt at the very first signal.

1856:

I asked Saheb for a few days' leave and he wanted to know why. I have worked for the last year without a break but that is fine. I am willing to work as hard as Saheb wants me to and even more. But I have to go to the Devi temple in our village for Dussera and I have to be there with my family. It is even more important that I go this year: it is with the Mai's blessings that I got this new job. But Saheb is Parsi and will he understand what we feel about the Devi? I am Dattu from Sophale village near Ratnagiri and worked in the mango farms there which are owned by Saheb. Saheb has always been happy with my work and even more so after I found the gold ring that his daughter lost in the gardens. Saheb was very happy with me that day and told me that he needed honest men like me to come and work at the new Mill he was setting up in Bombay. He has also put me in charge of the workers in our section and I have to tell the Supervisor Saheb about the work we have completed every day.

When he started the mill, Saheb told me that this was the first mill in Bombay using English machines. He wanted us to work hard and produce quality cloth like they produce in England, in that place called Lanka-shehar. We work hard – I make sure that my workers in the weaving section are busy all the time. We were all very happy when the first length of cloth came out of our mill this year. But Supervisor Saheb is still not very happy with the quality of our work. Frankly, not many of us have experience. We are famers like our fathers and our grandfathers before us. I told Supervisor Saheb it will take us time to get used to this new work and produce cloth like they do in Lanka-shehar. Supervisor Saheb thinks that the workers are lazy but I know that we are doing our best.

And we are new to this city. Life here is very different from what it was in the village. We have just one small room to live in. Even the food here tastes different. What my wife cooked in the village tasted much better. But she says it is because of the water here. We are used to water from the river and here we have to get it from a well. Anyway, she brings my lunch here to the mill every afternoon. When Nandu is a little older, I will ask him to bring the lunch because I don't like the way other men look at her when she comes here. We have to be careful in the city because its inhabitants are not only our people from Ratnagiri but others from places like Pune, Nagar and Gujarat.

The mango is not a fruit. It is a many-hued, multi-textured experience that connects deeply to your roots. The mango, for Ananya, was synonymous with her maternal home in North Calcutta. Summer afternoons in the cool, darkened living room of the old house were reserved for long post-lunch mango sessions with Indrani and Kaushik, her cousins. These were followed by story sessions with their grandmother and Ananya would often rest her head on Dida's lap as she imagined the kings, queens and sages that Dida would talk of. The summer air would be heavy with a fascinating mix of smells of the lunch, of the mangoes and of Dida's sari. There was nothing that Ananya found more comforting.

18:57: Masjid Station.

1857:
Dear Brothers and Sisters,
I am grateful to all of you, and especially to the organisers of today's event, for inviting me to speak to you. I would like to begin with a few words of clarification. When you invited me here today, you did so because of what little reputation I have acquired as a lawyer in this city. But, at the same time, I think I was expected to speak to you about matters connected with religion and spirituality for these are the matters that concern the members of your association. As you all know, my father was a scholar of Sanskrit and I was encouraged to study Sanskrit language and literature. From an early age, I had an interest in philosophy and have been a student of some of our

philosophical traditions ever since. On the other hand, I have also had the benefit of English education, here and in England.

When I sat down to decide what the subject of my talk today ought to be, I felt I should share with you my thoughts on what I feel is the most important, recent development in our city. This is the establishment of the University this year. This is important because many more of our students will be able to pursue higher education without having to go abroad. Some of you may even be sceptical of my espousal of the English system of education which the University will impart for it may seem that acceptance of their education may be tantamount to an acceptance of their lifestyle and culture, on the one hand, and their political authority, on the other. I believe that it is possible to avoid these pitfalls and combine the best of their science and literature with that of our own, ancient tradition. It is only the modern education that this University system will deliver that will help us examine the governance of our rulers critically and also expose us to the new political ideas of democracy and equality which are sweeping the world. Our journey into the future depends on how effectively we assimilate new ideas and the new education system will guide us through this journey.

For those of you who feel that I have not addressed matters of religion and spirituality as I was expected to, I would like to say that we are moving into an age where the Universities will be our temples and the new knowledge will be our scriptures. This will be form that the religion of the future is bound to take.

In Deepa's cupboard, tucked away with all her important documents, was a fifteen-year-old newspaper clipping. It was a photograph with the Rajabai Tower, the grand colonial structure which housed the University library, as its backdrop. Ananya knew this photograph intimately for she had seen it several times in the last fifteen years. As a four-year old, when she first saw it, she was struck by the Rajabai Tower even though it was only a backdrop for the photograph. The photograph focussed on the traffic junction just outside the University and marked a spot on the road with a white circle. That was the spot where her dad Subir had died. He had stepped out of his office to go to the bank and had stopped near the traffic junction to buy a pack of cigarettes. He had looked down to light one and started crossing the road. It all happened in a split second. A speeding bus hit Subir and he did not live long enough to make it to the hospital.

Within a couple of weeks of Subir's death, Deepa was back at work and people who did not know about the tragedy, would have hardly gauged the depth of her grief. Time did not heal; it simply blurred. Ananya remembered Subir only through his photographs. She was too young at the time of his death, but she knew the story of because it had been repeated to her so often by Deepa.

19:03: Byculla station.

1903:

Life in business is such that one hardly gets time to go out of Masjid Bunder. But this afternoon I had work in Colaba and I decided to meet Sadiq after I had finished my work. I have been intending to meet Sadiq for a long time now but with work being what it is, one doesn't even have time for dear cousins like Sadiq. I spent more than an hour at Sadiq's place and was planning to leave around sunset. But he insisted I go with him for a walk along the harbour at Colaba to see the new hotel that has been built there.

For the last two months since the Taj Mahal Hotel was built, I have been planning to see it so I did not refuse Sadiq's invitation. I have seen the Taj Mahal that Shah Jahan built in Agra for his Begum Mumtaz. I can imagine an Emperor building a monument like that for his beloved but what will a building built for a city you love look like? If the story I heard about Mr. Tata is true, it seems he built this hotel to express his love for Bombay. I didn't know whether to believe this story till I saw the building. But, now that

I have seen it, I know it must be true because like the Taj Mahal in Agra this is also clearly a work of love. What a magnificent building it is!

I have heard people wonder whether it makes business sense for an Indian to build a hotel like that. After all, they have had hardly twenty or thirty guests in the hotel so far and, people are saying, 'Love for the city is all right. But you can't invest such a huge amount of money for nothing.' But my feeling is that Mr. Tata has the right approach to business. Because to succeed in business you need heart. You need to believe in yourself and have the courage to go ahead with what you think is right.

When I visited Agra, Abbas insisted that we should see the Taj Mahal on a full-moon night. I thought Abbas would know best since he has lived in Agra all his life and I was happy that I followed his advice. The full-moon night is the best time to see the Taj Mahal. Today in Colaba I realised that the best time to see the Taj Mahal Hotel is after the sun has set and the darkness of the night begins to cover the city. For that is when you can see the lights of the Taj Mahal Hotel come on. And what a sight it is! The whole building is lit up with electric bulbs. We had not seen anything like this before. As I sat with Sadiq on the sea-front looking at Tata's marvellous hotel, I wondered whether there would come a time when the whole city would be lit up with electric bulbs.

Ananya had agreed to go to the Taj, but only reluctantly. In all her eighteen years, she had not once stepped into the hotel as she thought it was not in conformity with her principles. Her early exposure to the writings of Marx and her involvement with student politics had oriented her differently and she could not see herself partying at the Taj. But Deepa had put together a major exhibition of her paintings and the gallery had organised a dinner after the opening of the show. A show of this magnitude was what Deepa had been working towards over the last twenty years and she was happy with the recognition that the art fraternity was according her, even though somewhat belatedly. Deepa was very keen that Ananya be present for the evening and Ananya finally agreed. If she had been completely honest with herself Ananya would have recognised that, in spite of her convictions, there was an element of curiosity in her about the Taj Mahal Hotel and, at least in part, she was excited about the impending experience.

At the end of the evening, Ananya wondered why she had made the effort to attend. After trying and failing to make meaningful conversation with some of the guests, she had just sat in one corner with a glass of fruit juice in her hand watching the others descend into the depths of intoxication. As she had looked around the room, her eyes had come to rest on Deepa who was elated, exhausted and inebriated, all at once. A welter of emotions had racked Ananya but anger was the emotion which, overriding every other, had sparked from her eyes and seared her mother.

19:13: Dadar station.

1913:

I still remember the day I met Dhundiraj even though it was 28 years ago that we first met. We were young lads and had just joined the J.J. School of Art. But even then Dhundiraj stood out as an artist and as a person. He was not content, at all, to accept the given but was driven to find something new. The lectures at the J.J. School bored him and he found the art instruction there very limiting. He would look at his own paintings and would be distressed to find them lifeless. He moved to Baroda very soon but we would meet whenever he was in Bombay. We kept up this contact for more than twelve years and then we lost touch. I met him, quite by accident, in the Fort area in 1901. He was very excited about his new passion: magic. He had found himself a German teacher and was completely involved. It sounded to me exactly the kind of thing Dhundiraj would do.

But today I realised how all these elements have gone into making Dhundiraj – no, I should call him Dadasaheb Phalke as the world now knows him. He was very kind to trace me through friends and invite me to the screening of his debut film, Raja Harishchandra. I had only to see the first few scenes to realise that Dhundiraj had finally found what he always wanted: an art infused with life and magic. This new medium was the right amalgam of the elements he had been searching for. In spite of growing up as a Catholic, I have been exposed to Hindu epics and mythology to know and comprehend the story of Harishchandra. But, on film, this story came alive in a way I have never experienced before. When I stepped out of the projection room at the end of the first film made by an Indian, my eyes filled with tears. I felt touched to have been a friend of a person as great as Dadasaheb.

Books had been Ananya's companions through childhood and adolescence but films saw her through her passage into adulthood. On her sixteenth birthday, Ananya discovered cinema when the screen came alive with the Bogart-Bergman romance in Casablanca. Love as an emotion had never before appeared so real to her. Her exploration of the world of emotions through cinema began and she became passionately involved with the medium. The ephemeral play of light and sound opened up new worlds for her throwing up more for her to imagine, think about and explore than what the mundane actuality of life had to offer.

19:21: Kurla station.

1921:

1st August is only four days away. I have no idea what I am going to do. A few days ago when I attended this public meeting on Gunvant's insistence, I didn't realise what I was getting into. Gunvant is only a year older than I am but he is clear in his mind about what he wants to do. I can't understand why I am not like him, in spite of being his sister. When Gunvant came a month ago, dressed in khadi and saying he will never wear foreign cloth again, I was amused. He said that the use of khadi was the weapon with which to fight the British government. I didn't see how the government was going to get affected by what Gunvant chooses to wear. But since I didn't fully understand all this, I should have stayed away from the meeting.

The meeting was in Santa Cruz on the 26th and it seemed like any other political meeting till Gandhiji arrived on the stage. When he started talking, it was as though the atmosphere in the hall had changed. This was the first time I was hearing him and, after listening to him speak for a while, I realised that there was a gentle persuasive power that he possessed. His speech was simple and quite lucid. He explained how the use of khadi could be our key to Swaraj.

All that was fine – but why did we have to promise to give up foreign cloth right there in the meeting? I was not prepared for that, neither did I want to give up foreign cloth. I use it not because it comes from England but because it is of such good quality. The hand-woven khadi is simply not as good. So I don't see why I should wear something inferior when I can afford the better cloth. Also, Gandhiji wanted us to give up using coloured cloth and wear white instead. It is hardly a year since I got married. Won't people think it inauspicious if I gave up coloured cloth and started wearing white? You know how tongues wag. I really think that what a woman should wear should be decided by her household. Why should someone else decide that?

It was really awkward when, at the end of the meeting, Gandhiji wanted all those who pledge to use khadi to raise their hands. I did not want to make false promises. But, in that crowded hall, I did not want to be the only person not raising her hand. Now, by 1st August, we are supposed to give all our foreign cloth to the party workers who will light a bonfire with all that they collect. I can't bear to think of all my lovely saris being destroyed.

By the time Ananya was in college, *khadi* had become a stamp of exclusivity. It marked you as an intellectual especially if you took care to co-ordinate it with the right kind of denim. The *khadi kurta*-and-Levis-look was what Ananya cultivated and she carefully matched this look with an air of casualness. *Khadi* was a convenience and could be replaced with soft mill-spun cotton if the weather demanded it. The jeans had to be Levis and her uncle's frequent visits to the U.S. made sure that she always had them in stock. The freedom to choose the kind of clothes she wanted to wear was something Ananya guarded zealously and she wanted no one, not even Deepa, to interfere with that choice.

19:27: Ghatkopar station.

1927:

Parveen, did you see the look on Behram's face last evening? I was so amused to see the surprise on his face but I think I also saw envy. When you told me that you had invited Behram and Persis for dinner I decided I should let them experience the sound of our radiogram. No, no, it is not that I wanted to show off to Behram. But when I decided to buy the radiogram he told me mockingly that he would have thrown the money into the sea rather than spend it on buying such a useless gadget. You know, that was the time the British Broadcasting Corporation was set up in England and I had the feeling that it will not be long before we have a broadcasting corporation in India. But Behram thought that would happen only by the time of my grandson's Navjot! Poor fellow, he just does not realise how efficient the English are. Our Indian Broadcasting Company was set up within six or seven months of the BBC and the fact that the Viceroy himself came to inaugurate it means that the British realise how significant it is. And what pleasure it is to listen to the radio – sitting in the comfort of your living room and listening to the melodious voices of the Homji sisters! The world is changing, Parveen, but Behram has not even bought himself a new hat!

Bijoya had come to Bombay just a little after Subir's death. Deepa needed someone to take care of Ananya and her home when she was away at work. Bijoya's husband had died a year before Subir. After her husband's death, Bijoya had to find herself a job as a household help. But, in Calcutta, these jobs did not fetch enough money and when Deepa's mother approached her with an offer in Bombay she was quite willing. For Deepa, Bijoya was a godsend. She took good care of the house, was a good cook and very tidy. But, above all, she was wonderful with Ananya taking care of her as her own daughter. Ananya thought of Bijoya maasi as a dear friend: as someone with whom she shared her afternoons, secrets and raw mangoes.

Ananya and Bijoya's afternoons were not complete without the radio. The Akashvani station would bring Rafi, Lata, Asha and Kishore alive in Ananya's tiny bedroom. It was curious that they should listen so avidly to Hindi film music. Bijoya's knowledge of Hindi was just enough to help her buy vegetables and groceries. Ananya did study Hindi in school, but like most of the Bengali diaspora, her cultural roots were in Bengal. While she did watch the popular cinema that Bombay tirelessly churned out, very few of them made an impact on her as the cinema from Hollywood or Calcutta did. The only unexpected aspect to her cultural makeup was her passion for Hindi film music. She nurtured this passion over the years and it was something that she shared closely with Bijoya.

19:38: Mulund station.

1938:

I have been working with the Communist Party for a few years now, even though as a young student I was initially with the Congress party. But the Communist ideology and its goal of a classless society appealed to me as it did to many young people. It dawned on me that freedom from British rule is only the first step towards the bigger struggle of achieving social justice. This knowledge has been the stable base of all the political action that my comrades and I have been involved in.

I woke up this morning with a sense of elation because today we have called for the first major industrial strike in the country. To motivate and organise tens of thousands of workers in this city to agitate was no mean task but our party workers toiled over the last few weeks in order to make this possible. In my perception, this agitation made the masses, which were singularly focussed on the struggle for freedom from British rule, confront the issue of social justice. I felt that this gave our political struggle a moral superiority.

However, as I sit now at the end of a very long day, I am no longer sure that I can talk about social justice so glibly. No, let me tell you first what happened today. We had organised a huge procession of industrial workers which culminated in a meeting at Jambori maidan where many of our Communist leaders like Nimkar and Dange addressed the crowds. But, for this strike, we had also joined hands with the Dalits and the leader of the Dalits, Dr. Babasaheb Ambedkar also addressed the rally. Frankly, I did not know much about him except that he was a learned man who has a Ph.D. from Columbia University in the U.S. and that he had successfully organised the untouchables in Mahad to fight for access to water from the lake. I thought the issues he was fighting for, though important, were specific to a particular group of people. I was wrong. Babasaheb's speech was a revelation.

As I listened to him, I realised how my intoxication with the idea of a classless society had made me blind to the real issues that Indian society was faced with. In my entire political career, I had not once asked myself what my caste identity means. It is so much easier for an upper-caste Maharashtrian like myself to talk about a classless utopia with little thought to the problem of the lower castes and the untouchables. Our society has been rigidly and brutally divided for millennia and there is no abstract social justice we can work towards if we do not rid ourselves of the caste system. Babasaheb has made me see this so clearly that I cannot now wish it away. It will take me a while to figure out where I should go from here.

In Elphinstone College, Ananya came into contact with a group of students who were actively involved with the students' union. At first, Ananya was not keen to interact with them but when she became aware of their leftist orientation her interest was provoked. She soon found out about their Thursday afternoon study circle where they met to discuss Marx, Lenin and Trotsky. Ananya became part of the study circle and an active member of the union.

Some time later, the students' union decided to agitate against a fee hike that the University had proposed. When the letter that they sent to the Vice Chancellor was ignored, meetings were called, fiery speeches were made and it was decided that the students' union would storm into the Vice Chancellor's office to press for their demands. Ananya felt that the rhetoric and bombast around the issue did not reflect its seriousness. Nonetheless, being a part of the union, she had to go along with the course of action that had been decided upon.

The University had prior information about the union's plans and had prepared itself adequately. The gates were shut and policemen stood guard around the campus. When the students reached the campus, they found there was no way they could get in. Some students tried to distract the attention of the police by trying to open the gates while others then attempted to jump over the unguarded fence. The police got into action with their *lathis* and the students dispersed in a few minutes. A woman constable swung her *lathi* at Ananya and she got hit on her knee. It was not long after this event that Ananya quit the union.

19:42: Thane.

1942:

We are very close to our goal now. I have no doubt about that. Freedom – freedom from British rule. It is only a matter of time. Bapuji has categorically asked the British to quit India – to simply leave this land with no conditions attached. I am happy that we, as a people, are today in a position to say this to the British. We will follow it up with action: non-cooperation. 'Do or Die,' Bapuji said. That is the mantra he gave us when he addressed the meeting today at Gowalia Tank. 'Do or Die' because the British are not going to take it lying down. They are going to come down heavily on us and our leaders. I won't be surprised if our leaders are arrested tonight. But we are prepared for that. We will fight, even die, so that our children can live in a free India. This is the beginning of the end of British rule in India.

Ananya was in the first year of college when she went with a few classmates to Mani Bhavan, the house on Laburnum Road which was Gandhiji's residence in Bombay. Ananya had never been to Mani Bhavan before and it was for a project that she was working on in college that she decided to make this visit. It did not take her long to realise what a treasure-trove of history the place was and she got completely engrossed in the exhibits. It was only when she saw photographs of the Quit India movement in the exhibition that she realised how close she was to the famous Gowalia Tank where the movement was launched on 8th August 1942. Ananya was somewhat ashamed that she had never visited Gowalia Tank in spite of living in Bombay all her life. She decided that now was the time to make amends for her lapse. None of her friends were interested, however, and Ananya decided to go on her own.

August Kranti Maidan, as the Gowalia Tank ground was now called, was an unimpressive plot of land set in the midst of a very busy part of the city. A tall, white pillar that stood in the centre was the only sign that marked it as a historical site. As Ananya looked around the empty maidan, empty only because it was a weekday afternoon, to get a sense of the history of the place, it began to pour. Ananya ran and took shelter under a roof of thatch abutting a tea stall. She watched the rain and imagined the historical drama that had unfolded on the maidan so many years ago. To her left sat an old man, his body huddled together to protect himself from the cold wind that was blowing across the ground. His face was creased with age and his eyes stared aimlessly as he smoked a *bidi*. To Ananya's right was a young girl, seven or eight years old, squatting cross-legged on the ground, her frock adjusted over her lap to hold the *jamuns* she was eating. She went about the task of eating the berries very intently and when she finished she got up and stuck her hands out into the rain to wash the purple juice of the berries off her hands and mouth. She then brushed her frock down with the palms of both hands and looked up at Ananya, her face lit up with a happy smile.

3

Laila had been fascinated by signboards ever since she was little. To her, signboards chronicled the mythology of the city in a unique way. The names, the typefaces, the colours, the images and the icons were windows into the lives of the people who owned these small shops or restaurants.

There were ones which bluntly told you the owner's identity – displaying a family name which also announced the community he belonged to: C. Joshi and Brothers, or Tyrewala and Sons or M. Berman and Co.

Other boards chose to tell the story of the owner's roots: Great Punjab Restaurant or Sind Provision Stores or Mysore Coffee House, or some which traced their origins to historical antiquity like Light of Persia Restaurant or Bethlehem Bakery.

A cluster of shops all named after the same god was a clear indication of a temple in the vicinity.

Some signboards spoke of an era gone by. Victoria Restaurant and Stores, Britannia Bakery or Coronation Cloth Merchants, while others made a statement on the contemporary. A superhit film would help christen a hundred shops and events which made headlines were grist for the signboard mill. Skylab Readymade Garments was a reminder of the NASA space station that came crashing down on Earth.

A glimmer of humour appeared in Touch Wood Furniture or Hide and Chic Leather Goods. Restaurants could be classified and graded by simply studying their signboards – even a limited imagination was enough to judge what kind of food a restaurant that called itself Hindmata Restaurant and Milk Bar was likely to serve and how much it would cost.

Of these myriad names and images that the city offered to Laila for her semiological explorations, there were two which stood out and had fascinated her for quite some time. These two boards were adjacent to each other on the busy junction at S.V. Road just outside Andheri station and announced themselves as Ahura Bakery and Mazda Wines. The bakery and the wine shop belonged to the same Irani family and being Zoroastrians it was understandable that they would name their shops after the supreme deity of their religion, where Ahura and Mazda, the masculine and feminine principles, were eventually synthesized into a monotheism. Laila was struck by the other dualism that the signboards alluded to: bread and wine, the body and the blood of Jesus, the human and divine aspects of Christ.

At Elphinstone College, where she studied, Laila had been reading Jung which made her see a deeper connection in these signboards: Jung suggested that the bread and wine sacrament was, in fact, a residue of rituals from pre-Christian tradition especially from the ancient religion of Persia making a possible connection between Zoroastrianism and Christianity. These inter-cultural links, Jung felt, were the stuff of our dreams and delusions. Laila was intrigued by the sign-boards because they were not the Irani shop-owner's dream: they inhabited that portion of objective reality which through its din and chaos announced itself as an evening in Andheri.

Laila wondered whether, in the act of naming, we draw upon images from the collective unconscious, just as we do in dreams. The conscious mind takes a backseat in the process of naming something or someone and the mind draws upon a collective fund of words and images in what is apparently an unmediated process. The naming process evokes mystery and even fear and the process often digs deep into religion, numerology and the occult. What does it mean to give a name to something, wondered Laila, for is it not true that a rose is a rose no matter what we call it? No, she thought, the rose by any other name is not a rose for the name and substance stand in an essential relationship. When you call it by any other name, there is no rose even if it is a fact that the new thing called by the new name also smells as sweet as a rose.

It reminded Laila of the story of a Sufi saint who was told the name of a *raga* that he had never heard before. He disappeared into his hut and locked himself in all night and tried to imagine what a *raga* called Gaud Sarang would sound like. He emerged out of his hut the next morning singing a song in Gaud Sarang. The name of the *raga* was enough to evoke a complete description of it; the name of a person is sufficient to evoke memories of days lost in the mist of time.

Why was she named Laila, she wondered. On the day she was born, her father had suggested this name and her had mother liked it. The name Laila had sprung up in Gobind's mind as though out of nowhere and he probably thought he had settled on that choice of name for his daughter because it sounded good – the name had a nice ring to it. Moreover, Gobind had always been fond of Urdu literature which contained innumerable references to the love legend of Laila and Majnu. That may have been all that was there to it but it may have had a source somewhere in Gobind's past. For someone like Gobind, who had gone through the horrors of the Partition when he was eighteen, there was hardly anything in his life that did not go back to that past.

Gobind's memories of his childhood in Lahore were wonderful. He remembered the big courtyard outside his house where he would play with his friends. His siblings, a brother and a sister, were much younger than him but his memories of childhood were crowded with that of his cousin, Bimla, his mother's sister's daughter who lived in the neighbourhood. Bimla was just a year younger than Gobind and the two children grew very close to each other. Bimla's father owned an apple orchard in the outskirts of the city and Gobind and Bimla would accompany him there on weekends. The ride to the orchard in the stylishly-decorated red tonga was as exciting as the orchard itself. The children would run around the orchard or splash around in a small pond nearby and, when they were exhausted, they would sit under the cool shade of a leafy tree and eat apples. Years later, Gobind would look at the fruits Bombay had to offer with contempt, such were the memories of the apples from Masadji's orchard.

Gobind was about sixteen when he finished school. His father wanted him to study further and Gobind decided to work towards a B.A. degree in History at the Oriental College in Lahore. College life was exciting and intellectually stimulating. Gobind became a member of a poetry club in college: the great poet, Iqbal, had been a teacher in Oriental College and even though Iqbal had left the college decades ago, the college prided itself on its literary tradition and poetry was a passionate engagement with some of its young students.

Gobind was exposed to trends in modern Urdu poetry and his own writing was considerably influenced by these trends. He would fill up pages of his college notebooks with his poetry and, when he had an afternoon free, he would go to Bimla's house to read out his poetry to her.

For Bimla these afternoons with Gobind were valuable for it was her only contact with the world of intellect to which she was denied entry. Her father had been indulgent enough to let her complete her schooling but college education for a girl was unthinkable. Bimla lost her mother to tuberculosis when she was in the final year of school and her father was now anxious to see Bimla married. While she had resigned herself to a life where she would be married into a large, comfortable family with possibly a businessman for a husband there was a part of Bimla which craved for the life of the intellect. She had loved mathematics and literature in school and, though the world of mathematics was closed to her now, she did her best to keep her interests in literature alive. Her tastes in poetry were inclined towards the classical but she was still very interested in finding out what

Gobind and his friends were discussing. She liked listening to Gobind's poetry though she found it amusing that all his poems were about love and, more often than not, about the pain of separation from the beloved. She loved to tease Gobind about it and he would go red in the face when she said that in order to feel the pangs of separation he ought to find a girl to fall in love with in the first place. It was around that time that she started calling him Majnu.

A map is a dangerous thing, an invention of the Devil himself. It projects the three-dimensional space we inhabit on to a two-dimensional sheet of paper but in doing so it ignores many other dimensions. While it feebly attempts to capture the infinite variety of the geographical landscape in terms of texture and colour, it totally ignores the dimensions of culture which are necessarily associated with the space in which human beings live. It conceives of space as devoid of the people who inhabit it and it is, therefore, possible to divide a map into two by simply drawing a line through it. It is not possible to divide the space people live in without that line passing right through their hearts, ripping them apart.

Towards the middle of June 1947, Lahore was very tense. Gobind's father's business associates advised him to leave Lahore and go to Delhi or Bombay. They feared the worst for the Hindus living in the part of the subcontinent that was to become Pakistan. There were reports of mob violence coming in from different parts of the city and when stories of the abduction and rape of Hindu and Sikh women started making the rounds, Gobind's father decided that he should leave Lahore.

He liquidated his business assets for which he got a pittance but he desired the safety of his family more than anything else. He also spoke to Bimla's father offering him the same advice that his friends had given him. Bimla's father did not see reason in his brother-in-law's actions: he was convinced that even if the Partition were unavoidable it would not be necessary for the millions of Hindus and Sikhs in West Punjab and Sind to migrate. He could not see how any government, political party or group could even think that such a mass migration would be possible. A few days later his conviction about the impossibility of the exodus was shaken but he still felt that he should stay long enough to see that his assets fetch him a decent sum of money which would allow him to set up business in Delhi. Gobind's father tried to convince him to leave with them but to no avail.

When they finally left Lahore in early August, the city was already ravaged by riots. They encountered one such riot on their way to the station and, in their attempt to escape from the crowds and find a safe spot to hide, Gobind and his brother, Randhir were separated from the rest of the family. When they reached the station there was no sign of the others. They waited anxiously for three hours but the platform was now packed with people all waiting to take the next train out of Lahore to Delhi. Even as the train that they finally boarded got ready to leave, a hundred men armed with sticks and swords entered the platform. It was the alertness of the Anglo-Indian station master that ensured that the train left before they were attacked.

When they reached Delhi, the situation was even worse and they could not even step out of the station. A helper in the railway kitchen gave them shelter and Gobind and Randhir spent a day and a half hiding in the small storeroom adjacent to the kitchen. They slept on the sacks of potatoes and onions. The minute things in the city became a little normal, they took leave of the helper (and only at that time they discovered that he was a Muslim) and found their way to the house of the only relative they had in Delhi. They were happy to find their father and sister already there but their mother was not with them. She had been separated from her husband and daughter in Lahore and no one had any idea where to find her. It was more than two weeks later that a relative from Amritsar brought her to Delhi. It was not clear how Gobind's mother had landed up in Amritsar and there was little they could find out from her because she was in a state of shock and unable to speak coherently for months afterwards.

In the four months that they spent in Delhi and for quite some time after they were in Bombay the family made efforts to trace Bimla and her father. They contacted all the relatives and friends they could think of, searched for them in refugee camps and listened to the radio every night to find out whether their names were announced as part of the list of new refugees who arrived in the camps. They chased a couple of leads but those turned out to be false. In the course of their searches, they were offered three stories about Bimla and her father. The first story was that Bimla and her father were brutally killed and their house was set on fire. The second story talked about Bimla's abduction by the son of a well-known Muslim family in Lahore. It was claimed that this young man was smitten by Bimla and had made use of the chaos that prevailed in the city to abduct her. It was further conjectured that he kept her captive for weeks till her resistance broke down, had her convert to Islam and married her. Bimla's father, according to this account, died of the shock of losing his daughter. The third account talked of Bimla's father being killed in the riots while Bimla was helped by a Sikh family to escape from Lahore. She was now in Amritsar and married to one of the young men in the family. Somewhere towards the end of 1948, Gobind accepted the fact that he was never going to find out which of these stories were true or, indeed, if Bimla and her father were alive or dead. He never again spoke of Bimla.

This was the story about her father and Bimla that Laila had pieced together from all the snippets that she heard. Gobind's sister, her Bua, was her main source and she had also got some inputs from her mother who, in turn, had heard these stories from the family. The missing links in the story were supplied by Laila herself, but she felt no closer to solving the mystery of her name. Did it have something to do with the fact that Bimla used to tease Gobind by calling him Majnu? Laila felt that her name might have sprung out of Gobind's subconscious – an episode of the past which he had relegated to some forgotten, dark corner of his mind. On the other hand, Gobind might have chosen the name deliberately because it was secular. At some point when Gobind married Tahira he had decided that his children would be brought up with no specific religious identity. On the other hand, Tahira did not feel very strongly about this issue and it had to do with the fact that she was not religious at all. She had grown up in a liberal family and her parents had not been religious either. Of course, she had fond memories of the festivals they celebrated at home but she remembered them as joyous family occasions quite devoid of serious religious connotations.

After coming to Bombay, Gobind could not immediately resume his studies but had to find a job instead. It was about four months before he got a job as an office assistant in a lawyer's firm. It was not exactly an exciting job but it provided him enough money to supplement his father's meagre income. But after four years in the job, Gobind felt he ought to pursue his studies. His father had set up a small business and had a more stable income now and Gobind felt that this was the time to get back to studies. He could not give up the security of a job, however, and tried to negotiate with his boss for some flexibility in his working hours. He was frustrated to find his boss unwilling to accede to this very reasonable request and so when a new job offer from another lawyer came his way, he did not hesitate to quit his job.

Mr.Patel, his new boss, was not such a well-known lawyer as his previous employer but Gobind realised that he would learn more on the job with him and, more importantly, he was willing to let him pursue his studies. Within a couple of days of taking up the new job, Gobind discovered that his boss was a Muslim. After Lahore, this was the first time that Gobind was coming into close contact with a Muslim. In Lahore, most of his friends were Muslims but, where he now lived in Sion, his neighbours were Hindus – Punjabis and Sindhis – who had been displaced from Pakistan. Every house had a story to tell of fragmentation and rupture. It was not easy, in that milieu, to recognise that the Muslims in India had gone through the same hell as the Hindus had in Pakistan. Muslims were not seen as 'people who suffered like we did' but as 'people who caused our suffering'. Gobind felt tormented. He wondered whether he should quit this job. But he had no other offer on hand. So, after a great deal of soul-searching, Gobind decided to continue with Mr. Fazal Patel but keep his distance as an employee would with his employer.

It is not clear whether it was Fazal Patel's zest for life and generosity that won Gobind over or whether it was the fact that, at a deep-rooted level, Gobind felt integrated with the culture of Islam. But, in a few months' time, Gobind and Fazal Patel were more than employee and employer: they shared a warm friendship. Since Gobind was busy with college in the mornings, he often had to meet Fazal saab at his home in Bandra in the evenings. Fazal saab's family was large: he had two daughters and two sons and Gobind was made to feel very much at home when he went there. When the two had finished their work, Fazal saab's wife would be ready with food for them which Gobind relished not just for its taste but for the affection with which it was served. Very soon, Gobind felt very much a part of the Patel household.

About two years later, Fazal saab and Gobind were busy with their work one day, when someone brought bad news: Fazal's brother and his wife had died in a bus accident. The news shattered Fazal. He left immediately for his brother's house. When Gobind next went to Fazal saab's house, there was a new member of the family. Tahira was Fazal saab's niece, the only child of the deceased couple.

Tahira was about nineteen when she came to Bandra.

Her parents' death had shocked her into silence and she hardly uttered a word. For months, she remained silent and Fazal saab got anxious with each passing day. Like all large-hearted, garrulous people he was completely helpless when it came to dealing with silence. Gobind started spending some time trying to talk to Tahira every day and slowly she opened up. It was poetry that Tahira finally responded to and, in turn, Tahira managed to bring the poetry back into Gobind's life. By the middle of 1955, Gobind decided that he wanted to marry Tahira: he was totally in love with her.

Laila knew the story about how her parents met and, in fact, as a child she liked to listen to it over and over again from her grand-aunt. But her dual religious identity was never a problem for Laila: she felt that she had gained from the richness that was implied in this intermingling. She was never in a situation where she had to face the consequences of a mixed religious identity, at least never seriously. A good deal of this comfort with her dual identity had to do with her parents and the kind of life they had made possible for her and, in a way, that was epitomised for Laila in the name that they had chosen for her.

So there were two stories that the name Laila evoked: one which saw the name as emerging from the force of Gobind's unconscious and was rooted in the tragic and violent division of the Hindus and Muslims in the Punjab; the other which saw it as a conscious act of Gobind which had its roots in the coming together of the two communities symbolised in his marriage to Tahira. But there was a third aspect of the name that Laila became aware of.

When she was returning home from college, she saw a couple of boys from the neighbourhood standing near the corner of the street where she lived. When she neared them, one of them started singing a popular song from a recent Hindi movie: 'Laila, O Laila, kaisi tu Laila…' Laila stopped and glared at him and the boy stopped singing. As Laila walked towards home she realised how for this boy the name Laila meant nothing. He was aware of none of the history that she associated with the name. He had stripped it bare of its context and brought it out into the street. Laila was disturbed not because of the boy's innuendo but more because of the fact that it was possible to use the name Laila in a way that did not signify anything and, precisely because of that, she felt that her name had no intrinsic meaning. It was a game, after all, to read meaning – Jungian or otherwise – into the signboards.

In the last year, there had been many such instances. Laila discovered that the meaning she attributed to so many things around her was arbitrary and bore no significance that survived at a deeper level. This was the source of profound agitation for her; it was not an intellectual predicament for Laila but a philosophical condition.

Around this period, she had a recurrent dream. She dreamt that she was reaching out to something which she thought was solid but all that her fingers encountered was thin air.

Laila could not locate the source of her disenchantment with things for there was little she had to complain about in life. She was the only child of doting parents and she loved them very much, in turn. She got everything she wanted. In her early teens, she did quarrel with her parents for, at times, she felt cramped for space and felt that her parents did not allow her to do what she wanted. But these were no more than awkward expressions of the anxiety of transiting into adulthood. She had a large circle of friends of whom some were very close to her; she was passionately interested in poetry and films, she was very fond of reading and loved listening to music. In fact, she was a happy nineteen-year old who had a life to look forward to. And yet Laila was disturbed. Disturbed by the frailty of the human condition, disturbed by the shallowness of relationships, disturbed by the limits of reason, disturbed by the apathy of people and disturbed, above all, by the firm imprint that the absurd had left on all things.

She took to writing poetry to express her angst, but the poetry was more an expression of the condition and not a way out of it. The poetry was penned in her diaries and she hardly let anyone except her closest friends take a look at it. She related to her poetry so intimately that she was not comfortable with others, who did not know her well, reading it. At the same time, she felt that her poetry was not the kind to be of interest to others because she did not write for an audience. It was the expression of her self: a very private, inner world which would have no appeal to others.

The need to express the workings of her inner world was overwhelming in Laila: it was a tune playing incessantly in her head and she wanted to exhaust it through the medium of poetry. She wanted to play the record over and over again till the record, the stylus and the music all disappeared leaving behind a silence. She did not know if that silence really existed at the end of the music or if the music was getting louder in her head each time she played it. The music had to go on, the poetry had to be written.

4

It was at the moment when Laila looked down and the setting sun cast its rays across her face that Prahlad told her that he was in love with her. He blurted out his declaration of love somewhat awkwardly but felt relieved the moment he had uttered the words. It was an emotion that had disturbed Prahlad for weeks now and it was beginning to assume the dimensions of torment. Was love just an emotion – what was it, after all? Prahlad did not know but all he knew was that he had to speak about it to Laila. He did not know how she would react – whether she would reciprocate his love or reject it.

At some level, even Prahlad could see the absurdity in speaking to Laila about his love for he had known her only for a few months. They had first met at the Max Mueller when Ananya and Laila had gone to attend a lecture on Adorno by a visiting German professor. They were struck by the questions Prahlad asked at the end of the lecture. It was obvious that Prahlad was far from satisfied with the answers he got because he was still agitated when he came out of the lecture hall. Ananya and Laila stopped to talk to him and were somewhat surprised to find out that he was not a student but worked in a nearby typesetting firm. They found that they had so much in common with him that it was not long before they became very good friends. Prahlad would meet them for an hour or two when they had finished classes. When the girls went back home, Prahlad would go back to work but think only of Laila and Ananya and his next meeting with them.

When they met, they spent their time discussing literature and philosophy and, while between them, they had an enviable resource of knowledge, the inadequacies that, at times, showed up were offset by their passion for the life of the mind. The intellectual make-up of the page on which they were inscribing their relationship allowed them to define the margins of the relationship quite sharply so that they could keep, or at least pretend to keep, other dimensions out of it. But the compositor who composes the page is not the author who writes the story. The story is not constrained by the picas and points that the compositor measures his text with but spreads unevenly, spills over margins, crosses boundaries and, in short, does everything possible to mess up the neatly constructed world of the compositor.

Ananya did not come to college one day and this was the first time that Prahlad was alone with Laila. He suggested that they go to Samovar – the cafe in Jehangir Art Gallery. Over lunch the two talked, somewhat self-consciously, about Whitman's poetry but the conversation lacked vitality.

It was a different Prahlad that Laila saw after lunch when he started talking about Kamala: his memories of her as a child and her recent death. Laila did not see tears in his eyes but they betrayed a vulnerability she had not noticed before.

Laila also realised why Prahlad's engagement with the world of the intellect was so different from her own. She could not think of ideas, however abstract, without relating it to her own condition. The existential question held centrestage for Laila and ideas which did not connect with this primary question held no appeal for her. From the very beginning, she had realised that Prahlad's approach was different but it was only now that she could see why. Prahlad could engage in metaphysical discussions about death without relating them to his personal experience of it and now when he was actually narrating the story of his mother's death, it was a display of raw emotion unfettered by any philosophical trappings.

Like that day in Samovar, Laila again saw the vulnerable, helpless Prahlad proclaiming his love for her as the sun set over Marine Drive. As he turned his face towards the sea to hide the moistening of his eyes, he wondered what was going through Laila's mind. He wondered whether he had done the right thing because he did not want to lose Laila as a friend.

Laila had looked forward to this moment. She had been curious to find out what it would feel like to be told by someone that she was the object of his love. She had wanted just to experience that one moment. The moment had come rather unexpectedly but its matter-of-factness blunted its edge. It did not have the sharp, heart-piercing quality that millions of pages of poetry had attributed to it. What was she to say to Prahlad? The only thing that was clear was that she would not be able to give him any definite answer: neither an acceptance nor a rejection. She first needed to talk to Prahlad to find out what he meant when he said he loved her and to see how that corresponded with her own idea of love.

Laila was in love with the abstract idea of love. This was a love that she hoped would transform her life. There was a tiny part of her that hoped that love would help her recover meaning in life. But even that hope was transitory because the love that Laila conceived of existed only in a very rarefied, abstract realm. She did not think that she would ever discover anything like it in the real world. For, she argued, that if such a love were possible in any relationship it would have been possible in all relationships. Instead, love got tied down to relationships and could not break free of them. Like everything else it remained conditional and incapable of transcendence.

Thus when Laila finally spoke, it was not a simple refusal or acceptance of his love, as Prahlad had hoped for, but an attempt to analyse love, its meaning, about the possibility of its existence, about the limitations of the manner in which it is actualised in relationships and the general conditions which lead to a yes or a no answer. So was that to be taken as a maybe, Prahlad wondered. He felt like Trishanku suspended between heaven and earth, between the ethereal softness of a 'yes' and the tangible hardness of a 'no'.

It was getting dark and Laila had to leave. Prahlad walked her up to Churchgate station still hoping that she would react to his declaration. That was not to be. He walked back to Nariman Point and sat there staring at the waves lashing the tetrapods. He left an hour later but did not feel like going back to Johnson House. He landed up at the Nehru Planetarium instead where his friends Neila and Nitin worked.

Neila and Nitin had started working together at the Planetarium when they were still in the first year of college. They now had full-time jobs at the Planetarium and stayed back till very late. Prahlad would often go after work to meet them there and the three friends would listen to the music in the sky theatre. This was a very special experience because of the wonderful acoustics but the experience was even more dramatic when Nitin switched on the projector and the night-sky appeared on the hemispherical ceiling. Along the edge of the hemisphere was a silhouette of Bombay which highlighted the landmarks of the city.

As Prahlad lay down near the projector, the sky came on and the first notes of his favourite Led Zeppelin album floated across the theatre. Page and Plant moved into top gear and the music was measuring the diameter of the theatre, of Bombay and of the Universe in one giant leap, doing a non-stop to Andromeda, hitting the Bombay skyline, bouncing off Haji Ali and going straight to the Pleiades cluster. It mingled and mixed with the cluster and turned back to hit Chowpatty beach, spending just enough time there for a *bhel, kulfi* and *paan* and then heading straight for Orion: through these multiple reflections, the music, in the manner of primordial sound, was constructing Bombay as a mirror image of the Universe. And in the middle of all this, supine on the floor, lay Prahlad contemplating the unreality around him in the form of the projection of the sky and the silhouette of the city. Unreal city, unreal sky and unreal the horizon where the sky meets the city! The only thing that seemed painfully real for now was his love for Laila and with his love he was, as Plant was now singing, 'down on the killing floor'.

The planetarium sky usually induced a sense of calm in Prahlad. But, this evening, his inner world was in a turmoil. In this moment of angst he remembered Nietzsche and a line from Thus Spake Zarathustra flashed across his mind: 'What is love? What is creation? What is longing? What is a star?'

*****

Laila could hardly wait till the next morning to meet Ananya and talk to her.

She started off rather abruptly, saying: 'Prahlad says he is in love with me. He told me last evening.'

Ananya put down her cup of tea and stared hard at Laila.

'And?' she said, wanting to know more.

'And what? Aren't you surprised by this?'

'Well, not really. I could see it coming. It was clear from the way he was behaving with you. Don't tell me you didn't expect it! '

'No, no. I didn't,' said Laila, somewhat sharply.

'But what did you say?' Ananya wanted to know.

'What could I say? I mean, do you think I would have been able to say anything to him? I wasn't expecting Prahlad to bring this angle into our relationship. I can only think of him as a friend.'

'Yes, a very good friend,' added Ananya. 'But nothing more than that. Not possible. To begin with, when I close my eyes and think of a man I can be romantically involved with it is not someone like Prahlad. Far from it. I see a mature individual, a man – I see someone in an immaculate white *kurta* and someone with a beard, maybe. Someone who can light up a room with his presence, someone who can lend depth to the poetry he reads with his rich baritone. Prahlad is not all that.'

'You seem to have it all worked out, Ana,' said Laila.

'Don't tell me this is not the kind of person you imagine as your lover.'

'Imagine, maybe. But this is not imagination.'

'Yes, right. The reality is always a little short of all that. But come on, Laila, you can't be serious about Prahlad. I mean he is so naïve when it comes to things like politics. Frankly, I find that bit about him very irritating. He is a very intelligent guy, without any doubt. But it is almost like there are two different people: the Prahlad of the Head and the Prahlad of the Heart. The first of them is remarkable but the second Prahlad is quite pathetic.'

Laila couldn't help interrupting: 'But you can't judge a person just by the limited views on politics he may have. Prahlad may be naïve in these matters but there is so much else to him.'

'Of course, there is. He is intelligent and well-read. But it is all so unconnected with the world we live in. He is dismissive of any kind of political or social action.'

'But, Ana, we also know the limitations of these political movements – we have seen these closely and they are not what they seem to be.'

'Of course, but we have spent a few years working with organisations and with people before we realised their limitations. You cannot just write them off the way he does without knowing the first thing about them. What bothers me about Prahlad is that he reads a lot but it's like water off a duck's back. None of it seems to touch him. Look at the way he relates to poetry. Of course, he has read everything one should read and he has memorised so much of it. But the way he recites poetry is like a child reciting mathematical tables. He does it with just about that much passion and, much like a child, he feels so thrilled at his own ability to memorise and recall.'

Laila was silent, but Ananya went on: 'Even when he writes poetry, it is the same. He spends time trying to get his iambic quadrameters right rather than worrying about his self finding expression in the poetry. In fact, with all this stuff about meter and rhyme, I think he wants to hide rather than reveal himself through his poetry. I don't know but I feel that all the knowledge that he has is unconnected to the person he is. I can't imagine how someone could have read so much and still be so immature. It is like being an encyclopaedia but it's not true knowledge that he possesses.'

'I can see what you are saying, Ana, but, no, you are being too critical of him. I think we tend to look at people through these lenses of politics or poetry or passion. But that is our limitation because people like Prahlad have a different engagement with the world. It is different but that does not make it inferior. Even you talked about how much he knows and the amount he does know is impressive.'

'Yes, that I agree with. And maybe he has a different way of engaging with the world. Maybe. But that is not our way. And for two people to be together there has to be that intellectual consonance.'

'I agree, there has to be an intellectual sharing. But we do share some concerns with Prahald, don't we? I think we have tried to underline our differences with Prahlad without trying to see how similar we are to him. We need to see him differently. But, for me, it is much more than all these issues that you have brought up. I too can see that there is a gulf between the intellectual and emotional sides of Prahlad.

'But I have seen him vulnerable and that makes me want to protect him. Because I feel this need to take care of him, I cannot say no to his love. But I am unable to say yes either because I cannot accept a word called love at face value. I am not sure whether there is any meaning to that word at all and even if love exists I can never be sure that I am the unique object of his love. So I have to continue this conversation with him – have to talk to him about love and the impossibility of it.'

Ananya could not help noticing the finality with which Laila spoke these words.

*****

Tahira was concerned about the withdrawn, faraway look that she had seen recently on Laila's face. She knew that Laila would often go into a shell but it was always possible to draw her out of it. But now, she seemed to be so lost in her world that she did not respond to any of Tahira's attempts.

It was past eight when Laila returned home one evening and her face betrayed the state of exhaustion that she had worked herself into. She had spent three hours walking through the crowded streets of Kalbadevi and Girgaum with Prahlad. Prahlad had to drop off some typeset proofs at the office of one of his clients in Kalbadevi. Laila waited for him as he ran in and out. They had then walked aimlessly, engaged in their discourse about love. By the time Laila reached her home in Juhu, it was late and she was really tired. Tahira was worried about her and tried asking her what the matter was but Laila was in no mood to talk.

When her mother followed her to her room still asking questions, Laila made her sit on the bed and lay down, resting her head in her mother's lap. Tahira undid Laila's hair and gently massaged her head. As Tahira's fingers ran soothingly through her hair, Laila closed her eyes and thought of Prahlad. He must be at least as tired as she was but he was not going back to the comfort of a home at the end of the day. He did not have a mother's lap to rest his head on nor was a Kusum setting a hot dinner on the table. How she wished she could take care of Prahlad!

At the same time, as Laila thought of the events of the past few days, she clenched her fists in frustration as she had hoped that the immediacy of the experience of love would be very different from all her ideas about it. She had hoped for magic: a magic that would transcend language. She had hoped that the man who fell in love with her would look into her eyes and the instant magic would redeem her life. Why is it that only words are available to us when we seek magic, she anguished. But, paradoxically, the only way that Laila could respond to the situation was with words. And it was with words that Laila confronted Prahlad's notions of love.

'So you say you love me. I want to understand what you mean by it,' said Laila, for what was probably the thousandth time.

'What I feel for you – that emotion is love.'

'That doesn't say much. What I am asking you is a more general question: what is is this urge in human beings that makes them identify a set of emotional states as love? I need to understand that.'

'Come on, Laila. You are stating it as though it is a philosophical problem.'

'It is, isn't it? What could be a more important problem in philosophy than knowing what love is – what is this emotion that human beings feel for each other? '

Prahlad felt choked by a lump in his throat. All the wordy constructions which came so easily to him otherwise suddenly deserted him. It was with a struggle that he finally found something to say.

'You know, I am talking about my feelings for you. These you cannot analyse like a problem in science or philosophy. There are things in this world you simply have to experience – you cannot analyse them.'

'But, Prahlad, how do you know what part of the world can be analysed and what is beyond analysis? Where do you draw the line? Even to know where to draw the line you have to first attempt to analyse your experience.'

'No, there is a world of subjective experience which I think you cannot analyse. You can only analyse what is objective.'

'I don't agree. Maybe I don't even know what you mean by analysis. Maybe in the world that science deals with analysis means something different. No, but it can't be. It is about trying to understand the world around us and the world around us is as full of objective facts as subjective details. On the other hand, I think what we often describe as subjective experience has elements of the objective in it. So even that experience needs to be broken down and we have to figure out what it is.

'Let's try to see what your love for me could be in its elemental form,' she continued. 'When you break it down to its elements it is composed of the physical, the emotional and the psychological.'

'Physical?' said Prahlad, meekly disagreeing.

'Yes, come on. Of course, you cannot pretend that at some level it is not a physical attraction. But, coming back to what I was saying, if these were the only elements that love was composed of, then I don't see why you are in love with me. What makes me special? Is it just because we have been spending time together? Some chance brought us together; a combination of biology and psychology then made you fall in love with me.

'Also I cannot understand why it was only you who came up to me and announced your love. In the last few years, I have been close to a few boys from college and none of them fell in love with me. Maybe they did – and didn't tell me. No, I think no one did. And, if love is nothing more than a concatenation of these elements then the puzzle is: why am I not in love with you? Or equivalently, why are you not in love with Ananya?'

'Ananya! Come on, you are being absurd.'

'Yes, Ana. Why not Ana? You spend as much time with her as you do with me. You are very close friends. You may have some intellectual differences with her but so do you with me. In fact, in some ways she thinks a lot more like you do. Then, why me and not Ana?

Over the next couple of weeks, Laila asked him this question over and over again.

Even though she was nowhere in the picture, Ananya had suddenly been brought into the love story. Prahlad, who was already struggling with the strong emotion of love that he felt for Laila, was further traumatised because he simply did not understand why Laila insisted on talking about Ananya. He clumsily attempted to distance himself from Ananya in order to prove to Laila how much he was in love with her. Ananya could gather from Prahlad's behaviour that everything was not all right and she, in turn, started reacting to Prahlad. To complete the triangle, Laila felt she had only Ananya to talk to about her relationship with Prahlad. So she talked endlessly to Ananya about what Prahlad felt for her, about what she thought of love and how she had brought Ananya into the picture.

Ananya realised that over-riding all her reservations about Prahlad, was the possessiveness she felt for Laila as a friend. Ananya did not want Laila to reciprocate Prahlad's love because she would then be left out in the cold.

A few weeks later, Laila and Prahlad were back on Marine Drive for a walk. It was the time around sunset but the sky was cloudy and it was darker than usual. When they were halfway down Marine Drive, the sky opened up and it began to pour and they had to sprint across the road, through the rush-hour traffic, to get to the other side.

They took shelter under the parapet of a building. As they stood there huddled together, the force of the rain, the gentleness of the cool breeze that was blowing across their faces, the beauty of the last light that had not yet given way to darkness were all working their magic on them. Even as Laila realised how close to each other they were standing and attempted to move back a bit, Prahlad bent over and kissed her. The kiss was no ordinary kiss. It was Prahlad's first attempt to transcend the language of their relationship which was so bound up in words, an attempt to seek a resolution which words had not helped him find. Laila's initial reaction was that of surprise but her instinct told her to experience the moment fully.

When they finally moved apart, the rain had eased a bit. Prahlad, who had taken a small detour out of time, came crashing back to earth. He was anxious to gauge Laila's reaction. Laila didn't wait to talk to him but headed straight back to the station.

*****

When they met the next day, Laila did not show in any way that she was upset with what Prahlad had done. He felt more reassured. The kiss had changed things a bit. Since Laila had not reacted adversely to him after the incident she had, at least to an extent, accepted his love. Laila felt that she was somehow drawn closer to Prahlad – was it that a tiny ray of that 'magic beyond words' that she was so desperately seeking had shone through the clouds of disbelief?

Ananya could sense that Prahlad had reverted to his older self and was more relaxed with her. But things had changed only that wee bit. Prahlad was still struggling with the reality of unreciprocated love, Laila was still seeking the meaning of love as if she was seeking the meaning of life itself and Ananya still did not think that Prahlad was suited for Laila.

5

Mr. Nadkarni was pleased. The work on the catalogue for the Machine Tools exhibition was completed and the pages had already gone to the printer. He had been worried when taking on the assignment because he was not sure Omega would be able to deliver the catalogue in a short time. But Prahlad had put in a tremendous amount of work and, particularly, in the last week he had spent all day and night at the office with virtually no break. Now that the work was done Nadkarni was happy to give Prahlad a couple of days' leave.

Ananya and Laila had been away in Gujarat on a college educational tour so they hadn't met Prahlad for more than two weeks. It was about three in the afternoon on a Friday when they met and they decided to go to Wayside Inn, a place they loved going to because it allowed them to sit for hours at the tables by the window and look at the world outside. But today they entered the restaurant to find all the window tables occupied and one of them, in fact, by Ashok Bhende. Bhende was a friend of Deepa's and he waved out to Ananya. Ananya went up to him and gave him a warm hug.

'So, how're you?' asked Bhende. 'Where's Deepa? I haven't seen her in a long time.'

'Ma has gone to Delhi but she will be back in a couple of days,' said Ananya.

'And how's college? What are you young people up to these days?' he asked, looking at Laila and Prahlad.

'O, sorry not to have introduced them,' said Ananya. 'Laila is with me in college and Prahlad works at a typesetters' down the road.'

'Yes, I know him well,' said Bhende surprising Prahlad.

'Why don't you pull up some chairs and join us? ' said Bhende.

He was with a friend, a dark man with grey hair and bright eyes.

'My turn to apologise for not introducing my friend. Meet God,' he said, gesturing with his hand in an exaggerated manner.

The friend looked a bit embarrassed and said in a low voice, 'Hi, I'm Dorai.'

'G.O. Doraiswamy!' said Bhende, trying to explain his joke. 'We have called him God ever since we have known him. Well, in this city if you have to find God, you can only find him in Wayside Inn,' he added, laughing at his own clever line.

Prahlad was amused to see a Bhende very different from the one he had known.

Bhende said in a more serious tone, 'Dorai is a writer.'

'What kind of writing?' asked Laila, suddenly becoming interested in the conversation.

'I am happy to hear you call me a writer, Ashok,' said Dorai.

Turning towards Laila, he said, 'I used to be a freelance journalist. As for my writing, I attempted fiction but I have given up writing now. In my younger days, I wrote quite a lot but never published anything.'

'Well, it is only writers like me who have to publish and make a living out of writing. Your father made sure that you don't have to work for a living. So why would you publish?' said Bhende.

'I am happy that he didn't publish,' he said, winking at the girls, 'otherwise we less talented writers and poets would not have stood a chance.'

'You haven't changed, Ashok,' said Dorai, smiling.

Ananya couldn't help warming to his smile. There was something about Dorai she liked.

'It is amazing,' said Bhende, again assuming a serious manner. 'I was sitting here in Wayside Inn reminiscing about the old days and the afternoons that I spent here with friends and Dorai walked in through the door. I was seeing him after twelve years.'

'Thirteen,' said Dorai, correcting him.

'So, where were you all this time?' asked Bhende.

'Well, that's a long story. I will tell you all later,' said Dorai.

Laila got back to the point in the conversation that had gripped her interest.

'Why did you give up writing?' she asked.

Dorai's eyes had a deep intensity about them.

'I guess it was disenchantment with writing. I took to writing because I perceived it as a powerful medium. But slowly I found it lacked potency – at least, the kind of writing I was engaged in and the disenchantment started growing.'

'But did you not want to write about that disenchantment itself?' Laila asked, echoing some of her own attitudes to writing.

'I guess that is what it ends up being – as writers we merely chronicle the human predicament but are in no position to change it. I was not going to accept that. I wanted it to deliver the transformation and change that it once promised me,' said Dorai.

'But, by transformation, do you mean trying to change the system itself?' Ananya interjected.

'No, not really. I want to deal with lives and want to feel them tangibly.'

'Then, what do you think transformation means? Does it refer to an inner state? That I find is often nothing more than a shift in perspective,' said Laila.

'No, for too long I struggled with all these notions of an inner life and the outer world, the self and the other. I am a writer and I want to return to the potency of writing. I want to discover the power of the word and I believe now, after my thirteen year-long quest, that such a form of writing indeed exists.'

'What kind of writing are you thinking of?' asked Bhende, his curiosity aroused.

'I will tell you about it sometime, Ashok. But it is not

the kind of writing you will find interesting; no, you will probably think it is not even possible. The best we can do is to meet like this over beer and talk of the old days and pretend they were, indeed, the good old days. Then we can talk of some writer from some obscure land whose works we have not even read and then get down to our own exciting world of writers in the city and discuss who is scratching whose back to get which work published,' said Dorai.

Dorai's manner was not rude but his tone was such that an awkward silence descended on the table.

Bhende drained the last bit of beer from his glass and announced that he had to leave and Dorai left after him. Laila and Ananya were intrigued by the strange man they had met but Prahlad was unusually quiet. Even in the short time that they had spent with Dorai, it was obvious to Prahlad that he had caught Laila's interest and Prahlad could view no object of Laila's interest with compassion. It was a remarkably democratic manner in which Prahlad's jealousy operated: it chose its object with scant regard to age or sex. In spite of his age, Dorai was charming and Prahlad could see how both Laila and Ananya had taken a liking to him immediately on meeting him and that was enough reason for Prahlad to take an immediate dislike to him.

It wasn't long before they met Dorai again this time on Rampart Row as he was stepping out of Chetana Book Store with a pile of books under his arm. Soon they were sitting huddled together over pots of tea at Samovar. The girls were talking to Dorai quite excitedly but Prahlad again was quiet and this did not escape Dorai's attention. Dorai made an attempt to direct the conversation towards Prahlad. In their first meeting, he remembered it being mentioned that Prahlad worked at a typesetters.

'Is it a linotype machine you work on or is it one of these modern phototypesetting machines? ' he asked.

Prahlad realised that Dorai was not a stranger to the world of printing.

'I am quite fascinated by typography,' Dorai said. 'I still remember the first time I saw a linotype machine at work when I was about your age. That lines of text could appear from the molten, formless liquid that bubbled in the pot was like magic to me.'

'Yes, it is quite fascinating', agreed Prahlad.

'Well, to me the shining, black metal form of the linotype was not that of a machine but of a black goddess who was creating lines of physical metal from apparently innocuous keystrokes. When the page had been printed the line would be dissolved in the pot again and disappear and merge with the formless. I thought that this was the metaphor for the lila of creation and dissolution,' said Dorai.

'That is an interesting connection,' said Ananya. 'I think it is a riveting metaphor.'

'Only now, I think that I was wrong,' said Dorai to confuse Ananya. 'This was no metaphor. The game that the goddess is engaged in is that of the creation and destruction of the words. Typesetting is not just a metaphor – it is the universe. Words are primary and the worlds are only a consequence.'

As he paused for a moment in the course of this monologue, Prahlad said, 'You don't really mean that the world emerges from the play of words, do you?'

'Yes, I am convinced about the primacy of words. In fact, anything that exists is dependent on words for its existence. The mistake lies in thinking that there is a pre-existent world of objects out there and that we then attribute names to these objects', said Dorai in a emphatic tone.

He continued,'The creation and dissolution of the world is the creation and destruction of words. The Sanskrit word matrika means the letter of the alphabet and also 'little mother' – the atom from which everything emerges. These matrikas are also strung as a garland of skulls around the neck of Kali. These are the fifty letters of the alphabet and Kali wears it around her neck to tell us that typography is the secret of the universe and that with words everything emerges and with them everything dissolves. It is for this reason again that typefaces are called fonts, or even better founts, for they are the founts from which the world springs.'

'I don't think I understand what you are saying,' said Ananya but before she could continue talking, Dorai interrupted her saying,

'Yes, you won't. I didn't at one time and it has taken me thirteen long years to come to this knowledge.'

'For me, to think that words can create a world is fascinating as an idea. But I can't conceive of the world that way,' said Laila.

'Precisely,' said Prahlad. 'If what you are saying is true then two sets of contradictory words will bring into existence two sets of contradictory worlds.'

'There is nothing that tells us that such contradictions don't exist,' said Dorai. There was no hint of the impatience in his voice that he had displayed when talking to Bhende the other day.

'But what you are saying is only metaphorical, surely? With the reference to Kali and all that,' said Ananya.

Dorai looked at Ananya without saying anything for a while and then he said, 'It is not a metaphor. It is my experience.'

With that he got up and left.

'He is so strange,' said Ananya, breaking the silence of a few minutes.

'I don't know if he is strange. But his is a very different way of thinking,' said Laila.

'If you can call that thinking,' said Prahlad. He was getting impatient with what he felt was Dorai's rambling. 'I didn't see any logic in what he was saying. It was all so vague and deliberately so.'

'Well, I don't know if it was logic that I was missing but it all seemed so unsubstantiated,' said Ananya.

'I don't know. I think he sees it from a different perspective and he feels that his experience has offered him the substantiation he needs. I wonder what his experience has been. I am really keen to find out who Dorai is, what he has gone through and where he was when he disappeared for thirteen years,' said Laila.

The following Thursday when they met Bhende in Wayside Inn again it was no coincidence. Laila had been burning with curiosity to find out more about Dorai and the only person they could talk to was Bhende. Luckily, Bhende was alone and they sat down to talk to him. After a few pleasantries had been exchanged, Laila came directly to the point.

'Your friend, Dorai – tell us more about him,' she said.

'So you want to know more about God! See God does this to people. He reveals only so much of himself at a time so that people's curiosity in him is kept alive,' said Bhende, laughing. 'Well, I have known Dorai for years now. Almost twenty-five years. Before he mysteriously disappeared, we were all part of a group of writers and poets who met regularly, often in this very restaurant.'

'And when he disappeared, you have no idea where he went?' asked Ananya.

'All I know was that he had secured an assignment to write on Tamil Nadu for a foreign magazine and he went down to Madras to do research for this work. I still remember the party we had the day before he left,' said Bhende, trying hard to remember who were present at that party.

'Do you remember if he was normal at the party? Did he show any sign that he would disappear?' asked Laila.

'Yes, I remember clearly. Dorai was his usual self and none of us could have guessed that he wouldn't come back. In fact, I remember he had a couple of assignments to attend to on his return and he left for Madras promising these people that he would return in three months' time.'

'And when he didn't come back, did you and the others not get worried?' asked Ananya.

'Well, we all knew that Dorai had the spirit of adventure in him. We thought he had discovered something that had again caught his fancy and had decided to stay longer. Except we never thought it would be so long and neither did he get in touch with any of us when he was away all this while.'

'Did he not have any family here in Bombay?' asked Prahlad.

'No, Dorai was living alone and he still does. He has this wonderful flat on Marine Drive – huge and sea-facing – and he lives there all by himself. His father was a Tamilian who had settled down in Bombay in the early thirties. He was a very successful man and on the Board of Directors of several companies. He left his entire wealth to his son which included this flat in Marine Drive.'

'And Dorai's mother?' asked Prahlad.

'Dorai lost his mother very early in life. I think he was just eight or nine when she died. He had an aunt to take care of him but she also died when he was in his twenties. And his wife . . .'

'Is he married?' asked Laila, astonished.

'He was. For about three years. But they couldn't get along and they were divorced. I learnt later that she had gone off to London where she married again. So there he was in his mid-thirties, with no parents, no wife, no children, no job but with a lot of money. So what was to stop him from disappearing one fine day?'

'But you have no idea what he did in these years? He has not spoken to you about it?' asked Prahlad.

'No and I doubt he will. From his attitude I gathered he was not very keen to discuss the story of his adventures with me.'

There was not much else that Bhende knew about Dorai. For almost three weeks after this meeting with Bhende, they did not meet Dorai and almost lost all interest in him. One evening, they decided to do the ritual walk along the sea at Marine Drive. It was early evening and the sun was still some distance above the horizon but the walkers and joggers were already on the seaface for their round of evening exercises. The three friends decided to walk towards Chowpatty beach. As they neared the beach, the sun started moving closer to the horizon and the sky was covered with a resplendent red. Ananya and Laila wanted to watch the sunset, so they sat by the sea to soak in what remained of the evening.

They were so immersed in the beauty of the evening that they almost did not hear a low, deep voice behind them saying, 'Hello!'

Dorai stood behind them, flashing the smile that Ananya loved.

'So you are in my neighbourhood today,' he said.

They stood there talking for a while and then Dorai invited them home. Dorai's flat was a sprawling Bombay flat from the thirties and its size was matched only by the classy décor. Furniture of Burma teak, Chola bronzes, Tanjore paintings and antiques from different parts of the world filled the drawing room. But the study was much more impressive. It was a large room with shelves of books all along the four walls and a comfortable seating arrangement in the middle of a carpeted floor. There were a few thousand books on those shelves on literature, history, art, music and philosophy. Laila could see Prahlad's jaw literally drop as he saw the collection of books. In fact, it was for the first time in the weeks after they had met Dorai that Prahlad felt admiration for him as he would for anyone who possessed such a collection of books.

'You have a beautiful home,' Ananya said, after they had recovered from the overwhelming impact of the study. 'But how did you take care of this place when you were away for all those years?'

'I have Pandyan and his wife, Padma, who live here and take care of everything around this place,' said Dorai.

'Pandyan has worked in our house from when I was very small and he loves and takes care of this place as his own.'

Padma came in with hot cups of coffee.

'Why would you leave such a place and go elsewhere?' asked Prahlad, still feeling intoxicated by the books.

'Well, I didn't plan to go. It simply happened,' said Dorai.

'And are you going to tell us where you went and what you did for all these years?' asked Laila, grabbing her chance to get to the nub of the story.

'The coffee is getting cold,' said Dorai, pointing out to the cups. He picked up one cup himself and settled down in an armchair. 'I went to Thanjavur – that is where my family hails from. I hadn't travelled much in that part of the country before I went there for this assignment I was working on. I thought that the assignment was a good excuse to discover the land of my ancestors but I ended up discovering a lot more.'

'And what was that?' Laila asked.

'Well, it will take a long time to tell you about my experiences. Some other time, maybe,' said Dorai.

'Can we drop in again?' asked Prahlad, excitedly. He was thrilled with the prospect of exploring Dorai's library.

'Yes, of course,' said Dorai. 'I prefer to have my mornings to myself. But you can come any time in the afternoon.'

Looking at Prahlad, he said, 'And if it is my library that will bring you here, then do make yourself at home even if I am not around. Pandyan and Padma are here the whole day and I will leave appropriate instructions with them.'

Over the next few weeks, the three friends frequented Dorai's flat very often. For Prahlad, the library was the primary goal of these visits but the girls spent their time talking to Dorai when he was free.

Ananya was gradually beginning to realise that Laila was not wrong in her judgement of Dorai. Even though she was still not fully comfortable with Dorai's references to the occult, Ananya had begun to appreciate that he was genuine even when he was talking about these matters. It was just that she did not connect with him on any of these issues but then there was so much else they could talk about.

Laila looked forward to the conversations with Dorai not only for the literature and poetry they discussed with him but more for the references he made to this other world of his experience. She was not quite sure what word she would use to describe this world but she did not think that it could be described by the word 'occult'. But whatever it was, it really caught Laila's imagination.

Prahlad would also join the girls in their conversations with Dorai, partly because he did not want to appear to be rude to his host and partly because that gave him some more time with Laila. He was usually quiet and though he often did not agree with what Dorai was saying, he would wait till later when he was alone with Laila and Ananya to put forward a refutation of Dorai's position. Ananya would tease him saying that it was not clear whether he was refuting Dorai because he disagreed with Dorai or because he saw Laila agreeing with Dorai. While he didn't like Ananya saying so Prahlad knew deep inside that there was an element of truth in what she was saying.

In the weeks that they got to know Dorai better, it was becoming clear that he had stayed in Thanjavur all those years because of his encounter with this other world – the world that the girls didn't even have a descriptive phrase for. Each time they talked to Dorai they got a glimpse of this strange world which he seemed to have intimate access to. At times, when Dorai talked about this world they found him incoherent and even Laila, the most sympathetic of the three, would get impatient with him. But more often his descriptions were eloquent, possessing a rich texture and embellished with what seemed like metaphorical ornamentation, and would sound like poetry to their ears. Yet, it was only a very blurred picture of Dorai's world that Laila and Ananya were able to put together.

'I have something to show you,' said Dorai, one afternoon. 'In the first phase of my thirteen years away from home, I was writing quite regularly. It was a chronicle of my experiences as of the memories that events and places evoked. I hadn't taken a look at it for years and it was only recently that I had another look at these pages. I would like you three to take a look at it and see how you respond to it.'

This was quite unexpected and the girls looked at each other excitedly. Dorai had placed a thick notebook on the table in front of him.

'This book is precious to me so please handle it carefully,' he said, handing it over to Laila.

As Laila stepped out of Dorai's house, she wondered why Dorai had entrusted the book to her. They barely knew him but for some reason he wanted them to read the book. As she held the book in her hands she felt an excitement run through her being. She could hardly wait to find out what the book contained.

6

Probably the only way in which Dorai continued to identify with Gudalur was through the initial in his name. Gudalur, the G in Dorai's name, was the village his family originally belonged to; or put differently, some decades ago the village of Gudalur had belonged to his family. Gudalur was a village on the banks of the Kaveri in Thanjavur district.

Dorai had come to the town of Thanjavur to carry out research for an article a German magazine had commissioned him to write. The magazine wanted him to do a piece on Tamil Nadu and highlight how this ancient land was coming to terms with modernity and Dorai had to particularly concentrate on Madras, Madurai and Thanjavur. He had already spent a month each in Madras and Madurai and this was the last month of his research which he would spend in Thanjavur. He found the town fascinating even more so than Madurai and it had to probably do with the fact that his own roots were enmeshed in the rich culture of this place.

While in Thanjavur, he had taken time off to visit his ancestral village. Gudalur was not very far from the main town of Thanjavur and it had taken him only about an hour and a half to reach here. It took him more or less the same amount of time to walk around the village – through its main street, through the smaller lanes in the periphery, to the Shiva temple and along the Kaveri. He walked around as a stranger in his own village for it was the very first time after the age of six that he had come to Gudalur. As the breeze blew across Dorai's face, it carried with it the rich smell of the land that had once belonged to them.

Dorai's grandfather had been a much revered person in the village and in the surrounding district, but from what Dorai had gleaned from family accounts, it was fear rather than reverence that Vaidyanatha Iyer evoked in people. Vaidyanatha Iyer was an authoritarian person and possessed of an insatiable appetite for the good things of life. His volatile temper made it a lethal mix. Nevertheless, the villagers believed that beneath the tough exterior, was a soft, childlike aspect to him. Vaidyanatha Iyer had acquired the reputation of being a just person and, indeed, became the sole dispenser of justice in the village.

No eyebrows were raised when people became aware of his relationship with the temple dancer: it was thought to be becoming of a man of his stature and this relationship was just one more in a long list of such relationships that Vaidyanatha Iyer was involved in. However, when the woman transgressed the limits of decency and, while dancing in the annual procession had the audacity to turn and show her back to the village elders, Vaidyanatha Iyer had meted out instant justice with his whip. In the following year, he spent thousands of rupees for the treatment of the dancer's ailing mother. The temple dancer's story was often cited as an example of Vaidyanatha Iyer's noble and just behaviour.

As a young man, Vaidyanathan was keen on becoming a lawyer and was studying for his B.A. degree in the nearby town of Trichinopoly. But he had to give up his studies and return to Gudalur when his father took ill. His father died and Vaidyanathan had to take charge of the land that was his ancestral wealth.

But the three years in Trichy had left its mark on Vaidyanathan and, even as he tried to adapt to the life of a landlord like his ancestors, he had been transformed by English education in his stint at college. He had cultivated the friendship of a couple of Englishmen in Trichy and attempted to learn more about their ways.

When he heard about the new art of photography, he was so excited that he went all the way to Madras to buy himself a camera. He set up a small dark-room in his Trichy home and spent time learning chemistry which he thought would help him further his new passion.

On returning to the village after his father's death, Vaidyanathan found little time to keep in touch with the exciting developments in the world outside but, in spite of that, he tried to keep himself abreast of the events as best as he could. He found village life stifling sometimes because he had no one to share these interests with. He had been married to his second cousin, Meenakshi, at a very young age though it was only after he returned to the village that they started living together as man and wife. When they had children, Vaidyanathan found himself cloistered even more in the simple life that Gudalur could offer. But soon his domesticity became a licence to lose himself in the simple pleasures that cards and women offered him.

This tranquil rural existence was punctuated by Vaidyanathan's violent outbursts, with his retinue of servants being the most preferred targets though Meenakshi also had to bear the brunt at times. But with his daughter, Dharami, and his son, Omkareswaran, Vaidyanathan was always gentle and would calm down in their presence even when he was having one of his mad fits of rage. Vaidyanathan was a loving father even though he did not always know how to express his love for his children. Conventions in Gudalur dictated that there was only so much feeling that a father could demonstrate towards his children.

Moreover, even though he loved both his children dearly, Vaidyanathan could not afford to be soft with his son; he had to make sure that the boy understood the demands that transiting into manhood would place on him. But secretly Vaidyanathan hoped his son would settle down to a life in the city and discover the world the way he himself would have liked to. In his aspirations for his daughter, he was much more the conventional zamindar wishing for her to be married into a good family at an early age.

If he dreamt of an early marriage for his daughter, Vaidyanathan had the means to realise that dream. Dharami was only twelve when she was married to Natesa Iyer's only son, Swaminathan. Vaidyanathan could not have hoped for a better family for his daughter to get married into.

Moreover, Natesa Iyer's home was in the nearby village of Nemam and he could have her visit home whenever he wanted to see her. Meenakshi had been concerned that the boy was not keeping very good health and, when she dared to voice this at the time of the engagement, Vaidyanathan had silenced her with a look. Later, in one of those rare, tender moments, Vaidyanathan tried explaining to Meenakshi how fortunate they were in securing this match with Natesa Iyer's son and how the groom, who was only fourteen, was sure to grow up into a strong and healthy man.

When Dharami came of age two years later, she was sent to her husband's home in a procession the likes of which the villages in that region had never seen. However, Swaminathan's health only worsened with age and became a cause for concern for everyone around him. Dharami bore five years of an unconsummated marriage taking care of her ailing husband and when at the end of the five-year period Swaminathan died, Dharami was numbed into a lifelong silence.

Vaidyanathan never forgave himself for what he had done to his daughter. To see his dear Dharami with a tonsured head and in widow's garments tortured his being. But, just like he had found no way to express his gentler emotions, Vaidyanathan did not know how to express his grief. His unexpressed emotions found an outlet, as always, in violence and his assistants dreaded every moment that they spent with him.

Meenakshi was getting concerned about herself and her children. She felt that it would be a good idea for her to visit her brother for a few weeks. She planned to take Dharami and Omkareswaran with her. Her brother, Ramaseshan, was a senior official in the Port Trust in Madras and Meenakshi felt that her fifteen-year old son would benefit from the time he would spend with his uncle. Meenakshi was hesitant to make this suggestion to her husband because she knew that her husband and her brother did not get along very well. Vaidyanathan and Ramaseshan had been classmates at the National College in Trichinopoly and Vaidyanathan had been the better student. But it was eventually Ramaseshan who made it to a life in the city and Vaidyanathan could never get over the jealousy and rancour he felt for his brother-in-law.

Moreover, in a tradition where the word mama evoked collective memories of Shakuni and Kamsa, the maternal uncle was doomed by mythology to be the villain. Every action of the mama would be scrutinised, every word of his critically analysed and every mistake of his would find a place in the family's treasury of stories. The wife, torn between devotion for her husband and affection for her brother, would have to prove her loyalty to 'her house' by staunchly defending her husband. This story was simultaneously unfolding in a million different homes in the country: Meenakshi's was just one instance of it.

When Meenakshi finally mustered the courage to ask Vaidyanathan whether she could go with the children to Madras, even she could not have guessed that Vaidyanathan would react as violently and angrily as he did. The brutality of Vaidyanathan's reaction stunned Meenakshi: in fact, she found his violent expression so unwarranted that, for the very first time, she found it necessary to question the nature of his reaction. It was a woman saying, 'Enough is enough'.

Vaidyanathan felt deeply insulted by his wife's resistance and he would brook none of it. He couldn't have his wife do this to him and that too in front of his children. He rose from his chair and started thrashing her. Meenakshi pulled her knees up, curling foetus-like to avoid the blows but Vaidyanathan carried on savagely.

**

The idea of a soul must have first occurred to a woman. It is only someone whose body has been inhumanly brutalised who would seek to peg her identity on something other than the body.

**

Dharami and Omkareswaran watched in horror. At one point, Omkareswaran darted forward and held his father's powerful wrist even as it was moving downwards to inflict more pain on his mother's body. As the young boy struggled to subdue his father's hand, his father turned around and looked at him, shocked at his son's act of defiance. The next moment Vaidyanathan's left hand swung and landed with a sickening thud on his son's temples. The son reeled under the impact of the blow and fell down in a swoon.

Vaidyanathan staggered out of the room leaving Meenakshi and Dharami to take care of the unconscious boy.

When Omkareswaran regained consciousness, his body was hot with fever and he babbled in a delirium. His mother and sister could make no sense of his utterances but he continued talking. It was not until the third morning that his fever subsided but his body was weak and he could hardly get out of bed.

A week later, when he had recovered, Omkareswaran took the night train to Madras. His eyes filled with tears when the train moved out of the platform and he knew he would miss his mother, Dharami and his friends in the village. But he could not think of continuing to live in his father's house after what had happened. He did not have to run away from home as he had planned to, because he had Meenakshi's consent.

Meenakshi could think of no better plan than to send Omkareswaran to Ramaseshan in Madras. For years now, she had been putting away whatever money came her way into an earthen bowl in the kitchen. This money was now useful and as she thrust the money and a bag of sweets into Omkareswaran's hand, she invoked the blessings of all the gods she could think of with prayers and entreaties to them to take care of her son.

If years later Meenakshi could have visited her son in Bombay, she would have been convinced that her prayers had, indeed, been heard. Even a mother's love could not have asked for more. Omkareswaran had studied and trained with a Dutch company in Madras to become a talented engineer. He rose very quickly in his job and the rise necessitated his move to Bombay. In 1934, Omkareswaran moved with his wife, Maitreyi, and his two-year old son, Doraiswamy, to a comfortable flat near Five Gardens in Matunga.

Four years later, Omkareswaran returned home one evening to find a distraught Maitreyi with a telegram in hand, which had brought in the tidings of her mother-in-law's death. As Omkareswaran read the telegram, Maitreyi held him and cried inconsolably. She had been married for ten years but had not once met her parents-in-law. Omkareswaran had not returned to Gudalur after he left the village at the age of 15.

His uncle, Ramaseshan, would periodically give him news of his mother and Dharami but Omkareswaran had still not forgiven his father and never asked after him. When Ramaseshan had arranged his marriage to Maitreyi he tried to persuade Omkareswaran to invite his parents and his sister for the wedding. But Omkareswaran did not want his father to attend his wedding and so none of his family was invited. Neither were Meenakshi and Vaidyanathan present to celebrate the birth of their grandson four years later. Maitreyi knew her parents-in-law only from the photographs she had seen at Ramaseshan's house. She had tried hard to convince Omkareswaran to re-establish contact with his parents but he was unrelenting.

Omkareswaran and his family could reach Gudalur only three days after Meenakshi's death. A male cousin had lit Meenakshi's pyre and Omkareswaran did not even get a last glimpse of her. He had to stay back, however, for the thirteenth day rituals. The first evening that he was there, he exchanged no more than a furtive glance with his father. The next afternoon, as he sat in the courtyard, his father came and sat next to him. Vaidyanathan was 59 now, but his face was creased in a manner which made him look a lot older. His frame, however, was as broad as it was in his youth.

Omkareswaran couldn't help feeling that his father had changed in a way that had little to do with his age. There was none of the aggression and the violence that had characterised him in his younger days. There was a silence in him now which was indicative of peace. When Omkareswaran had spoken to Dharami that morning, she had talked to him of the slow transformation that had come over their father. After his son had left home, Vaidyanathan had become something of a recluse. He avoided the company of people and would be cloistered in his room. He would only step out of the house in the mornings to go to the river and the temple.

After a year, Vaidyanathan met a yogi who was visiting Gudalur and who offered to initiate him into the techniques of meditation. Having mastered these techniques, Vaidyanathan spent hours lost in meditation. He would wake up every morning before sunrise and, having taken a dip in the Kaveri, he would settle down in the silence of his inner quarters meditating till almost noon. His lifestyle went through a remarkable transformation: he ate frugally, avoided the use of any form of luxury and became even-tempered. He spoke softly and gently and, in fact, spoke very little except during his evening discourses.

The discourses started as small, informal gatherings but, over the years, Vaidyanathan's reputation as a spiritual person spread among the villagers of Gudalur and the evening discourses had started attracting fairly large crowds of people. Vaidyanathan would speak, in these meetings, of stories from the epics or from the religious texts. Legends of Vaidyanathan's intuitive powers had gained wide currency and the people who flocked to these discourses would stay back to discuss their individual problems and seek his predictions of their futures.

Omkareswaran listened patiently, but he was amused and exasperated when she finished her story. He did not quite believe what he had heard about his father. He was willing to concede, at the very most, that his father had changed his ways and was a calmer human being now. But he was angry that people had made him into some kind of a saint invested with spiritual powers. Were there really so many people who, in spite of knowing his father and the philandering ways of his past, thought of him as a saint?

All these thoughts flashed through Omkareswaran's mind as his father sat next to him. For the briefest of moments, he wondered whether he was being unjust to his father. Was he right in doubting his father's spiritual attainment? It was Vaidyanathan who broke the silence.

'When do you plan to leave?' he asked, in a halting voice. 'I hope you are here till the thirteenth day.'

'Yes, I will be here till the ceremonies are over.'

The words seem to stick in Omkareswaran's throat. It was difficult for him to bring words to a relationship shrouded in years of angry silence.

'I am happy to know that,' the older man said. 'It is an important day – the thirteenth day. Not just from your mother's point of view but also mine.'

He saw the puzzled look on his son's face and added, 'It is on the thirteenth day after your mother's death that I will cast away this mortal frame.'

'What? ' exclaimed Omkareswaran, incredulously.

'Yes, it is ordained that I will die then,' said Vaidyanathan, with a distant look in his eyes.

Omkareswaran felt the bile well up in his throat. He got up and walked away but his manner conveyed to his father his level of disbelief. How could his father allow people to revere him as a saint? How could he be so presumptuous as to predict the day of his own death? This was more than Omkareswaran could handle.

Moreover, this entire sham called astrology was something that Omkareswaran truly detested. Right from a young age, he was sceptical about the truth-claims of astrology but later, especially during his days in Presidency College in Madras, this scepticism found a more solid base in a scientific world-view. Omkareswaran had become a member of the science club in Presidency College and regularly attended its meetings. It was only through the talks and discussions in the science club that Omkareswaran began to appreciate that science is not simply a collection of interesting but isolated facts but a world-view and probably the only consistent and universal world-view available to us. It was not possible then to subscribe to a scientific vision of the world and also dabble in religion or spirituality. Astrology, in particular, Omkareswaran felt, was the most dubious of all systems, because either its 'predictions' were not precise or they were so specific that their claims could never be established in general.

The fact that Omkareswaran was now reminiscing about his Presidency College science club was not a coincidence. It had very much to do with the kind of prediction his father had made: a prediction of his own death.

'Is an extreme prediction of this kind sensible?' Omkareswaran had asked in one of his science club talks.

Prof. John Holt, who was their physics teacher and the founder of the science club, had encouraged Omkareswaran to present a talk on science and astrology. In the course of his research for the talk, Omkareswaran chanced upon a book on the Renaissance mathematician, Jerome Cardan, who was famous for his work on the solutions of cubic and quartic equations. Other than being a mathematician, Cardan was a physician of repute, a professional gambler, chess-player and astrologer.

Omkareswaran was amazed by the story he read. So many vicissitudes were clearly more than one life could bear. There were stories about Cardan's illegitimate birth;

his changing fortunes driving him to gambling over and over again; one son was a murderer and another a gambler always on the wrong side of the law; a daughter who was a prostitute and died of syphilis; his trouble with the authorities because of his outspoken nature; his fame as the greatest physician of Europe for effecting several miraculous cures; and the controversy with the Church for casting the horoscope of Christ.

While Omkareswaran could only admire the mathematical genius of Cardan, he loathed Cardan, the cheat, the conman, the card-player. In this image of Cardan, he could see his father and this made him loathe Cardan even more. From his reading of Cardan's life, he suspected that Cardan must also have been a womaniser like his father. The book didn't say so explicitly but which Renaissance intellectual was not a womaniser! But what shocked him most about Cardan (and to this aspect of Cardan he devoted most of his science-club talk) was what he interpreted as Cardan's perverse nature. This had to do with the legend of Cardan predicting the date of his own death. Cardan, indeed, died on the predicted date and the legend was that he killed himself.

Within the world-view Omkareswaran had grown to accept, this was the only way Cardan's prediction could have come true: through suicide. If he had died a natural death on the day predicted then Omkareswaran would have called it a coincidence.

In either case, for Omkareswaran, it was perversion: perversion of the individual who used suicide to 'prove' the system of astrology, or it was the perversion of nature which uses something called coincidence, something that defies rational explanation.

Omkareswaran's friend, Sundaram, was a student of literature in Presidency College. He was a gifted writer and was already making a name for himself by publishing short stories in journals and newspapers. Sundaram could only laugh at the way his friend was agonising over Cardan.

He argued with him, trying to get Omkareswaran out of his scientific strait-jacket. If Cardan died on the date he predicted, Sundaram felt, then his prediction should be taken to have been verified even if Cardan had taken his own life. For if it were not ordained that he would die that day, then such circumstances would have arisen as to prevent the act of suicide. Omkareswaran wilted under the force of his friend's irrationality but had no good answer.

Sundaram returned the next day with an obvious air of elation about him. He had spent the night writing a short story based on Cardan's life but written in the manner of a tale out of Hindu mythology. The more Sundaram had thought about the story of Cardan's death, the more convinced he had become of revisiting it with his imagination.

The gist of the story was: Sage Kardana was a renowned astrologer who was known far and wide for the unerring accuracy of his predictions. For someone so renowned, pride is usually his nemesis. Sundaram was going along with a canonical theme in classical Hindu mythology which revolved around the humbling of pride, garva bhanga. At some point, Kardana aspired to immortality and undertook severe penances and austerities in order to propitiate Lord Shiva. The power of penance in mythology is such that the god invoked has no power to ignore it or not be bound by it. Shiva had no choice but to appear before Kardana and grant him whatever he wished. Kardana, who was waiting for just this moment, asked for immortality. Again, the mythological ploy, when confronted with such a request, is to grant it conditionally. Shiva argued with Kardana that life is uncertain and immortality is a condition that is beyond uncertainty and, therefore, not possible within the normal conditions of life.

'Is there any phenomenon you know which gives you grounds for certainty?' Shiva asked his devotee.

The proud Kardana immediately cited his predictive ability as such an example of certainty.

'Very well, then,' said Shiva, smiling. 'You will not die as long as your predictions are verified to be true. If, however, your prediction fails even once then you will die at the very end of the day your prediction is found to have failed.'

At this point, Sundaram departed from the traditional story-plot and provided the unexpected twist. Kardana, a Tamil Brahmin of the kind Sundaram himself was, cunningly realised that it was logic and not astrology that would now grant him immortality. He selected a date at random and predicted that as the date of his death. If he were to actually die that day, his prediction would be true and, therefore, by virtue of his boon, he would not die. On the other hand, if his prediction were false and he did not die on that day then he would die at the end of the day making his prediction true again. The story ended with Lord Shiva quickly granting the wicked sage immortality unconditionally and making a silent promise to himself that he would never get into these deals with Tamil Brahmins again.

Sundaram's story was largely motivated by the desire to demonstrate to Omkareswaran how there were approaches other than that of science to the story of Cardan. Omkareswaran, however, was not convinced. He accepted that his friend had made an interesting story out of the life of Cardan but he did not think that this rewriting constituted an 'understanding' of Cardan's life or his perversion. He felt that, in a sense, Sundaram's story glorified the perverse attitude to the question of death. It was already unclear how much of Cardan's story was true. To take that story and make fiction out of it meant going further away from reality. What if someone really predicted the date of his own death? This was the question that Omkareswaran felt Sundaram had no answer to.

After all these years, Omkareswaran was revisiting the argument he had had with Sundaram and even repeated this question out aloud: What if someone really predicted the date of his own death? The prediction could be ignored, unless the person is bent on taking his own life. If he thought someone was capable of a perversion of that kind, it was his father. He wished he could meet Sundaram today and tell him how wrong he had been. Life is real and not material for fiction and, Omkareswaran felt that if Sundaram had been confronted with a real situation of the kind he was faced with, even he would have changed his attitude to the issue.

*****

There was not much conversation between father and son over the next few days. In fact, Omkareswaran avoided contact with his father as much as he could, and at the same time kept a watch on him from a distance. The rituals following the tenth day of Meenakshi's death were completed and the long lunch ceremony was done with. It was a hot afternoon. Omkareswaran was amongst the last to eat and the smoke-filled rituals of the morning, the heavy lunch and the sweltering heat made him drowsy. As he lay down on the verandah, his eyes fell on his father sitting under the shade of a tree in the distance. He could also see his son sitting on his father's lap. Omkareswaran's immediate reaction was to go and snatch his son away from his father but as he approached the two he saw his son get up and walk up to Dharami who was also approaching them at the very moment.

'He is a good boy,' he heard his father tell Dharami. 'He will follow in my footsteps when he grows up.'

Omkareswaran did not know what to make of that pronouncement but resolved to make his son as unlike his grandfather as was possible. At the moment, he was more worried about the thirteenth day and wondered what drama his father had planned for that day.

The thirteenth day is one of *Shubha Sweekaram*, the day when the bereaved family puts its grief behind and accepts the new auspicious phase ahead of it. No expense was spared on the occasion and the family, the servants and the labourers who worked in Vaidyanathan's fields were given garments, grain and gifts.

That afternoon, Vaidyanatha Iyer lay down on the verandah for a nap. Later, Maitreyi brought him his coffee but he had not woken up. Later when Dharami tried to wake him up, she found he was not breathing. Omkareswaran wanted nothing to be done till his doctor friend from Trichy could come and examine his father. The doctor's examination resulted in a brief certification of death due to natural causes during deep sleep.

Within the next few months, Omkareswaran liquidated his ancestral wealth, sold most of their lands, gifted some of it, sold his family house and brought Dharami to Bombay. Gudalur, his father and his mysterious death were never mentioned in his house again.

7

Saraswati Mahal library was Dorai's favourite haunt in Thanjavur. The library's rich collection of manuscripts had him captivated and Dorai spent a good deal of the initial part of his Thanjavur visit in the library. It was getting to a point where he knew he had to get on with the interviews that he had planned but somehow he couldn't extricate himself from the library. The visit to Gudalur introduced a break in the rhythm of his daily visits to the library and he decided now to start meeting his contacts in Thanjavur and fix up time slots for interviews.

Vaithiswaran was one such contact who had been recommended by a friend in Bombay. Vaithiswaran, or Vaithi as he was known, was a short man with oily hair dressed always in an immaculate white *veshti* and shirt. Vaithi carried a small pouch under his arm containing everything from his betel-leaf and betel nuts (*vettalai-paaku*) to a who's who list of Thanjavur. It was almost as though he derived his sustenance from chewing the *vettalai* for he chewed it all the time.

When he spoke, with his mouth full of red juice, he had to hold his chin up so as to prevent it dribble from his mouth. The fact that Vaithi never stopped talking meant that he was usually walking around sticking his chin up in the air exuding every bit of the famed Thanjavur arrogance. It is a reflection of the miserable times we live in, Vaithi felt, that we cannot keep our body and soul together just on borrowed money. If he could have done that, Vaithi would never have cared to work. But he had to work to survive in this heartless world and so he decided he would work whenever he needed the money.

He was what one may roughly describe as a specialist tourist guide who worked either with foreign tourists or wealthy Indian visitors. He was not a guide who would bother explaining to the tourists the history of the places they visited – he simply hired someone else to do that job for them – but he who would arrange schedules, get special darshans organised in temples, get access to places to which the visitors would have otherwise been denied entry, organise special music or dance performances and put his clients in touch with artists and sculptors.

When Dorai got in touch with Vaithi asking him to help set up interviews with people, Vaithi couldn't believe his luck. He had been promised a big amount of money by Dorai and for a job which was really a piece of cake. He drew out a long list of people who Dorai could meet and interview. He understood the nature of Dorai's project and he put in every effort to see that Dorai would get to meet the right kind of people who would give him a real feel of what Thanjavur was all about.

It was one such appointment that saw Dorai and Vaithi waiting in the outer room of Sadasivam's home. Dorai had not been very sure that he wanted to meet Sadasivam: he had a vague idea that Sadasivam was some kind of godman and he was not so keen on spending time interviewing him. He was more interested in meeting normal people who, he felt, would give him a truer picture of the day-to-day life of this town. But Vaithi had been insistent on setting up a meeting with Sadasivam. In fact, Dorai noticed that Vaithi's arrogant manner would disappear completely when he was talking of Sadasivam. It was only Sadasivam who came close to evoking anything like respect in Vaithi. From what he knew of Vaithi in the last few days, Dorai felt that anyone who could affect this change in Vaithi definitely deserved to be met.

Dorai was quite fascinated by the old house. The walls of the house gave the impression of belonging to some hoary past. The house wore a deeply mysterious look which somehow seemed to fit in with the kind of character Sadasivam himself was reputed to be. The rest of the family, however, seemed not to fit in. Two young boys, probably Sadasivam's grandsons were playing marbles in the small courtyard outside the house while a young girl, who looked like a daughter of the family, was busy hanging clothes on the clothes-line. Sadasivam's son was sitting in one corner of the room where Dorai and Vaithi were waiting. Vaithi had made an attempt to introduce Dorai to him but the son was not very interested in having a conversation glued as he was to the radio listening to the commentary of the Australia-India cricket match. He had studied to be an accountant, Vaithi explained to Dorai later, but had not been able to find a job where he could work for more than a few weeks. Women's voices could be heard from what was probably the kitchen.

Even as Dorai tried to get a feel of the house and its people, the door to Sadasivam's room opened. An elderly couple emerged accompanied by a young girl. The girl was about twenty, tall and fairly well-built, her hair tousled and her mouth shut in a palpably tense manner as though she was somehow holding herself back from screaming. The look in her eyes mirrored the state of her troubled mind. Just one glimpse of the girl's face was enough to tell Dorai that her parents had brought her to the wrong place: she needed a good psychiatrist's help. He leaned forward and shared this opinion with Vaithi but Vaithi held up his hand in a gesture to silence him because he could hear Sadasivam's voice beckoning them in.

The room was fairly large but crowded. There was a small idol of Kamakshi in one corner of the room and a big brass lamp next to it. The rest of the room was filled up with books and *puja* accessories piled up against the wall. A canvas easy chair occupied another part of the room. Sadasivam was sitting cross-legged on a slightly raised stool supporting his elbow on a wooden shelf in front of the only empty wall in the room. He looked like he was about seventy. He wore his grey hair in a dishevelled pigtail and his smile revealed teeth which had turned brown with age. He wore a *veshti* but his torso was bare except for the sacred thread which ran diagonally across it. He wore a necklace of *rudraksha* beads with a small gold locket attached to it.

Dorai and Vaithi sat on the floor in front of Sadasivam and the old man greeted Vaithi warmly.

'Dorai saar is visiting from Bombay,' said Vaithi. 'He is planning to interview several people in Thanjavur for an article that he is writing for a magazine. When I told him about you, he was very keen to meet.'

Sadasivam's face lit up with a smile.

'People come to me asking questions about themselves, their lives, their problems. It is a welcome change when someone wants to ask me questions about myself,' he said.

'Yes, I thought it will be interesting to talk to you and find out more about what you do. I must begin by apologising for my poor knowledge of Tamil so some of my questions will be in English. Can you begin by telling me what you do?' Dorai said.

'Well, that's simple. I do my *pujas*. I go to the temple. I hardly ever visit anyone at their home. When people want to meet me they come here,' said Sadasivam, rather matter-of-factly.

'And what is it they seek from you? ', asked Dorai.

'People are always seeking something or the other,' said the old man, narrowing his eyes as he spoke. 'It is in the nature of human beings to be discontented with their lives. They come to me seeking help and advice on these issues. But there are a few others who are true seekers. They come to me seeking nothing but I know what they are after.'

Dorai frowned trying to make sense of the cryptic remark about the true seekers. But he decided to come back to that later.

'Tell me about the first set of people you were talking about. You said they come to you with specific problems. Do you have the answers to these problems? '

'No, I don't. Never. I am only there to lead them to the answer. If someone tells me he has lost a diamond and I tell him that he will find it on the night of the next full moon, it doesn't mean that I have given him an answer. If he finds the diamond then it means that he has found the answer. I only tell him when he is likely to find it.'

'So does that mean it is equally likely that he may not find the diamond?' asked Dorai.

'When I tell him that he will find the diamond, I am showing him the way down a road. If he takes that road, he will necessarily find the diamond. I can help him by showing him the way but he is the one to finally decide which road to take.'

'Forgive me for saying so, but that sounds to me like the easy way out,' said Dorai, and Vaithi looked at him somewhat anxiously. 'I think you are not accepting responsibility for the truth of your statements.'

'I certainly accept responsibility for that,' said the old man, smiling. 'It is obvious that there won't be so many people wanting to meet me if that weren't true.'

He paused for a moment as though he were trying to recollect something and then continued, 'You know, you were worried about the girl who was here before you. You felt she ought to have been taken to a doctor.'

Dorai wondered how Sadasivam had heard him say this. He had made sure to lower his voice down to a whisper when talking about this to Vaithi.

But Sadasivam continued talking. 'I do feel very responsible for someone like that. She is so young and this is not the kind of illness she should be suffering from.'

He turned to Vaithi and said, 'Do you know Dr. Ranganathan who has his clinic near the Tank? Yes, of course, you do. She is Ranganathan's niece. They have tried everything that the English medicine has to offer. Ranganathan even took her to the best doctors in Madras but nothing has worked. That the English system did not work for her does not mean that it invalidates the truth about that system. The truth is not in the system but how it applies to individual people. It didn't work for her.'

He paused and then continued, 'I have taken responsibility for making her better.'

'What if she does not walk down the road you map out?' asked Dorai, persisting with his line of questioning.

'With experience, you learn that too. You know who will and who won't.'

'But, I want to understand something else,' said Dorai. 'In what you call the 'English system', if someone has an illness he will visit a doctor. If it is a condition of the mind there is a different doctor who will take care of it. Someone who has lost a diamond is likely to go to the police. You seem to be saying that you have the solution to all these problems ...'

'Well, if people discovered that the police inspector has a better cure for a stomach ache why would they go to a doctor? It is just we who have designated people and given them different tasks to perform. That is only a convenience. Dr. Ranganathan, for example, is an accomplished veena player. He has performed at several concerts. So is he a doctor or a musician?'

'But the police inspector who cures stomach aches has to first diagnose his patient and know that he has a stomach ache. Do you know, for example, what kind of mental illness this Ranganathan's niece is suffering from?' asked Dorai, getting a little impatient with the self-assured manner of his respondent.

'That again depends on the system,' said Sadasivam. 'In the English system, you may call it a mental illness. For me, she may be possessed by some spirit.'

'My God! We cannot be talking of spirits in this day and age, can we?' said Dorai, making no attempt to conceal his irritation. 'Three Americans landed on the moon four months ago and we are still talking about spirits here.'

Dorai's outburst led to a very awkward silence. It was finally an embarrassed Dorai who broke the silence.

'I am sorry. I did not mean to be offensive. It is just that I reacted to the talk about spirits. This kind of talk is very alien to my understanding of the world,' he said.

'No, I don't dabble in these things myself. It is just that one ends up being like a radio aerial, sensitive to all the signals that are floating around. How much importance one attaches to what signal is, of course, up to us,' said Sadasivam.

He looked at Dorai closely and continued, 'You know, several years ago there was this lady who was brought to me who was said to be possessed by a *Brahma-rakshasan*. People were really scared of this spirit that had possessed her. When they brought her to me, I asked my cousin to go to the temple to look for the oldest nadaswaram player there. The man he found was probably eighty-five and had lost all his teeth so that he made a dreadful noise when he attempted to play the nadaswaram. Well, it took just a few minutes of that noise and the *Brahma-rakshasan* was at my feet pleading with me to make the old man stop playing!'

With that he laughed loudly and Vaithi joined in the laughter. Dorai smiled, amused at the manner in which Sadasivam had tried to defuse the tension. He did not believe Sadasivam's story at all because he knew this to be an old Tamil folk tale. But, with the story, Sadasivam had certainly managed to lighten the atmosphere in the room.

Sadasivam's daughter-in-law walked in with hot coffee in steel tumblers. Sadasivam invited his guests to have the coffee with a gesture of his hand and continued, 'You know, we spend a lot of time analysing things around us – breaking them apart and trying to understand them. But that is no substitute for experience. Here is a tumbler of coffee. One can ask what it is and go on to say that it is just the decoction, milk and sugar in the right proportion. But these three things alone do not make coffee. I cannot decide to have the experience of coffee by consuming the decoction today, the milk tomorrow and popping a spoonful of sugar in my mouth the day after. The three elements that go to make coffee have to blend together at the same time and that is when I experience it. Ultimately, it is my experience of these three things together that makes it coffee.'

He paused dramatically for a moment and continued, 'It is not enough to ask questions. Things have to move into one's realm of experience.'

'Experience of what? ' asked Dorai.

'Experience of the reality that is not available to the senses. You have to simply drink the coffee to experience it. That is not the kind of experience I am talking about. There is a reality which is not available to your sense organs.'

'Even if I do accept that such a reality exists, what happens when you experience that reality?' asked Dorai.

'The possibilities are endless because you look at the world from a different perspective. So even the world that is available to your senses can be changed because of the new experience. It's like the group of hunters who were searching for a pond in a part of the forest they were not familiar with. They went off in different directions through the dense forest but were not successful in finding a pond. It is only the one who had the wisdom to climb up a tall tree who was successful in finding it.'

After a moment's pause, he added, 'But sometimes the tree takes you to a height which you realise is more important than seeking any pond. Once you are there you don't want to climb down.'

It was getting close to noon and Sadasivam was getting tired.

'Why don't you come back this evening?' he asked. Dorai looked at Vaithi who said he would not have the time.

'Fine. I will make it on my own,' said Dorai, who, in spite of all his initial scepticism, was now keen on spending more time with Sadasivam.

When he went back to Sadasivam's house that evening, Dorai found him to be in a very different state of mind than what he had been earlier in the day. There was a distant look in his eyes and he was clearly not paying any attention to Dorai's questions. Dorai tried to see if he could get Sadasivam to talk like he did in the morning but soon gave up. They sat silently for a few minutes, Sadasivam still distant. Dorai wondered whether he should excuse himself and leave but it was Sadasivam who broke the silence. It was as if he had woken out of a reverie. Dorai was somewhat taken aback by his question:

'Tell me about yourself. Where is your family originally from?'

'Well, we are originally from a village near Thanjavur. But I have lived all my life in Bombay and know very little about this region,' said Dorai, in almost an apologetic tone.

'Which village was that?' asked Sadasivam.

'It's a place called Gudalur on the banks of the Kaveri and not very far from here,' said Dorai.

'Gudalur? Yes, I have been to Gudalur. What was your father's name?' he asked.

'My father was called Omkareswaran but he was in Gudalur only as a child. It was my grandfather who lived there. He was a zamindar and his name was Vaidyanatha Iyer,' said Dorai.

'My God!' exclaimed Sadasivam. 'You are Vaidyanatha Iyer's grandson! I should have known. I should have known.' He kept shaking his head as though it was his mistake that he hadn't figured out the connection.

'I met him when I was young. My uncle was travelling around this region and I decided to go with him. We spent a few months in Gudalur and it was from my uncle that your grandfather received his initiation,'

Dorai realised that Sadasivam was referring to his grandfather's initiation into meditation. He had heard these stories from his aunt, Dharami.

'So you see how these things are. There is an order in all this which we miss when our vision is small. It was ordained that we meet.' Sadasivam was getting really excited.

'Well, in a way it was a small coincidence. It was all due to Vaithi,' Dorai offered in way of an explanation.

'Vaithi! No, no these things are beyond Vaithi and such people. He is only a vehicle in the whole process. Like the magazine that you are working for. They have all materialised only because we had to meet,' Sadasivam exclaimed.

Dorai felt a bit embarrassed by the way the old man was reacting to what he felt was a very ordinary situation. But he did not want to be rude to him.

Sadasivam could hardly contain his excitement. It was like a 'Eureka' moment for him. Then, as though he had made some great effort to calm down, he suddenly quietened.

'I will have to consult the goddess,' he said. 'I have to ask her what she has to say.'

Dorai could make no sense of this and he wondered what the old man was up to now. He was already regretting this second meeting with Sadasivam.

Sadasivam, in the meantime, got up and went towards the Kamakshi idol in the other end of the room. Next to the idol was a small wooden box. He opened the box and pulled out a small packet wrapped in a red cloth. He sat down now next to the idol and put the packet in front of him. He then sat in a meditative posture, his eyes closed, his frame erect and his hands resting comfortably on his lap. It was a few minutes before he opened his eyes. He unwrapped the packet lying in front of him with the care that one would reserve for a most precious thing. Dorai moved up closer and sat in front of him curious to see what he was doing.

'If nothing, this is interesting material for my article,' he thought to himself.

By now, Sadasivam had spread out the red cloth in front of him and placed the contents of the package in the centre of the cloth. Dorai could see that it was a book of palm leaves.

He had seen similar books at the Saraswati Mahal Library.

Sadasivam opened the cover of the book and Dorai bent forward to see what was written in it. He could not see anything at first so he moved even closer. Seeing his curiosity, Sadasivam lifted the book and held it in front of Dorai. The book had several leaves bound together and the leaves looked old, though how old Dorai could not say. But there was nothing written on the leaves – it was an empty book!

'The book has nothing in it,' said Dorai, surprised.

'It has everything in it. You will see now when I read out of this book for you,' said Sadasivam.

'Read out of this book?' Dorai wondered silently. 'Why am I referring to this object as a book? Is a set of leaves bound together worthy to be called a book?'

Sadasivam, by now, had again assumed an erect posture, had closed his eyes and was meditating. Dorai's mind was abuzz with several questions and conjectures. One can read only something that is written - otherwise it is only speech. Dorai was telling himself. But, yet, here the speech was being presented as though it was the reading of a written text.

Sadasivam began to read from the book in a low and gentle voice. He started with an invocation to Kamakshi and then to Shiva. To reaffirm his Smartha tradition, he then chanted a small mantra to Vishnu and Lakshmi. At this point, his voice changed and so did his manner. It was as though he, as Sadasivam, had invoked some power and now it appeared that this power had taken over.

Words in chaste Tamil flowed out of him like the Kaveri in full glory. He started by narrating the story of Kannappa Nayanar and extolling the virtues of his selfless devotion to Shiva. Dorai sat transfixed, admiring the lyrical flow of the story. More references to the lives and works of Tamil saints and mystics followed only some of which were comprehensible to Dorai.

Even as Dorai was being gently transported along this main flow, a tributary seemed to show up suddenly. This tributary touched upon Gudalur, Vaidyanatha Iyer and incredibly about his remarkable prediction of the date of his death. Dorai was listening very intently not wanting to lose the thread of the story in the very complex metrical forms of Tamil. When the story of his grandfather's death appeared he was surprised. He had thought that it was a secret and unknown to anyone expect close family and an inner circle of friends. He had himself heard about it from his aunt who had told him the story after exacting a promise that he would never let on to Omkareswaran that he knew.

Consequently, Dorai had never spoken to his father about it till much later. It was only a couple of years before his death that Omkareswaran told Dorai about his childhood, his memories of his mother, his father and his death. Omkareswaran could neither understand how his father's prediction had come true nor could he accept it as something supernatural.

Even as he wondered how Sadasivam knew the story of his grandfather's death, a new story was unfolding. Again it took Dorai some time to figure out who was being alluded to but soon it became clear that this was the story of Omkareswaran, about his life in Bombay and his meteoric rise to riches. The poem went on to talk about Omkareswaran's one great sorrow - the death of his wife, Maitreyi.

Maitreyi had succumbed to cancer when Dorai was only eight years old. She had suffered from acute pain in the abdomen for several months before the doctors put their finger on the cause - cancer. There was little they could do even to help relieve her pain. Dorai had vivid memories of his mother through her illness and the months that she spent in bed. He remembered her efforts to smile at him even when she was writhing in pain. Her last days of acute pain and suffering were deeply etched in his mind and had wrought his personality.

As Sadasivam's poetry painted pictures of Maitreyi's suffering and her eventual death, tears rolled down Dorai's face. He had by now stopped thinking about the source of Sadasivam's information: he was now really going with the flow. More followed: Dorai's marriage and the separation. The poem ended by saying that Dorai's divorce was one more step towards Dorai's spiritual attainment, and he had already started his journey on the path of such attainment.

When the poem ended, there was a silence that lasted several minutes. Then Sadasivam said, softly, 'I now know why you are here.'

He wrapped his book in the red cloth and put it away in its box. He then sat in front of Dorai and asked him to close his eyes. After a few minutes, Dorai could feel Sadasivam's fingers rest on his forehead but only for a few seconds, after which he had the sudden sensation of a massive flow of energy through his being. His eyes were closed but he felt no need to experience anything with his senses. He was one with the Universe.

When, a few days later, Dorai tried writing in his notebook about his experience in Sadasivam's house that evening, he could only write: 'The whole world seemed to be my subjective experience.'

8

Exactly two weeks after Dorai had given them the book, Ananya and Laila were sitting at a table in the Army and Navy Stores. Laila had not finished her cup of tea which had gone cold. The waiter hovered over the table wondering when the girls were planning to leave. Ananya looked up from the book she was reading and asked him to get two more cups of tea.

Ananya had read the book a few times already, especially the part that detailed Dorai's meeting with Sadasivam.

'I really wish that he had written more,' said Ananya, with a touch of exasperation in her voice. 'Somehow his story seems to end with his second meeting with Sadasivam. The few pages that follow contain inconsequential details about his days in Thanjavur but nothing more.'

'Yes, you're right,' said Laila. 'Unfortunately, there are no dates in this book. If he had recorded dates then we would know how long Dorai continued making notes after he met Sadasivam. I guess too much was happening in Dorai's life suddenly for him to keep track of it in the form of writing.'

'One would think that as a writer he would have felt compelled to keep a written record of these events which were changing the course of his life,' said Ananya. 'But I guess his life was completely overpowered by this new force he had encountered.'

'But, Ana, what do you think this 'force' was? Even now I have only a vague idea of what it was about.'

'I don't know whether I should label it. But his writing suggests that he came face-to-face with some force which was about to transform his life. From what else we know of his life, like his thirteen-year disappearing act, it is not too far-fetched to presume that his life was, indeed, transformed.'

'What do you mean when you describe it as a force?' asked Laila.

'Well, not something physical but something operating at a psychological level, I guess,' Ananya ventured.

'But the genuine problems of our existence are so deep-rooted that I find it difficult to accept that this 'force' can do anything to it, whatever the nature of this force is.'

'Well, I guess, Dorai will argue that the problems you are grappling with are not genuine,' said Ananya.

'I know. I have gone through that kind of argument with Prahlad so often even though Prahlad's position seems to be diametrically opposite to that of Dorai. I think my problems are genuine if I experience it as that. One cannot argue these problems away because it is so much a part of the world that we experience.

'After all the long debates that I have had with Prahlad, ironically I find that the nature of his 'problems' is not very different from my own. But he doesn't give it the primacy I do. The genuine problems, as far as he is concerned, have to do with our knowledge of the world or with the tools that we use to seek that knowledge. The paradoxes of logic or of physics are the 'problems' that he finds engaging. I find it a device by which he simply places the origin of all the paradoxes to a location 'out there' rather than finding the location somewhere within.'

'But that is Prahlad,' said Ananya. 'We were discussing Dorai.'

'Yes, I know. For some strange reason, I see them as being very similar. I see them as the people who don't talk about problems like I do but about solutions. They claim that answers exist and they have found the answer, each in their own way. The world is so much simpler if one can accept that there are answers. I wish I could. It would be so much easier if I could just sit for a few minutes with someone's hand on my forehead and feel an overpowering flow of energy through me which resolves all my problems. If I did believe in that possibility, I would not even be talking about it like this.'

'You then don't believe what Dorai is talking about?' asked Ananya.

'To the extent that it is a chronicle of his experience, I guess I believe it. I don't doubt his intentions at all. But I don't know whether a similar experience will do the same for me.'

'How would you know?' asked Ananya.

'I don't. But it is my hunch. I think this experience, whatever it is, will be written elsewhere. It will not be written on the pages that I am obsessively reading and re-reading.'

Laila paused a while and continued, 'It is like the experience of sex. One expects so much out of it before one actually experiences it. One grows up believing in its redemptive power. But, even at its best, it does not touch every aspect of you. There is a brief moment of complete release. With eyes shut one surrenders the self to the ecstacy of touch and feel. But, even in that moment, I find a part of my self asserting its identity as something untouched, as something that is never going to be touched.'

After a moment's reflection, she added, 'On the other hand, Dorai's experience may be the kind to touch every aspect of your self. I just don't know but I would like to observe it, understand it and see what potential it has.'

'But for that you will have to spend more time with Dorai. And I can see Prahlad is already not very pleased with the amount of time you are giving Dorai,' said Ananya.

'I am sure I will be able to talk about it to Prahlad and explain why I am spending time with Dorai. But I don't think Prahlad is right in expecting me to fall in line with his expectations.'

'But are you right in what you are doing to Prahlad?'

'What is it that I am doing to him? I think, from day one, I have made it clear to Prahlad that it is not possible for me to accept his love. I am not playing any games with him. But, anyway, why are you so concerned about Prahlad, all of a sudden?'

'O, for God's sake, Laila! If you don't want me to be part of it then so be it. But you were the one who wanted to talk to me about it all the time. I am sick and tired of this love saga of yours. It will be best if you make a clean break with him. Tell him it is not possible and save him and everyone else a lot of trouble.'

Ananya's face had turned a bright red with indignation. 'If only I had the clarity to say no to him, I could easily have said yes,' said Laila.

'God! You are enjoying this whole damn thing, aren't you? It must be so wonderful to be loved by Prahlad and must feel even better to say I am above all this. How you infuriate me!' cried out Ananya.

Ananya's outburst was quite audible over the noise of the restaurant and the men sitting at the table across them turned to look. Ananya picked up her bag and stormed out of the restaurant.

******

A year later, Prahlad was sitting on the steps outside the library in the University campus at Kalina. On any other day, Laila and Ananya would have also been sitting with him. But Ananya was away in Calcutta to attend a cousin's wedding and Laila hadn't shown up at the University that day.

Prahlad had missed laboratory work to sit in the library all morning to read a new book on quantum mechanics. But when he had spent an hour with the book, Prahlad found his mind wandering.

Often, when he experienced these lapses of concentration he would stop being a physics student and revert to being a typesetter. The pages of mathematical formulae, with arrays of complex symbols, would not have the meaning a physicist would attribute to it. It would be the misaligned line, the broken serif, the wrong line-breaking or the inappropriate indent that would start troubling Prahlad.

The physicist had no time to waste on a symbol; his concern was with what the symbol denoted. To the typesetter the symbol and its denotation were bound in an organic unity. There was a meaning to the symbol itself which only the typesetter could appreciate. The physicist had declared all connections between the form of the symbol and its content to be arbitrary and his concern was with the content, the soul. The typesetter celebrated the body, the form, which for him encrypted all the secrets of the soul.

It was only after lunch that Prahlad started worrying about Laila. Why had she not come today? Was all well with her? When he had called up her home, no one had any idea where she was. It was around half past three when he called up Laila's house again. This time it was Tahira on the phone.

'No, *beta,* she is not home,' said Tahira.'She left for the University at nine in the morning. Where are you calling from?'

Not wanting to make Tahira anxious, Prahlad did not quite answer the question but put down the phone saying he would call later.

When he went back to the library, his mind was restless and he could not concentrate on his reading. That is when he decided to sit on the steps outside the library and listen to some music on his Walkman.

Prahlad had taken admission to the M.Sc. programme in physics some eight months ago. Laila and Ananya had graduated from Elphinstone College at the same time. Laila continued with literature but Ananya decided to do a Masters in Sociology even though she had graduated with Economics.

It was at the time when the girls were busy with their B.A. exams that Prahlad realised that Laila would soon move out of Elphinstone College and the Kala Ghoda area. The desire to be with Laila, his love for physics and the security of the money he had saved over the last two years made Prahlad want to quit his job and go back to college. After Kamala's death, Prahlad's heart was somehow not in his work. His mother had wanted him to pursue his passion and their last conversation had deeply impacted him. Her death had also awakened a disdain for money in Prahlad: he had hoped to save enough to provide her a decent life but now he thought it was futile to earn and save more money.

It was with these thoughts that Prahlad had downed a cup of coffee at Madras Cafe and walked into Nadkarni's office. When he stepped out of the office ten minutes later, he had submitted his resignation to a distraught and stunned Nadkarni.

Prahlad wanted Laila to see it as a sacrifice he had made in order to be close to her and to prove his love for her. It was a year and a half now since he had told her about his feelings but Laila's position had not changed even a little. She was clear that she was not in love with him, she was not sure that what he felt for her was love and she did not still accept that something called love could actually exist. In the time they had known each other there were delightful moments of togetherness but at the heart of their relationship was Prahlad's blind assertion of love and Laila's denial of it. This had led inexorably to a deadlock from which they had no idea how to extricate themselves.

The situation only worsened with Laila's need to spend more time with Dorai. Prahlad just could not bear to spend time with Dorai anymore. He would retreat to the seclusion of Dorai's library after a few minutes of desultory conversation. When he saw that Laila wanted to spend more time with Dorai, his resentment grew and he stopped going to Dorai's house altogether. When Laila was with Dorai he would prefer to be at work but that was when he was still working at Omega.

Since he had joined the University, Prahlad suffered every moment of his loneliness when Laila was away with Dorai. There were times he would park himself on a ledge in front of Dorai's building and wait for several hours for Laila to come out. At other times, he would be sitting at the corner of the street near Laila's home waiting to meet her before she reached home. He would sometimes call up Dorai and ask to speak to Laila but become stubbornly silent when Laila came to the phone.

While he waited for Laila, Prahlad would imagine himself engaged in long debates with Dorai. He would put forth eloquent refutations of Dorai's positions and demonstrate to Laila, in his imagination, how hollow Dorai was. In the early days when he had spent time with Dorai, he had heard Dorai talk about how truth could only be discovered through experience and intuition. To contrast with that position, Prahlad would project himself as an advocate of reason. He did not think he would be able to put forward a sufficiently convincing refutation of Dorai if he confined himself to the Western philosophical tradition and so he would use everything he had read and understood of Indian philosophy to support his arguments.

Prahlad admired the rigour and the logical exactitude of Nagarjuna and Gaudapada: it was armed with their syllogistic ammunition that he attacked his imagined enemy. How often had he destroyed his opponent with his superior logic and reason and how, thus humbled, his enemy had knelt in front of him in acknowledgement of his superiority!

There were times when he tried to put forward a cogent sequence of his arguments to Laila but even though she would listen to him attentively she was not convinced by his arguments.

'You know, Prahlad. Forget all these complicated arguments. I am not interested in them. Ask yourself why you are doing this. That will probably tell you more about yourself,' she would say.

Prahlad remembered these words as he sat outside the library listening to Abbey Road on his Walkman. Her words replayed in his head even as McCartney and Lennon were singing, 'O! That magic feeling, nowhere to go'.

He started missing Laila again and switched off his Walkman. He went down to the phone booth for the third time but this time he dialled Dorai's number. Laila did not tell him she was meeting Dorai today but where else could she have gone?

'Aiyya is not at home,' he heard Pandyan saying from the other end of the phone. Pandyan always used this deferential term when referring to Dorai. Apparently, Dorai had left home early in the morning.

'Did Laila come there at all?' asked Prahlad, his voice betraying his worried state.

'No. She didn't', said Pandyan. 'Is everything all right?'

Prahlad murmured a quick yes and put down the phone. He was more worried now.

'Where on earth is she?'

With the passing hours, Prahlad's restlessness grew. He decided to go to Juhu and wait outside Laila's house. He knew Laila did not like him to wait there. She made sure to meet him elsewhere if she planned not to go to the University. But then there were times she would not be able to meet him and she would find Prahlad waiting on the kerb. For him it was important to see her before he went back home for the night.

But something made Prahlad very uneasy today. He couldn't quite understand it. Usually, Laila would tell him where she would be spending the day. Could she be at the Max Mueller library, he wondered. But it was already eight and she wouldn't be at the library at such a late hour.

As another hour crept by slowly and the light of the lamp-posts became brighter against the increasing darkness of the night, Prahlad's mind flooded with morbid images. He could see Laila in a train on her way back home from Churchgate, standing close to the entrance and holding on precariously. He could tangibly feel the moment when her grip on the handle loosened and as she fell from the moving train he watched it as though it had been filmed in slow-motion. He imagined how Laila's parents would be informed by the railway police, how he would hear about it, how they would set out in the night to the spot where she had fallen. He imagined his future without Laila etched against a backdrop of heroic sadness. He imagined his life as a grieving, reclusive lover who, through his singular devotion to Laila after her death, would prove to her how much he loved her.

It was a sudden pang of hunger that ended the train of thought and Prahlad checked the time on his watch. It was nine-thirty now and suddenly, and quite inexplicably, Prahlad felt a surge of confidence. He argued with himself that it was very late now and it was not possible that Laila was not back home yet. She must have slipped in when he was not looking – possibly when he went to the paan-shop by the street corner to make a call. All he had to do now was to go to Laila's house, meet her for just a minute and then go back home. It was only when he had climbed the flight of stairs that led to Laila's house that he wondered whether he was doing the right thing.

Wasn't it too late? Laila's father was likely to be home by now. What would he say? But then there was no way he could go away without seeing Laila. He decided that if Laila's father were around he would pretend that he came over to pick up a book which he needed urgently. With this thought, he rang the doorbell. It was Tahira who opened the door.

'Laila – is Laila there?'

'No. She hasn't returned. Where is she? I thought you may all have gone out together somewhere. It's so late,' said Tahira.

She continued talking but Prahlad could hear nothing more. He had been so convinced that Laila had reached home that he couldn't believe what Tahira was saying. His mind immediately reverted to all the morbid thoughts that had haunted him through the evening and even before he knew what was happening tears flooded his eyes and he broke down crying.

Tahira could make nothing of this but tried her best to handle the situation.

'What's happening? Why are you crying? What's going on here?'

Prahlad heard a voice say this and turned around to find Laila standing behind him.

9

Seventeen months had gone by since Laila had read Dorai's book but Dorai's description of his first meeting with Sadasivam continued to intrigue and fascinate her. She needed to find out more but Ananya was not with her in this exploration. Ananya's interest in Dorai had waned and, in fact, she chose to distance herself from Laila's obsessive involvement with him. But, inspite of the time she spent with him, Laila could not comprehend Dorai's world: it was too alien for her. She did not give up making the effort to understand Dorai and tried very hard to make sense of his abstruse statements.

`What do you mean when you say that Sadasivam would read out of blank leaves? How is that even possible?' she would ask Dorai but would never get answers to direct questions like this.

So, all these months later, she was delighted when she got another unexpected peep into Dorai's strange world. She was browsing through the books in his library when she chanced upon Sir John Woodroffe's *The Serpent Power*. When she opened it, an unaddressed envelope fell out. It was an old letter Dorai had written to a friend but had apparently never posted. It had lain there gathering dust. Among other things, the letter described Dorai's last conversation with Sadasivam. Laila read it avidly, again and again...

*****

Sadasivam was tired when he had finished with the last of the visitors that morning. It was well past noon and he was late for lunch. His morning had been busy with a long line of people who had come to meet him and seek his advice on a whole variety of matters. Sadasivam had already done three separate readings that morning.

'You know people don't realise this but each reading takes its toll of this body,' he told Dorai. 'I am pouring myself into it like ghee in a yajna. But there is little I can do to change this situation. People come with so many expectations that they will be crestfallen if I say I cannot do a reading for them.'

'No, you can't refuse them. But, at the same time, you have to worry about yourself. You are not getting any younger,' said Dorai, settling down in front of the banana-leaf that was spread out for lunch.

'I wish someone else would take over from me. When my uncle reached this age he entrusted this job to me. But who will take over from me?'

'I had initiated Ramanathan at a very young age,' he said, referring to his son, 'in the hope that he will be the person who will continue this tradition.'

Dorai was silent. He avoided talking about Sadasivam's family members, especially Ramanathan.

'He is a good boy,' Sadasivam continued, 'but his destiny is different. He wanted to get an English education like the other boys in our neighbourhood. Which boy these days will want to keep a *kudumi* (tuft) and sit in a *pujai*-room all day long? The world is changing and people do not respect these traditions any more.

'But this *pujai* and this reading are not superficial things. There is a lot to it,' he said, in a tone which sounded like he was trying to console himself rather than convince Dorai about it.

Dorai, of course, needed no convincing. After his first encounter with Sadasivam, he had stayed back in Thanjavur and he had now been there for three years. He lived in a small house not very far from Sadasivam's and spent most of his days with him. He would come in every morning at around six and leave only late in the afternoon. He devoted all his time to learning and practising the rigorous techniques of meditation that Sadasivam taught him. He spent his evenings reading books mainly on philosophy and religion.

His single-mindedness, which stemmed from a feeling that he had lost a good deal of time before he had discovered his true calling in life, had impressed Sadasivam.

'But tell me,' said Dorai, 'I have spent quite some time following the path that you have shown me and I can see it as a path of self-realisation. I cannot see where the readings and the predictions fit in, though.'

'Yes, you are right. You have focussed single-mindedly on the right goal. The whole point of walking down this path is to realise one's true nature and the nature of the world around you. See this *rasam* that we are eating now. When you make the rasam you squeeze out the essence of the tamarind but what remains can still be used to scrub vessels. You are, at the moment, devoting yourself to squeezing out the essence of the tamarind. But even after the essence has been squeezed out there are some uses it can be put to.'

'I am sorry but I don't think I follow you.'

'Okay, you are a writer. There is no point explaining this by taking the instance of cooking *rasam*. Let me take the example of a story. I have not read any of the stories you have written and I am not sure I will even understand your stories.' He paused to laugh softly at this point.

'But let's take a story of the kind that I used to like in my childhood. Typically these stories would have a king and his two queens and the king would love the younger queen more and this would make the older queen jealous. Am I right? You can't have just a king and one queen; that would not make for a good story, right? Then you put in a prime minister who is very wise, a hunter in the forest nearby and, maybe, a parrot with a ruby for a heart. Now you have all the ingredients for a story – the kind I love. And the story would develop in the usual way. But imagine that one of the characters, maybe the prime minister, because he is so wise, suddenly realises that all this is not real at all. This is all a story and it has been written by Dorai.'

To make his point, he repeated, 'This is all a story and he realises that it is our Dorai who has written it. What happens then? With this realisation, the prime minister has two identities – as a character in the story and as a realised person who is now not in the story'.

Sadasivam paused again, a little longer this time, and in a more subdued pitch, continued, 'You see what I am saying now. The prime minister has the advantage of seeing the whole story from the outside so he can see the story like any reader does and see the past, the present and the future all at once. He lives in a different *kala,* he is not in the same time-frame as the others. So he is in a position to advise the others, do a reading for them. But he can go even further – he can take the place of the writer and write his own story.'

He continued: 'In our journey on the path of self-realisation, we also become aware that the world as we see it is not real. And our own self, as we see it, is not real. We realise it is all a story. When that realisation is complete you get the full picture. That is when you can do a reading of the kind I do, or possibly even write. But it is very difficult, especially the writing. Not only does it require a great amount of *sadhana* but the process of reading and writing also consumes you. As I was saying earlier, it is like pouring ghee into fire. The more ghee you pour in the bigger the fire gets and wants to consume even more ghee.'

'Okay, I am tired now. I should go and rest.'

Saying this he got up to wash his hands. As he walked to the well, he told Dorai, 'I think you are moving ahead in the right direction. Don't get distracted though. These are small things, really.'

Sadasivam's words always made a deep impression on Dorai but the impact of this conversation was more, partly because of a vision he had a few hours later. In his vision he could see his house in Bombay. He could see himself standing by his window looking at the sea. Suddenly, strong winds started blowing and there were dark masses of low clouds in the sky. Flashes of lightning sparked across this dark setting. The sea was violent and the waves kept getting higher. Dorai tried focussing on this violent image in an effort to calm it down. The sea paid no heed to him – it raged ferociously and the Earth seemed to quiver in the face of such ferocity.

'This is me, my creation, my dream,' Dorai kept reminding himself.

He extended his hand all the way to the sea and caressed it gently attempting to calm it down. The waves kept fighting him asserting their identity but Dorai did not let a hint of fear creep into his heart. He held out resolutely against the waves. Suddenly, the dark clouds disappeared and the sky was lit up with a splendid light. When Dorai moved his hand to pat the waves again, he found himself moving his hand on a sheet of paper. A book had taken the place of the sea.

*****

Dear Ana,

Don't know if I will see this letter through to its end or whether I will then post it to you. I have written several such letters over the past few weeks each of which I abandoned before I could write more than a few lines. It took me some time to even want to write to you because when you left for Calcutta so abruptly; my initial reaction was one of anger. I felt you had no idea what you were up to. I have had time to calm down and the anger has subsided but I still don't understand you…after all these years of being together. But that is probably my own limitation.

When you left for Calcutta, I was more than surprised at the ease with which you left Bombay behind. You were not moving to Calcutta – you were simply going back home. This is the first thing about you that I cannot comprehend, because it is so unlike my own notions of 'home'. Ana, you and I share a common history: we have more in common than we care to acknowledge. We are both children, or should I say grandchildren, of the Partition –

progeny of the displaced people of East Bengal and West Punjab who settled down in Bombay. This is the city where we have grown up in and the only city that we know. At least, that is how I feel. But maybe it is different for you.

Or rather, it is different. Calcutta, for you, has been so much home that you always stood a little distance away from Bombay, I think. You were never part of this city the way I am and certainly not the way Prahlad is. Of course, you had your mother's home in Calcutta – your grandmother, your Mama and Mami, and your cousins who have lived there for a very long time. But is that the only reason you feel differently about Bombay? I, too, have a Bua living in Delhi but it has never filled me with the same nostalgia as Calcutta does for you. It may be that, because we Punjabis have a complex and ancient history, the trauma of our recent displacement has been more difficult for us to come to terms with. And that is why we have sought a sense of home in the land that the present offers us rather than in the one to which our past beckons.

But I didn't mean to write about Calcutta and Bombay but rather about you and me. And Prahlad. It was so uncomplicated, in a way, before Prahlad came into our lives. It would have remained uncomplicated if Prahlad had chosen to fall in love with you rather than with me because you would have given him a simple yes or no answer. Or would you have? But Prahlad did not seem to have any choice in the matter. He simply let himself fall in love with me – with someone who, in spite of caring so deeply for him, cannot give him the simple answer he seeks.

You slowly grew to hate the fact that I complicated matters even more by bringing you into the picture. But how could I not do that, Ana? We were so bound together at that time when we were experiencing all this that was happening. Do you remember we had once taped our readings of 'The Death of a Salesman' and 'The Four Quartets' when you had come over to spend the night at my place? When I listened to this cassette now it amazed me how, about halfway through the reading, we sounded so alike. There was only one voice! I can still hear our voices merge together as we were reading out of 'The Four Quartets':

Home is where one starts from, As we grow older
The world becomes stranger, the pattern more complicated
Of dead and living.

We were just one person and everything we did, we did together: recording our readings, filling up notebooks with our poetry or, even, wearing each other's clothes. Then how could I keep you out of what was happening to me with Prahlad? If I had kept you out of it, or even tried to, it would have been like moving away from you. And I just didn't want that.

I could see it was eating into our relationship but there was little I could do either. I had to go along with my explorations even though, like you, I could see no end in sight. You are, however, capable of withdrawing when you really see no end in sight – withdrawing from Prahlad, from me and from Bombay. I cannot, I am so inextricably bound to all of it and the knots seem to be getting more tangled with each passing day.

Do you remember how a few months ago Prahlad had broken down in front of my mum at home? I had met Dorai that day and got involved in some discussion and hadn't realised how late it was. It was not that this was happening for the first time but somehow Prahlad had really driven himself to the extremes of anxiety that evening waiting for me. I turned up home just when he burst into tears and, of course, I had a lot of awkward explaining to do to my mum. But Prahlad has also moved some distance away since then – that evening effected a definite change in him. He can't yet extricate himself out of this mess completely but he has moved away as much as he can because he cannot bear to see me spend time with Dorai. He has immersed himself more in physics now and hopes to continue doing a Ph.D. after the M.Sc. A few months more and Prahlad would have moved away from here like you have – each with your definite plans about the future. I will continue to remain here . . .
. . . As we grow older,
The world becomes stranger, the pattern more complicated . . .

Love,
Laila.

*****

Laila, my friend,

I was so amused to read your letter. I can't believe that someone whom I think of as my dear friend can write me a letter like this. Not so much that it was accusative – because that kind of accusation is acceptable in friendship. But because it was so self-absorbed, so completely blind to the life of another who is thought of as a friend – as a very special friend, in fact. It has taken me all these years and this long journey to Calcutta to be able to say this to you, Laila.

But don't make the mistake of thinking that I came all the way here just so that I will have the space to say this to you. What you are going through with your life, with Prahlad and with Dorai is something I have seen very closely and have empathised with you and felt with you. But that is not the sum total of my life. I have my own life even if you did not see it.

It sounds almost silly to say this, Laila, that you have been my closest friend. We were everything to each other. However, all that changed in the last couple of years. There was suddenly Prahlad and Dorai around you all the time and I was just displaced. You accuse me of withdrawing from the scene but I was not even invited to stay. Suddenly I became nothing more than an appendage. You became so caught up in your own problems that nothing else seemed to matter.

That is why I am not surprised that you had no clue what was happening in my life. When I tried bringing it up in conversation with you, you seemed to be totally disinterested – well, at least, distracted.

For a whole year before I left Bombay, everything at home had begun to feel unbearable. I had to suffer Ma's twin anxieties – anxieties about my life and about her own. She wanted to give the impression of being successful on both fronts and the world probably lives with that impression. But I know how far from the truth that is – I know the price we had to pay for that impression to be created.

Ma has been involved in a relationship for some years. Tapan Uncle has been her friend for a long time but I have never liked him. He is the kind of person who makes me feel very uncomfortable when I am alone with him. I suspected all along that something was on between them.

It was when I got home one afternoon, rather unexpectedly (after an argument with you, no doubt), that I discovered them at home together in circumstances which were embarrassing to all of us. Ma, in her usual style, tried to pretend nothing had happened. She did not even think it necessary to talk to me later and tell me about their relationship. It is simply because she had no way to – there is no channel of communication open between the two of us, however clichéd that may sound. Even worse, this incident spurred them on to think that since I was now in the know they do not have to be so discreet about their feelings for each other with the result that Tapan Uncle became more or less a permanent fixture at home.

I did try to tell Ma how I felt about him and she laughed it off saying that he knew me from when I was a kid. I really hated the way he would creep up behind me at unexpected times. I lost the feeling of security in my own home. That is when I decided to leave for Calcutta. I don't have any definite plans of how long I am going to be here but I will wait for a few more months till the M.A. exams are over.

After I read your letter, I listened to our reading of 'The Death of a Salesman' and 'The Four Quartets'. Yes, you are right that in 'The Four Quartets' our voices come together and merge in an amazing way. At some point, it is only one voice. But, somehow, after all that has happened over the last two years I cannot help thinking that it is your voice. I will come back, Laila, sometime ... sometime, when I can see it as our voice.

Love,

Ana

PS: Miss you so much.

*****

It was Thursday afternoon, and unusually hot for the middle of February, when Ashok Bhende walked into Wayside Inn for his ritual glass of cold beer. The image of Bhende sitting in Wayside Inn with a glass of beer in his hand was a source of great solace to anyone troubled by the impermanence of things – this was one great constant in this Universe, this Universe of which Kala Ghoda was the centre. This image seemed to be unperturbed by the flux of things around; it was eternal and immutable.

It was a little more than two years ago that Laila, Ananya and Prahlad had first met Dorai sitting with Bhende in Wayside Inn. So much had changed in the period that had elapsed since: Ananya had moved away to Calcutta and even the last letter that Laila and Ananya had exchanged was over three months ago. Prahlad still struggled with his love for Laila but had, in the meantime, got more involved with his second love, physics. Laila had probably changed the least but even she had been considerably affected by her experiences with Prahlad, on the one hand, and her interactions with Dorai, on the other. It was not that she was not still groping but her explorations were more considered and more tempered now. Dorai, himself, seemed to have changed in a way – he had never before involved himself with the lives of others. Now, through Laila, he felt intimately connected to all three of them and also felt he had indirectly contributed to some of the tensions between the three friends. In this changing world, only Bhende's beer ritual remained the same.

As he settled down today with his beer and a book, one of the waiters walked up to him.

'Sir, this is for you,' he said, handing Bhende a big, brown envelope. 'Dorai Sir was here last evening and asked me to give it to you.'

'Dorai did?' said Bhende, somewhat surprised. 'Very well. Thanks.'

Bhende had not expected Dorai to leave anything for him.

What could it be, he wondered. He opened the envelope to find what looked like the copy of a manuscript to him. There was a letter from Dorai.

Dear Ashok,
I am sure you are surprised to see I have left behind a manuscript for you. This is a novel I have been working on for the best part of the last two years. I am sending it to you because you were the person who first introduced me to the protagonists of this book – yes, this book is about our young friends: Laila, Ananya and Prahlad.

I have been observing and interacting with them, paying attention to their stories as much as sharing my own ideas with them, withdrawing and watching them from a distance to see their individual existences and the life they share with one another. I have been struck by their intelligence and their commitment to a life of the mind. And yet they are very young and their knowledge is not tempered by age and experience. They are prone to judging people, sometimes a bit too harshly and, often I discern a tension between what they live and what they have learnt from books. But they are an interesting trio and have so successfully managed to capture my imagination that there was no way I could not write a book about them.

To write a book about real-life characters is a very difficult task, almost impossible and you may well wonder why I even took up this enterprise. To imagine what is going to happen to these characters is difficult enough but to bring a subjective imagination to bear upon their past is the toughest aspect of this writing. Yet, for me, it allows for a blurring of boundaries of the real and the imagined and of the possible and the probable and that is my reason for persisting with this impossible task.

I have called my book Palimpsest *because it is an over-writing of the lives of my characters that I have attempted. There is also a certain ambiguity that is implied in the notion of a palimpsest which is something that characterises my book, too. Of course, I couldn't help playing around a bit – you know my fascination for such games – and so I decided I will write a novel of ten chapters, one chapter for each letter of the word 'palimpsest'.*

I thought I would use a pseudonym but I couldn't think of a name or an identity which I found appropriate. I eventually decided that the author of my book will be God, which is what you and other friends have always called me. For that reason and for the reason of God's omniscience, he is simultaneously me and my pseudonymous identity: bringing in an 'and' into a Kierkegaardian Either/Or. Just as this novel plays with reality and imagination, this pseudonym allows me to both accept and renounce responsibility for what is written.

As an old friend and fellow-writer, you have always encouraged me to write and admonished me for letting my lazy self get the better of my instinct to write. Knowing me as well as you do, you will probably be happy that I have finally shown the commitment to write a novel. But I must let you down, friend, as always because I have not been able to complete it. I have only been able to write nine chapters of a planned ten. I have to leave tomorrow and I decided I might as well leave you a copy of the nine chapters I have completed.

I will be also leaving a copy of this novel for Laila. Since I have time till tomorrow, I will try to see if I can type in the last chapter before I leave it for her tomorrow. If you meet her, you may be able to discuss this book with her.

Salaam!

Dorai

At the same time as Bhende finished reading the letter, Laila was walking up the stairs to Dorai's house. She rang the bell but no one responded. It was only on ringing the bell a second time that the door opened. Pandyan was at the door but Laila could see from his face that something was terribly wrong.

'What happened? Is something wrong?' she asked.

She could see Padma at the far end of the room in tears. It took a while before Pandyan could say anything at all.

'Aiyya . . .,' is all that he could eventually manage.

'What happened to Dorai Saab? Is he well?'

'Aiyya is dead,' she heard Padma say.

Laila felt dizzy and the world swam in front of her eyes. She collapsed in a chair behind her. Gathering herself slowly, she got up with Padma's help.

Padma told her that Dorai had gone into his study after lunch and had slept on the sofa there as he usually did. When Pandyan went to wake him up for coffee, he did not wake up. It was only after a while that Pandyan realised that he was, in fact, dead.

It took Pandyan some time to recover from the shock after which Laila helped him make calls to Dorai's friends. She waited till some of them arrived before she decided to leave. She was almost at the door when Pandyan called out to her.

'Before he went in to sleep, Aiyya gave me this and asked me to give it to you,' he said, his voice still choking. Saying this he handed her a brown envelope.

PALIMPSEST

God

Time

'Put that down differently. I am not sure that paragraph conveys the meaning we want it to,' Gobind told his colleague, Nikhil. Gobind had been down with fever and had decided to work from home that afternoon.

'Yes, sir.'

'And let's not spend all afternoon over it. Do it quickly while I go over this agreement that we drafted the other day.'

Nikhil was already sitting on the edge of his chair. Gobind was a good boss in many ways but he had a short temper and Nikhil was in no mood to test it today. The fever had left Gobind quite weak and he was more irritable than ever. Moreover, he was not used to working at home – he found it distracting. So as Gobind tried to concentrate on understanding the legal niceties of the agreement, Nikhil set about working on the offending paragraph.

'Tahira, can you open that door and let in some fresh air? This room is getting stuffy.'

They could now see Laila playing in the balcony adjoining the bedroom. She was talking to herself, singing songs and rhymes but Gobind was too busy with his work to pay attention to Laila, at least not until he heard her chanting, *'Galli, Galli mein shor hai, Pakistani chor hai!'*

Gobind looked up, his face betraying shock and anger. Again, he heard Laila say, *'Galli, Galli mein shor hai, Pakistani chor hai!'*

'Laila!' Gobind thundered. 'Will you stop saying that this very moment!'

She was not quite what he said but it was his tone and the look on his face which Laila caught a glimpse of. That was enough for her to burst into tears. Tahira came rushing to see what had happened. Laila ran to her mother and buried her face in her mother's sari.

'What is wrong, Gobind?' asked Tahira.

'You are asking me what is wrong?' Gobind was still in a rage. 'Where the hell did she learn to say things like that?'

'Gobind!' Tahira had to stop him by raising her voice because Laila was sobbing uncontrollably. 'She is only a child.'.

'It is terrible that she should be saying things like that,' Gobind persisted. 'I have no idea where children pick up such things.'

'You know where she has learnt to say it. So please don't pretend you don't. Anyway, she doesn't even realise what she is saying so don't blow this whole thing out of proportion. You have to stay at home just two days to bring the roof down,' Tahira said in an exasperated tone trying to console Laila.

Nikhil looked uncomfortable at being witness to a domestic squabble. Gobind seemed to sense his discomfort or in an effort to handle his own awkwardness he told Nikhil, 'I guess the child has heard it from my mother. You know my mother is very ill. She behaves like a child and with each passing day she seems to be getting more childlike. There is a lot she says that she doesn't understand and Laila picks it up from her, I guess.'

'Y..yes…s…s sir,' Nikhil stammered.

He couldn't think of anything more appropriate to say at this juncture. He was quite surprised at the candid manner in which his boss was talking to him.

When, later that evening, Tahira brought Gobind his khichdi for dinner she was very silent.

'You still seem to be very upset, Jaan,' said Gobind trying to start a conversation.

Tahira did not reply.

'You know how these things upset me – all this India-Pakistan, Hindu-Muslim sentiments really stir up the worst memories.'

Tahira still did not utter a word.

'Okay, I am sorry. I didn't mean to shout at Laila.'

'It's not enough to say sorry, Gobind. Laila is our child. She is everything we have. I can't take it when you shout at her like that.'

'Yes, I know.'

'It worries me too that she spends so much time with your mother. I am trying to figure out what else she can do outside school hours so that she can put her time to good use. But if she is at home she is going to have your mother's company and there is nothing you or I can do about it. This may create situations which may make you angry but don't take it out on our baby. I won't stand that.'

'Yes, but ...'

'No buts, Gobind. I want to be very clear about this. I am taking care of your mother as best as I can and with all the resources I can gather. But it is not easy. Like you said, she is another child to take care of and I am trying my best with her. But I will put up with none of this if it is going to hurt my daughter.'

'Do you think I would hurt my daughter?' asked Gobind. 'I am sorry again about what happened today.'

The events of the day made a deep impression on Laila but what captivated the seven-year old's mind was her father's cryptic remark about Daadi – about how she was becoming more of a child with each passing day. How is that possible, Laila wondered? But then she knew that Daadi was somehow different. Maybe she had some secret, some magic which was making her younger.

The next morning she decided she would talk to Daadi to find out more about her secret. She remembered the orange jujubes that Tahira had bought the other day. Daadi and Laila both loved jujubes especially the ones that were sour. If she shared some of the jujubes with Daadi, then Daadi might tell her about the secret. She slipped some jujubes quickly into her pocket and ran to Daadi's room.

Daadi's room was small but it had a nice balcony overlooking a garden. Also the balcony was hidden from the rest of the house and when Laila and Daadi played there no one ever disturbed them except Tahira who would peep in from time to time.

'Arre, Lilo, where have you been all morning?' Daadi called out from the balcony. Lilo was her name for Laila. 'What is it that you have in your hand? '

'See, I got these jujubes for you. Orange jujubes.'

'Mmmm. I love those jujubes. But I hope that wicked witch didn't see you get these jujubes. That horrid Shamshad.'

Shamshad was the help who worked in their house and had the job of taking care of Daadi.

'No, I got these without anyone seeing me.'

'That's good,' said Daadi and fell upon the jujubes with gusto.

'Tell me, Daadi, is it true that you are becoming younger every day? Yesterday, Pappa was telling us that.'

'Why did he say that?' asked Daadi, narrowing her eyes.

'He said that you behave like a child and that you were becoming more like a child every day.'

Daadi's face broke into a smile. This idea of becoming smaller seemed to appeal to her.

'Yes! I am becoming more of a child every day.'

'But how do you do it? Everyone else is getting older.'

'Ah, that is a secret! You should not tell Shamshad.'

'No, I won't. Promise,' said Laila, excitedly.

'I put a rose petal in my milk everyday. You see the roses from that plant there, those roses.'

'And that makes you younger? I don't believe you. You are not telling me the truth.'

'Yes. That rose plant is special. Every night two tiny fairies sleep on those petals. And every morning they leave just before the sun rises.'

'Really? '

'Yes, and that is why I am becoming younger and tinier. One day I will become as tiny as those fairies.'

'And then?'

'Then, when I become even smaller, I will go back into my mother's tummy.'

Saying this, Daadi laughed loudly.

'How will you go back into your mother's tummy? Your mother is dead,' said Laila in all innocence.

Daadi's face darkened.

'O God!' she said. 'My mother is dead.'

Laila sensed her Daadi's mood changing.

'Have one more jujube, Daadi.'

That had the desired effect. Daadi was chirpy again.

'Yes, yes, one more, one more.'

It was another eight years before Daadi died. A combination of ailments plagued her body in the last few years of her life and Daadi could do hardly anything on her own. It was the combined efforts of Tahira and Shamshad that helped her see through her last years. Towards the end, she could barely utter a word or two at a time: it pained Laila to see Daadi like that especially when she had grown up listening to Daadi chatting all the time.

The day after the funeral, a gloom descended over the house. The relatives had all left and only Laila's Bua stayed behind. Tahira was busy setting the table for lunch.

'Arre, where is Laila? Shanti, can you look for her? The food is getting cold.'

Tahira was clearly making an effort to sound normal because she was concerned about Gobind and Laila and how they would miss

Daadi. Laila's Bua walked around the house looking for Laila and found her sitting in Daadi's balcony. Laila was looking down at the rose plant with tears in her eyes.

'Ari, Lilo!' Shanti called out.

'Bua!' Laila had tears running down her face.

Shanti held Laila close to her.

'Don't cry, my child.'

'Bua, you sounded so much like Daadi when you called me.'

'Yes, I know, dear. I know she always called you that.'

'Do you know, Bua?' said Laila, wiping her tears. 'When I was a child I believed Daadi when she told me that she was getting younger every day and that was because she put petals from the rose plant there into her milk. She told me that one day she would become so small that she would go back into her mother's tummy. Isn't that where she is now, Bua?'

'I hope she finds peace wherever she is. Come now. Your mother is waiting for us for lunch.'

It was later that afternoon that Laila got talking to her Bua again about Daadi. She couldn't get Daadi out of her mind: she had pecked disinterestedly at her food at lunch, and then she tried hard to catch up with some sleep she knew she could do with but had ended up getting frustrated when all she could do was to toss and turn in bed. Shanti came into Laila's bedroom a little while later and the conversation inevitably turned to Daadi.

'There is something that happened to Daadi a long time ago that I don't seem to know about. What was it that had disturbed her so much? I want to know about what happened to our family at the time of the Partition. I tried talking to Pappa about it a few times but he just didn't want to tell me anything.'

'Maybe it is better you don't know about it. We don't talk about it because we all want to forget it,' said Shanti, laying a comforting hand on her niece's forehead.

'But it is not possible to forget it like that. I don't think any of us has really come to terms with what happened then.'

'Yes, maybe. But when we came here after the Partition we just wanted to rebuild our lives. That was the only thing that was important. We didn't want to keep looking back at the past and remember all that we had lost. That way there would have been no moving ahead.'

'But the past doesn't disappear because we look to the future. There was Daadi around all the time reminding you of that past.'

'You surprise me with the things that you say – at your age,' said Shanti.

She could not still think of Laila as anything more than a child.

'No, you are just getting away from this again, Bua. Today you have to tell me what happened at that time and, more importantly, what happened to Daadi.'

'Well, there is a lot I don't know myself. I was only thirteen when we left Lahore. What I know is what I recollect from that age and what else I pieced together from snatches of conversations at home. But, especially about your Daadi, we know very little.'

'But tell me all that you know.'

'What I remember very clearly,' began Shanti, 'was the day we left Lahore. It was the 3rd of August. For more than a week before that the city had been ravaged by riots. Stories of Hindu and Sikh men being murdered in broad daylight and of the horrible stories of what was happening to our women . . . it was frightening.'

'I remember we were on our way to the station hoping to find a train to get to Delhi. Someone had told Bhauji that it was better to go to the Cantonment station because there were hardly any trains leaving from the main station. We were in two tongas: Bhauji, Maaji and me in one and Gobind-bhaiya and Randhir-bhaiya in the other. I am not sure now but I think it was near this place called Moti Bazar that our tongawala asked us to get down hurriedly. He didn't even wait to collect his fare but hurried with his tonga into a small lane away from the main road. I can still remember the huge crowds of people in the main chowk – people with sticks and swords, shouting slogans. Some were throwing stones at the shop windows nearby. We were all frightened but Bhauji tried to keep his cool. He had a bag in one hand with some of our valuables and his other hand was tight around my wrist. Nothing was more precious to him than his daughter.'

'The crowds came rushing and the only thing that we could hope to do was to find shelter inside the nearest building. Bhauji was holding me tight but in that panic we lost track of Maaji. An old

Muslim lady opened her door for us and Bhauji let me inside while he went back to see where Maaji was. We had also lost track of the other tonga where Gobind-bhaiya and Randhir-bhaiya were.

'Bhauji came back almost immediately..The crowds were right outside the building and there was no way he could step out. For the first time, I saw Bhauji look completely helpless. He was trying to figure out how he could find Maaji but there was just nothing he could do. The old lady showed us an exit through the rear of the building which opened out into a small secluded lane. Bhauji was trying to work his way back to the main chowk to look for Maaji and my brothers. We walked through lanes so silent that we could hear our hearts beating. But there were road-blocks everywhere and the police had imposed a curfew. We were stopped by a police van. It was a Sikh police officer – I still remember his face so clearly. Bhauji pleaded with him to be allowed to go to the main chowk so that he could look for his wife and for his sons. But the officer refused to let him go because he feared that he would not come back alive. He convinced Bhauji that the best thing for us to do will be to go to the Cantonment station and hope that we would meet our family there.

'But when we reached the station, there was no sign of any of them. There was a train waiting but Bhauji did not want to go. He thought we should wait for the rest to show up. It was only when the station was again attacked by a mob that he decided to run into the train with me. No sooner had we entered the train it started moving. We did not realise at that time that Gobind-bhaiya and Randhir-bhaiya were in the same train. But in the crowd and the confusion there was no way we would have found them.

'When we reached Delhi we left the station quickly and were lucky that we could get out of that area before major riots broke out there. Gobind-bhaiya and Randhir-bhaiya got stuck in Delhi station because of the riots. But we were so relieved when they finally arrived at Mamaji's house the next day. I have never felt happier in my life.

'But there was no news of Maaji for more than two weeks. A distant relative of ours spotted her in a refugee camp in Amritsar and brought her to Mamaji's house. But she was in no condition to speak when she came.

'You probably know bits of the story so far – I am sure you must have heard us talk about it.'

Laila nodded.

'Well, after a short stay in Delhi we came down to Bombay – you know, we were in Sion-Koliwada. After the kind of life we had in Lahore, it was not at all easy to come to terms with life in Koliwada. Bhauji had set up a small grocer's shop, initially, but it was only several years later – just around the time I got married – he could afford to buy a shop in Gandhi Market – you remember his cloth shop in Gandhi market, don't you? You have been there when you were very young.

'For the first couple of years in Koliwada, Maaji's condition was not good. She would throw things sometimes in fits of rage but that was not so often. Most of the time she would be muttering to herself, sometimes sounding very angry but, at other times, she sounded like she was just having a conversation. She didn't really recognise anyone except the four of us and, in fact, only when Bhauji was around in the house did she seem more like herself. Bhauji was very patient with her, putting up with everything that she did and helping her out in every way. He tried several doctors, treatments, medicines but none of it worked very well.

'But after about five years, she became a lot better. She had occasional lows but nothing very serious. She started talking and became more cheerful and it seemed like she was getting back to being her old self.'

Tahira came into the room at this stage of the conversation.

'You two have been in this room for such a long time. Why don't you come out and get some fresh air?' she said, interrupting the conversation.

'Mamma, please.'

Laila wanted no interruptions at this point.

'What are you telling her, Shanti?' asked Tahira.

'Laila wanted to know about the days after the Partition and about Maaji.'

'Why talk about those days . . .?' Tahira started to say, but she stopped when she looked at Laila. Laila just wanted to go on with the story.

'Go on, Bua. Just ignore Mamma,' she said.

Tahira smiled at Laila and decided to join them in their conversation.

'As I said, Maaji was getting better. That was about three years before I got married. I was around eighteen then.'

'Yes, I remember, Maaji was quite all right even when Gobind and I got married,' said Tahira. 'It was only after Randhir . . .'

'That's right. When Randhir-bhaiyya died in that accident, Maaji relapsed into her old state. After that there was never any coming back.'

'But, at our wedding, I remember Maaji was fine and took part in all the ceremonies,' said Tahira.

'Yes she was all right then though she was still very vulnerable. We had to take care of her a lot and, at home, we especially avoided conversations about Lahore and the Partition. Though, at times, she would herself start talking about Lahore but I always felt she wasn't talking about a past – for her it was very much the present. She would ask me about our neighbours in Lahore or about my cousin, Bimla, as though I had just met them.

'Tahira, I am not sure whether I ever told you about this. No, I don't think you know. This was again a couple of years before I got married. Bhauji had to go to Delhi to meet some of his suppliers and Gobind-bhaiyya was also away somewhere on work – I think he had to go Nagpur or some place like that.

'Only Randhir-bhaiyya, Maaji and I were at home. It was sometime in June, I remember, because the rains had just arrived and that night there was a lot of thunder and lightning. We were always a bit worried about Maaji on nights like that because she would get upset if she were startled by a sudden bolt of thunder.

'But we got into bed early that night and I was relieved to see Maaji fast asleep. It was not very much later that I went off to sleep too. It was probably a couple of hours later. The sky was still lit up by lightning and the winds were strong. Suddenly Maaji started screaming in her sleep. It was really scary. Randhir-bhaiyya and I woke up immediately and tried to calm her. I held her in my arms and – I still remember this so clearly – I felt like I was holding a small child in my arms. She was frail and weak anyway but it was more than her body. It was the way she held on to me in her fear. Even though I was scared till then, I suddenly found myself becoming stronger when she held me like that. I knew that, at that point, I was her mother.

'You know, Gobind-bhaiyya often said that we missed out on our youth altogether. He had a very poetic way of saying it, of course, but what I remember him saying was that the Partition did not just take our homes away from us but also a decade of our lives. But it is true that I who was barely eighteen felt like a mother – the realities of that life hardened us more than just age did.

'But that was also the night I got a glimpse into what Maaji had gone through in the days that she got separated from us. Because even though I was trying to comfort and calm her, she was trembling with fear. And she couldn't stop talking. What she said didn't make sense, at first – it all seemed confused. But then she kept repeating something and I tried to pay attention to what she was saying. From what I gathered that night, when she was separated from us in Lahore, she had tried hard to reach the Cantonment station on her own. But she couldn't and, in her attempts to get to the station, she met a woman from a Sikh family. This lady took her into her own house where she seems to have stayed for two weeks. This I am guessing because she seems to have crossed the border on the 17th of August at Kasur. That was the day there were horrible incidents in Kasur – you know, the place where kasuri methi comes from. She probably waited to cross the border with the Sikh family.

'She seems to have been on the train to Delhi and they were stuck in Kasur because the tracks were blocked. There was a young woman, in her twenties probably, with a 3 year-old child in their compartment. Four or five men suddenly appeared and tried to drag the mother away. One of them, a tall one with bloodshot eyes Maaji said, pulled the child away from her mother while the others dragged the mother out of the train. The tall man then stepped out of the train holding the child in his hands and, in public view, strang. . .'

'Bus! Stop, Shanti. I can't listen to this anymore,' Tahira said. She had not failed to notice Laila shudder. Laila remained silent, though.

'You know now why we don't talk about it,' said Shanti.

Later that evening Laila was rummaging through an atlas to look for a detailed map of Pakistan. She wanted to figure out the possible route that the train may have taken from Lahore to Delhi and where Kasur exactly was. She found out from another book on Punjab history that Kasur was an ancient city and legend had it that it was built by and named after Kush, the son of Rama. His twin brother, Lav, was supposed to have built Lahore. It was ironic that the two cities that had so completely taken over her Daadi's mind were inextricably linked, like twins, through the Ramayana.

Three days after Daadi's death, on 19th November to be precise, India lost to Pakistan: a cricket match, of course. They lost the match and the series, that is, the battle and the war. The match had been played in Karachi and this was the first cricket Test series that India was playing against Pakistan after a span of 17 years. The expectations from both sides were very high but the Indian team struggled in difficult conditions and could not cope with the pace bowling of Sarfraz Nawaz and Imran Khan. Only one Indian batsman stood among the ruins: Sunil Gavaskar, who notched up two centuries in Karachi but even his valiant efforts were not enough to save the match. As the young Javed Miandad and Imran Khan hit up the winning runs for Pakistan with consummate ease, all of India went into a state of collective depression and gloom.

The score-cards of the match published in the newspapers the next morning were, somehow, incomplete: they forgot to add that seven people were injured in riots in Mohammed Ali Road – the heart of Bombay's Muslim district. They were not to be blamed for the riots, said an evening newspaper, because they were provoked by the Muslims cheering every run that Miandad and Khan scored. The Muslims, the paper bluntly stated, were made to pay for their unpatriotic behaviour.

That evening Laila took a bus back home from her friend's and found herself sitting behind two men, who looked like bank officers or company junior executives. It was inevitable that they would be talking about the match. While one waxed eloquent for a while about Gavaskar's batting technique, the other was keen to turn the conversation to the riots in Muhammad Ali Road.

'These Muslim bastards don't belong here. Why don't they just go away to Pakistan and leave us in peace?' he said.

Laila was shaking with anger when she heard this and was almost provoked to shout at the man. But then she checked herself – she was only a young girl and she was too conscious of herself to create a scene in as public a place as a bus.

That night as she lay in bed she wondered who she was and where she belonged. Was she a Punjabi Hindu or a Gujarati Muslim? Was she displaced from the Lahore her family once inhabited and had come to live in Bombay as an outsider or was she someone who had a 150-year long history of living in Bombay but was still being shown the door?

She was troubled by disturbing images when she tried to sleep: images of riots in Lahore, in Delhi and in Bombay, a child being strangled to death, her Daadi's meaningless patter, a woman being raped by four men. She saw her grandfather holding on dearly to his daughter's wrist even though it seemed to slipping away from his grasp and when he started calling out to her, asking her to hold on to him, he was shouting 'Laila!' and it was not her grandfather but her father.

Hunger

At around 1 o' clock every afternoon, the small window in the kitchen, overlooking the patch of marshy land at the back of the building, had to be closed. In spite of closing the window, black smoke would fill up the kitchen, the living room, the corners of the house and coat every inch of the walls. Kamala could feel the dense blackness enter her nostrils, fill her lungs and choke her insides. The smoke burned her eyes and when they watered she was not sure she was not crying. Her throat felt dry and parched all day long. Everything around her looked black: the walls, the doors, the clothes hung out to dry, and even when she closed her eyes she saw black, smudgy clouds.

In the last six months since Kamala moved here, she had had to suffer the smoke everyday. The men, around twenty of them, were there every afternoon without fail, to prepare bonfires of used rubber tyres. Huge drums were placed on the burning tyres and a lethal brew of jaggery, decaying fruits, bleaching liquids, varnishing solutions and remains of used batteries was cooked over the fire. The stench of the brew competed with that of the burning rubber and the combination of these aromas would make Kamala sick and leave her retching for a good part of the afternoon.

At times, she would long to go out for a walk but it was difficult to do so because, except for the big tract of marshy land behind their building, the rest of the neighbourhood was made up of small lanes crowded with pedestrians, bicycles, scooters and cars. Then there were shops which overflowed onto pavements – pavements which materially did not exist but were identified as the spaces occupied by hawkers, squatters and hangers-on. Walking through these lanes meant avoiding not just all these obstacles but also women cooking or washing clothes, or children playing cricket, or people engaged in every conceivable form of ablutionary rituals, or the products of these rituals – you blinked for just a moment and if you did not walk into someone's lunch you had your foot in their shit.

A young Dalit poet, who had grown up in this neighbourhood, wrote about it in an expression of angry eloquence:

'We have no place of our own,
except the roads,
No time to ourselves,
except that dark moment
before the city wakes up.
No water to drink,
But the streams of illicit hooch,
No air to breathe,
Save the stench choking us.
Only the rich, upper-caste dogs
Enjoy this city, this bitch.'

It was a world that Kamala did not dare engage with; it was difficult enough trying to cope with it.

Tarabai, who lived down the corridor, could not help sympathising with Kamala and her family. It was clear to everyone that this family did not belong here. Some believed they would "get used to the place" but others were sceptical. This new family spoke English and looked different, so how could they belong here?

'But it is good that they have moved in here,' argued Tarabai with the rest. 'We need more people like these to come in here to make our chawls respectable.'

She did her best to put Kamala at ease. She would wait for Kamala's door to open so she could talk to her. She tried to help Kamala by pointing out ways she could deal with the smoke.

'You can come out and sit out on the corridor in the afternoons,' she explained. 'You see, by six in the evening, the smoke is much less. The good thing about the smoke is that keeps the mosquitoes away.'

Kamala was not so easily convinced but appreciated the efforts Tarabai was making to help her. But, deep inside, she was miserable at having made the move to Koliwada though there was nothing else they could do. Kamala and Prabha had decided on it because they could no longer afford the rent they were paying in King's Circle. The entire process had been simple because their possessions had been reduced to the bare minimum so they could leave one morning without even letting their neighbours know.

Prabha's asthma had worsened very soon after they moved in to Koliwada. The doctor advised her to move to a new place and

Prabha was lucky that her office could get her a transfer to Surat. The move to Surat did her health good but it was difficult to maintain two establishments on the meagre salary that she was earning. At some level, Prahlad was coping better with the new surroundings than either of them. He did not have friends in this locality but had several in school. His grades in school were as good as they had always been so, at least apparently, the move to Koliwada had not affected Prahlad in any serious way.

Kamala, however, still worried for her son. This was hardly the place for a boy to be growing up and neither were their circumstances. There was no way Kamala could think of providing her thirteen-year old son all that she would have liked to but she was not even able to provide him the bare minimum. They struggled through the month but the last week was particularly miserable. The food would run out and so would the kerosene for the stove and there was only so much credit that the grocer's shop would allow.

At times, she would plead with the grocer and, at other times, she would borrow money or food from Radhai who lived in the next building. Radhai was the only friend Kamala had in that neighbourhood and though she lived in equally strained circumstances she was generous to a fault. It was only Radhai's help that helped Kamala cope and it was at Radhai's behest that Kamala decided to provide tuition in English to a few neighbourhood children. Teaching was not easy but even the little money it brought in was a big relief: the day her fees came in she would indulge in the luxury of buying pastries for Prahlad from the bakery at the end of the road.

It was around half past four in the afternoon that Prahlad returned from school that day. He had stayed back in school rehearsing for a play that they were putting up for the Founder's Day programme in school. It was a play based on the story of Krishna and Sudama and Prahlad was excited because he had been chosen for Sudama's role. He was still thinking about his role on the way back home from school and going over his lines.

As he turned into the narrow corridor on the second floor, Prahlad realised he had made a mistake. He was so immersed in thoughts about the play that he did not notice Anilbhai standing outside his flat. Prahlad immediately realised that Kamala was not at home and that he should also turn around and disappear as fast as his legs could carry him. But as he turned around in one quick swivel he found himself crashing into someone just behind him. Dattu was much bigger than Prahlad so it was Prahlad's nose that collided with Dattu's shoulder. The suddenness of the impact had Prahlad reeling for a moment and before he could gather his senses again he found Anilbhai standing next to him.

Anilbhai was his father's acquaintance – one of those people who had been foolish enough to lend large amounts of money to Krishnan. Many of them had written these off as bad debts for they had no idea where Krishnan was after he had been thrown out of his job in the printing press. They knew he lived in King's Circle but had no idea that the family had moved to Koliwada. But Anilbhai had somehow discovered their new address.

'So, you were trying to run away from me? Beta, it is not so easy,' said Anilbhai, his mouth dribbling paan as he spoke. The buttons of his multi-coloured shirt were open all the way down his chest to where his immense paunch started and a big pendant dangling from a gold chain accentuated the black hirsuteness of his chest.

'Don't try to run away like your father. Do you have any news of him?'

'No . . .,' stammered Prahlad.

He was speaking the truth. They had no news of Krishnan for months now. They would hear rumours from time to time from relatives and friends who derived great pleasure in sharing their speculations about Krishnan's whereabouts with Kamala. But the family really didn't know where he was.

'And your mother? Did she also run away with someone, then?' asked Anilbhai, his lips twisted in a crude smile.

Prahlad shot an angry glance at him.

'So, that hurt, eh? You feel insulted when I talk like that. Your family's honour, eh? Bah! Where was the talk of honour when your father came asking me for money?'

There was something about the way in which Anilbhai spoke his lines: it did not seem real at all. It felt like they were out of some movie.

A few of the neighbours gathered around. This was exactly what Anilbhai wanted. What was the point of a performance if there were no spectators? He had come here a few times earlier but never had the benefit of a live audience. Anilbhai decided he should address his audience now to garner some sympathy from them.

'This boy's father has borrowed more than forty thousand rupees from me. And then he disappears. These people leave their flat in King's Circle and come here. I was lucky to find out they have moved here because they left in the middle of the night from King's Circle without telling anyone.'

'We came here in the morning,' protested Prahlad.

'Oh! Shut up! Did I ask you when you came here? I just want my money and I am not leaving till I have it.'

'So he ran away with the money, did he?' asked Pandoba, delighted at this opportunity to feel morally superior because, most often, he found himself at the receiving end of these ethical discourses. Pandoba's drunken escapades were the stuff of the mythology that people in this part of Koliwada shared. 'His father does not ever show up here. I knew all along that there was some problem.'

Anilbhai was happy with this kind of support.

'It's not just me. There are many others who have given him their hard-earned money and he has disappeared,' said Anilbhai.

'Wonder what he did with all that money? Was it some woman?' ventured Pandoba.

'It was all of it – women, horses, matka – you name it and he was into it. I don't even think we should be mentioning all this in front of these sisters here,' he said, pointing out to the women who had gathered around.

Prahlad had lowered his head, his eyes pointed ground-ward. His ears felt hot with embarrassment. He shuddered to think what the neighbours thought of his family now, with their darkest secrets out in the open. Prahlad was cursing himself for not being alert enough to the danger that lurked outside his house. He had taken the short-cut by the railway tracks and had got in through the back of his building.

If he had taken the road to come home, he would have gone past Radhai Mami's house which is where Kamala would be now. Radhai's kitchen window opened out towards the main entrance of the block of tenements so she could see people entering or leaving the compound. As one who had spent a lifetime dodging people she owed money to, Radhai could sense instinctively that Anilbhai was one person Kamala did not want to meet, so whenever she saw Anilbhai enter the compound, she would send her little son Shiva running to Kamala's house warning her of the impending danger. Kamala would then disappear down the stairs in the back of the building and stay inside Radhai's house till the coast was clear.

As though it wasn't bad enough getting caught like this by Anilbhai, it was worse that this entire drama was being enacted in front of the neighbours. Prahlad was beginning to wonder how long this drama was going to last. He was getting very hungry now.

Just as he was wondering what to do, Tarabai's daughter, Champa, walked past. Champa was considered something of a beauty in that neighbourhood and walked with the confidence of a nineteen-year old who was aware of it. As she walked past Anilbhai, he followed her motion all the way down the corridor with a lascivious look.

Tarabai, who was sitting nearby, did not fail to notice Anilbhai's leer. With no warning whatsoever, she lashed out at him.

'Why are you standing here on our corridor? This is a place where respectable people live, not some street-corner for people like you to hang around!'

'Hey! It's nothing to you. I am waiting outside this boy's flat and I won't leave till I find out about his father,' shouted Anilbhai

'You bloody well get out of here! If people like you start hanging around outside our houses, it won't be safe for us,' shouted Tarabai. 'You can go and look for his father wherever you want. He is not here and you are not going to get anything from here. You just want to come and scare this boy and his mother. They didn't take the money from you, did they?'

'But he doesn't know where this boy's father is. That man has vanished,' said Pandoba, in Anilbhai's defence.

'You keep your trap shut!' yelled Tarabai. 'I know you well enough and I know what people like this man here are about. It is we women who have to worry about our daughters and young women. If it had been left to you men, God only knows what would have happened.'

'Why don't you go and look for his father elsewhere,' she said, turning to Anilbhai. 'I am sure you will be familiar with the places his father frequents. This chawl is not that kind of place, I am telling you that. And I don't want to see you hanging around here again under any pretext.'

Hearing the commotion, Mahendra came up to the second floor with a couple of his cronies. When there were arguments or disputes to be settled, Mahendra was always there.

'What is it, Mausi?' he asked Tarabai. 'Why are you getting so upset?'

'Upset! What do you expect me to do?' Tarabai was still hitting the high octaves. 'This stinking corpse decides to come and deposit himself on our floor in the middle of the day and it is becoming difficult for us women to even walk down this corridor.'

Mahendra was not amused and made that very clear to Anilbhai by looking him straight in the eye.

'All right. Mausi has spoken and you have heard her clearly. Now just bugger off,' he said, in a low, and what was supposed to be a menacing, voice.

Anilbhai did not move and Mahendra felt compelled to rest his muscular biceps on Anilbhai's shoulders and fix him with another chilling stare. This time the message seemed to sink faster into Anilbhai's head. He decided it was time to beat a retreat.

Anilbhai's departure brought a sense of relief all around. Mahendra put his hand on Prahlad's shoulder in the manner of an ancient bonding ritual and said, 'Don't ever worry. If you have any such problem, just let me know.'

This did not go unnoticed in the neighbourhood. The boys suddenly saw Prahlad in quite a different light: as someone who had won Mahendra over.

Over the next few days, new friendships were forged and new acquaintances were made and Prahlad became more a part of the neighbourhood. He went down to play cricket with the boys in the evenings and spent time getting to know them.

Suddenly, the fact that he was different, that he spoke English or that he went to a different school did not seem to matter so much. He became comfortable enough with his surroundings to go down on Saturday nights to watch the free movie-screening down the street. These open-air screenings were so much more fun than seeing films in theatres. The audience sang, danced, recited the dialogues and whistled all through the movie. The participation did not stop there; they would shout out to the hero and the heroine warning them about the villain who was hiding around the corner waiting to deliver a blow on the hero's head; they would egg the heroine on to accept the hero's love; they would shout oaths of disapproval when the villain plotted and schemed in his evil ways and cheer enthusiastically at the slightest hint of eroticism.

A year went by and Prahlad had moved to Class X, his final year in school. He had to do his best because everyone around him told him how much his future depended on it. He had heard it said so often that he believed it. But, at the same time, he did not devote himself to studies to the exclusion of everything else. He still found time to go down to play cricket and watch movies with his friends – or for his new-found passion, carrom.

There was something about the precision of carrom that immediately appealed to Prahlad. He was not yet a very good player, nowhere in the class of Mohan or Rajan or any of these stalwarts but, of course, he could never hope to spend as much time as they did playing carrom. But it was also great watching these experts play. Rajan was the kind who would work up a huge amount of nervous energy before playing any shot. As he placed his fingers behind the striker he would move his head and torso back till the upper half of his body was entirely tensed up. In the analyses that would inevitably follow every game, Rajan's technique was always argued to be suspect. It was not right to move one's head the way he did but, yet, Rajan was a brilliant player. Mohan was a total contrast and was as good a player as Rajan, if not better. He would settle his bulky frame firmly on the small stool in front of the carrom board and then he was rock steady. He would not spend a moment aiming his shots – he knew exactly where he wanted to strike and he always got it right.

It was just past sunset when Prahlad stood at the door of the carrom room watching Mohan and three others play. The room was right opposite Muktabai's home and, as was the practice every Tuesday evening, women had gathered inside to take part in a weekly ritual dedicated to Goddess Bhavani of Tuljapur. The room was so packed that the door had to be left open so that some of them could sit near the doorstep. It was a scene that immediately attracted Prahlad's attention. A small picture of Bhavani rested against one wall and the women sat around this picture, huddled together, dressed in reds or greens or flaming oranges. They had all let their hair loose and had red kumkum smeared on their foreheads. They were chanting and singing in praise of the Goddess but not very loudly and were swaying gently to the music.

'Look at him,' said Mohan, raising his head after playing a shot. 'He is more interested in looking at those women there.'

The boys laughed and Prahlad embarrassedly looked away and tried to focus his attention on the game. But he couldn't help turning back to look into Muktabai's room a little later. The goddess had made her appearance now, she was somewhere in the room. Of course, she was not visible but she was making her presence felt through the bodies of the women there. Here she struck one old woman, there a young sixteen-year old. She was moving through the room possessing these women at will.

Not unlike the striker hitting the coins on the carrom board one after another, the goddess moved from one corporeal location to another but while the mechanics of the carrom striker and coins was clearly spelt out, the logic of the Goddess' ways was inscrutable.

Without even being conscious of it, Prahlad was occupying a very interesting location – a threshold that offered him a simultaneous view of two events. It was a location in between two opposing worlds: one, a deterministic, enlightened, modern world; while the other a pre-modern, dark, chaotic world of the Goddess.

The woman sitting near the door in front of Prahlad stirred. Prahlad didn't notice her moving. It was only when she suddenly rose that he saw her. In a flash she turned around and Prahlad found her standing inches away from him. She was, in fact, of the same height as Prahlad so her eyes met his directly now. Prahlad did not recognise her at all. He could only see her eyes which were blood-shot and matched the vermillion on her forehead. There was a look in her eyes which sent a shiver down Prahlad's spine.

He tried to move his gaze away from her eyes and only then did he realise it was Shailesh's mother. But the realisation that she was the mother of one of his playmates did not help him get over his fear. Her contorted face, her rigid body and her arms, stiff and raised, all looked fearsome. Her lips were pursed and she had to make an effort to speak.

When she spoke, her voice sounded strange. 'You will leave this place. You will go away. To live by the sea,' said the possessed woman.

Prahlad could feel his legs shaking with fear. Mohan noticed what was happening and he and his friends abandoned their game to rush to his side.

Prahlad could barely understand what she was saying because his heart was beating so loudly.

'Do you hear what I am saying?' she asked angrily..

'You will go to live by the sea,' she said, swaying wildly.

'Touch her feet,', said one of the women. 'Touch the Goddess' feet, quickly!'

Prahlad was too stunned to react.

'Touch her feet,' some more voices shouted.

The Goddess was not happy that Prahlad was not bending down to touch her feet. The woman tensed. A strangled cry emanated from her lips.

Prahlad could feel two hands on his back trying to push him down.

'What are you doing?' he heard Mohan say. 'You have to touch the feet of the goddess otherwise she will get upset with you.'

Prahlad bent down and touched her feet. The Goddess seemed less agitated.

'You will soon go to live by the sea,' she repeated.

Prahlad could make no sense of what was going on but he stayed glued to her feet. He did not dare look up and meet her eyes again.

*****

It was some weeks later and Prahlad was busy preparing for his exams which were to start in less than a month. It was a Sunday morning and Prabha had come down from Surat for the weekend. It was her day to indulge herself with a long bath and hair wash before she settled down to eat her favourite food that Kamala was busy preparing in the kitchen. Prahlad was sitting crouched at a table near the window immersed in his chemistry textbook.

When he got up to take a break after a couple of hours of work he looked out of the window to see a car pulling in. It was not the kind of car that he was used to seeing in their neighbourhood. A few minutes later there was a knock on the door. He opened the door to see a stately, well-dressed old man at his door. It took him a few seconds to recognize this person as his grandfather.

‘Can I come in?’ his grandfather asked.

‘Yes. Yes. Amma, look who is here. It’s Thatha,’ Prahlad shouted out.

Kamala was quite taken aback to see her father-in-law. They had not been in touch for years and she had only seen him briefly a few months ago at Krishnan’s brother’s funeral. She held out a glass of water to him but her eyes were rooted to the ground. Thatha looked around the room and that made Kamala feel even more uneasy. She pulled a chair in his direction so he could sit down.

‘So, how’re you all doing? This boy has really grown up, hasn’t he? I guess I am seeing him after ten years or so. So what class are you studying in now?’ Thatha asked Prahlad.

‘In the tenth. I will be done with school in a couple of months.’

‘Japa was right. She figured out that you must be in the tenth,’ said Thatha.

Japa was Krishnan’s brother’s daughter.

‘Yes. I remember she was a year older than me. So she must be in college now.’

‘Yes, in Xavier’s college. She may have made it to science but…,’ his voice trailed off.

He turned to address Kamala and said, ‘It has not been easy for that child. She has grown up hardly knowing her mother and now Raman’s passing away has made it so much worse. She is brave, though.’

Prabha came out of the bathroom just then.

‘Oh! Thatha! When did you come? This is quite a surprise. We are seeing you after ages.’ Prabha was trying to sound as sarcastic as possible.

‘Yes. It has been a long time. It is all because of my wayward son – your father. I tried reasoning with him, scolding him, warning him but nothing worked. He did not change his ways. He left me with no choice but to cut off from him completely. Unfortunately, I had to cut off from all of you too.’

‘And then what made you change your mind?’ asked Prabha.

Kamala was worried. She placed a hand on Prabha’s arm.

‘No. Don’t stop me today, Amma. Let us speak our minds today.’

‘I guess you are right. You are also justified in being angry with me. But if you think about it carefully you will see how it was all your father's fault. But let us not get into that now. I have come today asking for your help. When Kamala came to Raman's funeral I realised that Krishnan was no longer living here. From that very day, I have been toying with this idea of coming and talking to you to ask for help. I hope you will not let me go disappointed,' said Thatha in almost a pleading manner.

'Help! What help can we offer you? We live in a hole like this and have hardly enough to eat. There is nothing we can help you with.' Prabha was getting impatient.

'Well, I thought you can help me. That is why I came here. And I hope you will agree.'

He again looked in Kamala's direction.

'Kamala, I am old now and am not sure how long I will live. I am worried about Japa. I am not sure I can take care of her all on my own. She is a young girl and needs the loving care of a mother or an aunt now. I want you to do this for me, Kamala. I want you to help me.'

'Amma has to take care of Prahlad,' Prabha interrupted. 'And me. When I come down from Surat.'

'Are you in Surat now?'

'Yes, but I do need to come and be taken care of by my mother whenever I can afford to.'

'I appreciate that. I also realise Prahlad needs Kamala's care more than anyone else does. Especially now that he is busy with his exams. But I have this suggestion. Please consider it seriously. Kamala and Prahlad can move in with me after Prahlad has finished his exams. Prahlad can go to a townside college and I will take care of all his expenses. They can stay with me till he finishes his college and then I can easily get one of my contacts to give him a job in the printing industry, if he is so inclined. When Prahlad completes his education, Japa will do so too. I will get her married soon after she is out of college and then I would have taken care of my responsibilities. After that, you can continue to stay with me or set up your own home.'

'I can't believe how you can think of only yourself; you, your favourite son, your granddaughter. Where were you on all those evenings when we went to bed without food? Where were you when we had to leave our King's Circle flat and come here? You are not even aware of what we have gone through and now you expect us to feel for you and your granddaughter,' said Prabha, angrily.

'Prabha, my child, I would not have let anyone else say so much to me. You are too young to know how much I have done for your father. I have blown up a fortune taking care of paying his debts and getting him out of trouble. After years of doing it, I realised that if I did not make a clean break it will just go on for ever. I did not want strangers turning up at my doorstep claiming that my son owed them money. I know I have been unjust to the three of you in the process but there was little I could do. Also, if you come and live with me now it may give me a chance to make up for that. I think what I am suggesting is the best course of action for all of us. Beyond this, I am not going to say anything at all. I will leave now and you can discuss this and call me this evening to let me know your decision.' Saying this, Thatha left.

A couple of months later, Kamala and Prahlad moved into Thatha's flat in Haji Ali – a sea-facing flat of the kind that the Goddess had predicted Prahlad would move into. Prabha was not entirely happy with the decision that Kamala finally took but Kamala felt she should not fail in her duty as a daughter-in-law. Somewhere, she felt that this would also ensure that Prahlad will at least complete his college education.

As for Prahlad, he had maintained a silence on this issue but, deep inside, he was very excited about the prospect of moving to Haji Ali. He hadn't ever imagined that this would happen to him but he felt that it would not be appropriate on his part to betray his excitement. He was hoping that Prabha would finally give in to Kamala and he was thrilled when she did.

It was a new world for the fifteen-year old and a complete contrast to his Koliwada neighbourhood. Prahlad, of course, loved the fact that some of the things had changed in his life, like not having to worry about food or clothes, about school fees or money-lenders. He did not even have to worry about the air: he could now breathe freely. But there were so many new things to get used to here, so much to figure out – it was only Prahlad's basic intelligence that helped him cope with all the changes. In spite of his intelligence, there were situations in which he felt helpless. He found it very difficult to answer phone calls, for example. To speak coherently to a voice that one couldn't put a face to was very difficult.

He had found it equally difficult to talk to his cousin, Japa. As it is, it was the first time that he was interacting closely with a girl who was more or less his own age. But her manner and her confidence were also daunting. The English she spoke was so different that Prahlad found himself struggling for words when speaking to her. It was very similar to the way some of his Koliwada friends had felt when he spoke English.

Where did she learn to speak like that, Prahlad wondered. It was not just her language that impressed Prahlad but also the things she knew and talked about. It was a world he had no access to because it was a world that one could not access through books. Prahlad had implicitly assumed, or he had been taught to, that every bit of the world could be gleaned out of books. It was only after meeting Japa that he realised that this was not at all true. A lot of it depended on where you were; where you lived, which school you went to and whom you talked to. He had studied grammar from Wren and Martin as Japa had and knew that book as well as Japa did. But he would never have guessed that hyperbole and litotes were pronounced the way they were. If he had even suspected that he did not know the pronunciation he would have consulted a dictionary but his grammar teacher, his friends, his school or anyone around would not have known that they were pronouncing these words incorrectly.

It was through Japa that Prahlad was beginning to discover the world beyond books.

Perfection

'Look! That's so beautiful,' exclaimed Indrani, pointing out of the moving car to a pond full of lotuses. 'Isn't that lovely?'

'Yes,' said Ananya, rather sleepily. It was only around nine in the morning but the sun was already way up in the sky and it was rather hot. Sunrise in Calcutta was so much earlier than in Bombay and like the sun the people here were also up early; so much so that already at that early hour it felt like it was noon. Ananya's mami had dished up a rather heavy breakfast in anticipation of the day's travel and it ended up making Ananya feel even drowsier.

'Wake up! You sleepy-head,' said Indrani poking her in the ribs.

'God! I don't know why we are doing this,' said Ananya.

'Doing what, Ana?' asked Deepa, somewhat sharply, from the front seat. 'You know how much Dida wanted us to go to this temple. You can do it for her sake, at least.'

'Yeah. I am doing it because Dida wants it.'

'Stop whining, Ana. Behave your age. You are almost an adult now.'

'I know. I know.'

'Look at Indrani. She is not complaining. I don't understand what your problem is.'

Ananya did not reply but she was sulking.

'You might as well enjoy it if you have to do it, Ana,' said Indrani.

'Well, you don't mind going to temples. But I do. I never go to one. Ma does not go either so I can't understand why she is so keen all of a sudden.'

'Ana, that's enough.' Deepa was quite irritated. 'If you do not respect traditions, you should at least respect your elders. Dida was so happy when you finally agreed. It was not easy for me either to come away from Bombay leaving my work. I have so much work to complete for the exhibition in November. But Dida has been planning this for such a long time. She was waiting for you and Indrani to be sixteen, so that she could take you both to this temple.'

'Thank goodness, we are the same age. Otherwise we would have had to go there twice,' said Ananya.

'Dada has taken trouble organising this trip. He has been running around for the last two days. Just organising these two cars took so much of his time,' she said, talking about her brother.

Turning to Indrani, she added, 'It has been a lot of work for him, don't you think? And it is good that he has brought his friend along.'

'Yes, Tarakeswar uncle will have a lot to tell us about the temple, I am sure,' said Indrani.

'That's right. Your father has asked Prof. Sen to come along because he feels that you girls should benefit from this visit. I want you to remember that too, Ana. This can be a learning experience.'

Ananya didn't look very convinced.

Her mami, Indrani's mother, was fast asleep. She had woken up at four in the morning to prepare breakfast and the packed lunch for the journey. It had been a lot of work and she was exhausted. The rhythm of the journey had lulled her into sleep and very soon her head was all over Ananya's shoulder. The sweat running down her aunt's forehead made Ananya squirm.

Half an hour later, they reached the temple – the Hanseswari temple in a small, sleepy town called Bansbedia. Ananya was quite surprised to see the temple – it didn't look like a temple at all but rather like a grand castle which with its thirteen minarets had a distinct Islamic feel. The other car with her Mama, Prof. Sen, Dida and Kaushik arrived. Dida was keen to go in and start the puja right away.

'Yes, she is right,' said Mama. 'Let's go in and do the the puja first. We can take a look around the temple later.'

The striking, bright blue idol of the goddess rested on a lotus which emerged out of the navel of a reclining Shiva. It was an image that Ananya found both strange and captivating. Dida and Mami spread out plates of offerings before the goddess. The priest chanted *mantras*, smeared *kumkum* on their foreheads, lit a lamp and performed an *arti*, and chanted some more *mantras*. He went through the routine in a mechanical manner, his face betraying no emotion whatsoever.

Indrani and Ananya were pushed ahead, pulled back, made to prostrate, join hands, close eyes at various points of this ritual. Neither the actions nor the words made any sense to Ananya but she went through the motions obediently. She had decided to go through this if it made Dida happy.

Dida was choked with emotion, her eyes filled with tears. She had planned this ever since someone had told her that this special puja done when a girl child attains the age of sixteen brings peace and prosperity to the family. Having completed the rituals of the puja for both her grand-daughters she felt a tremendous sense of achievement.

'Now that the puja has been done to everyone's satisfaction, I can rest,' Dida told the others. 'I will sit here while you go around and see the temple.'

Prof. Tarakeswar Sen was a small man with an animated face. His bushy moustache added to his comic appearance. His voice, in contrast, was deep and grave and almost startled Ananya when he started to speak.

'This is not a very old temple. Early 19th century. It was built by the zamindar of this place – a man called Raja Narsimha,' he started saying.

'But it doesn't look like other temples. Why did he build it this way?' asked Ananya.

'That is, in fact, what it special about this temple. Raja Narsimha wanted to build this temple in the image of the human body- a map of the gross and the subtle elements of which our body is made up. The temple as body!'

Prof. Sen seemed pleased with the manner in which he summed up his thoughts in that last sentence. He beamed from ear to ear.

'The outer structure with its thirteen minarets is made to resemble a lotus.'

'Yes, of course, it is a lotus!' thought Ananya. 'Why did I not see the lotus to begin with?'

'But the inner structure of the temple resembles the human body the way it is understood in our *sastras*. You see these six levels,' he continued, pointing to the six stories of the temple. 'These are supposed to represent the six chakras through which the *kundalini* rises. These five ladders represent the nervous system,' he went on, excitedly.

'And, notice the sixteen *lingas*. The linga represents the male generative principle.'

Indrani nudged Ananya gently. Prof. Sen's reference to the linga had tickled her imagination.

'Why sixteen?' asked Ananya, trying to ignore Indrani's giggle. 'What is the significance of that number?'

'Sixteen represents perfection,' Prof. Sen started saying.

But before he could proceed, Ananya butted in saying, 'Perfection? In what way?'

'See, sixteen is a perfect square.'

'So is four. Or nine.'

'Yes, that's true. But, in this case, sixteen has a special meaning. Notice that of the sixteen *lingas* here, only one is white while the rest are black. The fifteen black *lingas* represent the phases of the moon from new moon to full moon but the sixteenth is the invisible moon that completes the fifteen. That is why this goddess is also called Sodasi, the one who is eternally sixteeen years old. The age sixteen is when a human being transits into adulthood and so a person is at the threshold of experiencing the world through mind and body.'

'And that is the reason we have come here because Indrani and I are sixteen?' asked Ananya. 'I don't understand any of this, frankly. There seems to be no connection except that the number sixteen crops up in many different places and, to begin with, I don't understand what is special about this number.'

Prof. Sen was quite taken aback with this outburst. Mama seemed to notice that the situation needed handling.

'So, Tarak, tell us about the architecture of this temple.'

That was all that was needed to get Prof. Sen into his lecture mode again.

'You did a good thing to stop Tarakeswar uncle,' said Indrani, later when they found themselves alone in the car. The rest of the company had got down to have tea at a roadside tea-shop. 'Otherwise, he would have gone on and on.'

'I don't mind him talking if I can follow what he is saying. What he said didn't make sense.'

It was only after they got back to Calcutta later in the day that Ananya had time to think of Prof. Sen again. Had she had been a bit too hasty in judging him? After all, he had been trying to do his best to explain to them what he could and maybe he would have made more sense if she had let him continue. She remembered his one-line summary: 'The temple as body' which had seemed silly at the time he said it but now sounded a lot more interesting. For all her atheism, she still associated a sense of the sacred with the temple and the body seemed to have very little to do with the sacred. Or, at least, that is they way she had come to think of the body.

And, in fact, the body hardly ever occupied her thoughts. It was something that had all along only asserted itself through hunger, pain, discomfort, fatigue or fever or through those moments of pleasure that it felt when cuddling under a warm blanket on a chilly night or under a cold shower on a hot summer day. But even those sharp experiences of pain or those fleeting moments of pleasure seemed to be connecting elsewhere – some other domain of experience which seemed so mental that the body again was relegated to the background.

From time to time, the body would reassert its existence – as on those occasions when Ananya would stare at her fingers or her feet and wonder who they belonged to.

Are these my fingers? Are these mine because they are connected to the rest of my body? And what is this body connected to? What if my finger were to be chopped? Would I look at the finger and then say that is my finger? How much of the I goes away with the cut finger? Some bit of it, surely, if the I were distributed evenly all over one's body. Or maybe it is not. Maybe all of that I is located somewhere in some small corner of the body. But then what would happen if that part of the body was removed? Would the rest of the body be left with no identity?

Indrani had laughed – tossed her head back and laughed, as she always did – when Ananya talked to her about her confusions.

'Chopping fingers? Why would you want to do that? But there are times I feel I could do with a different set of toes. My toes are so ugly. Yours are so little and nice not ugly like mine. . .'

Seeing that Ananya was not very interested in this conversation about toes, she said, 'What do you mean – who am I?'

Pointing out to her with her hand, she said 'See, that. That is you.'

'This?'

Maybe that is it. I am just this body. Not the fingers or the toes or the eyes or the ears but all of it. The body as a whole. But then, what happens when I grow taller or gain weight? Is there that much more of me then?

'Of course, there is. Your body has grown. Everything changes with time and so does your body,' said Indrani, in her crystal-clear manner.

Indrani will never get it. She just doesn't see it my way. Maybe she is better off that these questions don't bother her.

It was ironical that just when Ananya had entered her teens and had discovered the fascinating world of books and ideas, her body had also demanded attention around that very time. It had fought hard for a place for itself and did not want to be relegated into the background. It was Mind staking its claim on Ananya and Body refusing to give up.

It was as though Mind and Body were engaged in a one-to-one combat. Mind's moves were replete with lightness, swiftness and dexterity. Body, on the other hand, was slow on his feet but attempted to use raw force to match Mind's subtlety. Well aware of the power that Body could pack into his punches, Mind kept moving swiftly trying to stay of Body's reach. He landed two hits on Body's abdomen and then followed it with a sharp jab under his chin which caught Body completely off-guard. As Body reeled under the impact, Mind put his hand on Body's shoulder and heaved with all his might. Body staggered and fell flat on his back. Mind pounced on top of him and, pushing Body's jaw with his left hand, he reached for the knife in his pocket. It was an elegant, black-handled automatic knife with an extremely sharp edge and it was this edge that was resting against Body's throat now. It would have required just one quick movement of his hand to end the fight but Body was not an opponent to give in so easily. Even as he held the knife against Body's throat, Mind felt something sharp against his abdomen. Body had allowed himself just that much space by wriggling under Mind and had managed to pull out his *rampuri* and had dexterously unsheathed the 9-inch long blade using just his left hand. Mind did not need to look at the weapon to realise how deadly it was.

So, that is how they were locked in combat: Mind's knife-edge on Body's throat and Body's *rampuri* sticking against Mind's abdomen. They were both aware that one false move from either of them, one momentary lapse was all that the opponent needed. This was an equilibrium of Mind and Body, no doubt, but a deadly one: an equilibrium that rested not on one but on two knife edges.

Ananya was about eleven years old when she experienced a bodily sensation that stayed with her as an indelible memory.

It was an unremarkable afternoon sometime in April: hot and humid. Ananya's school had closed for the summer and she was at home devouring the pile of books that she had borrowed from the local library, all those books that Deepa would not allow her to read till she had finished her exams. An electrician had come to fix the geyser in the bathroom and Bijoya was supervising him. Having finished his work the electrician came out to the living room waiting for Bijoya to give him his money. Ananya looked up from the book she was reading to see the electrician waiting near the door. He was a young man in his early twenties, tall and dark-skinned. Bijoya got him his money and some water to drink. The young man tilted his neck back with his face looking ceiling-ward and respectfully held the glass a good six to eight inches away from his lips and started pouring out a gentle stream of water into his open mouth. He would not defile the glass by putting his mouth to it.

Ananya was always fascinated by people who could drink water like that for when she tried doing the same she would only manage to get her clothes wet. The stream of water went down the man's throat, his Adam's apple moving up and down as he drank the water. As he was half-way down the tall glass, his hand shook just a bit and the stream missed his open mouth and trickled down his chin instead. The young man quickly adjusted his arm so the stream was again directed straight into his mouth. But the little water that had come on to his chin now flowed as a tiny rivulet down the dark skin of his throat. As she watched the trickle of water against the electrician's skin, Ananya experienced a strange sensation in her body which she could not identify and left her confused.

That was, of course, when she was just eleven. When as a sixteen-year old she first set her eyes on Sahil, it was quite clear to her what she felt for him. Sahil had come down to Bombay to spend some time with his aunt, Madhu Arora, who was Ananya's neighbour. Ananya had got back somewhat early from college and was climbing up the stairs leading up to her flat when she met Madhu aunty with Sahil.

'Ananya! Where are you these days? I don't see you only,' she said.

'I have been busy, aunty. College work.'

'That day I had made some pakodas. You like, no? But you were not there and Bijoya said you will be late.'

Ananya wasn't quite listening to what Madhu aunty had to say. She looked in the direction of Sahil who had, in fact, climbed down the stairs and was waiting at the bottom of the stairs for his aunt. He was such a good-looking guy: he was tall, had broad shoulders and wavy hair. These were the three somewhat disjoint things that she noticed about him at first glance but it was enough to convince her about his looks. She found him looking at her and avoided his glance by turning to look at Madhu aunty again.

'Haan, that is my nephew – my Pune-wali elder sister's son, Sahil,' Madhu aunty went on. She completed the introduction by telling Sahil, 'And this is Ananya. She is like my daughter.'

'Hi, Ananya,' said Sahil, in a very confident manner.

Ananya liked his voice, too.

'Sahil is joining Merchant Navy. He has just finished his final exams and he has come to Bombay to do some interviews-shinterviews,' Madhu aunty said. 'Chalo, beta, we have to go now. But we will meet you later.'

Ananya could not help thinking of Sahil. She knew it was a little absurd to get so taken up by someone she had only vaguely met. She knew very little about him but, on the other hand, why bother? He looked so good and she was quite sure, as a person, he was everything that his looks announced he was.

She met him again the very next day and it was a meeting she had not left to chance. She had returned home early from college. Bijoya was surprised she wanted to have eggs – Ananya was not very fond of eggs and there were no eggs at home. Bijoya offered to go down to the grocer's but was even more surprised that Ananya volunteered to go and ask the neighbours if they had eggs. It was Sahil who opened the door and suddenly Ananya felt very silly. She was struggling for a good opening line but Sahil managed to beat her to it.

'Hi, Come in.'

'Hi! How're you? I am sorry to bother you but I just came to check with Madhu aunty if I could borrow some eggs.'

'Yeah. Sure. Maasi-ji!' he called out and went back to the program he was watching on TV. Ananya had to listen to a ten-minute account of Madhu aunty's attempts at baking before she could get the eggs out of her hand.

'But good you came today,' Madhu aunty said. 'I am wanting to call you and Deepa for dinner on day after tomorrow night. So tell your mother – she comes so late, no.'

Ananya heaved a sigh of relief as she stepped out of Madhu aunty's flat. She was cute but Ananya could take her only in small doses. But, in spite of Madhu aunty, this egg-seeking mission was very satisfying. She had managed to get just a glimpse of Sahil, but he was so wow! His forehead! Yes, she had taken good notice of his forehead today and it was clear that he was so intelligent. It was a forehead that betrayed all the wealth that lay hidden under it.

Day after tomorrow night took its own sweet time to come, or that is what Ananya felt. Deepa managed to get back early enough for them to present themselves at the Aroras in time for dinner. Vinod uncle had also just got back from work, and having showered and readied himself for dinner, he preferred to spend a peaceful half-hour downing a couple of large pegs of whisky as he listened to old Hindi movie melodies and sang along in an irritating monotone. He offered to pour Deepa a drink who decided against it. Madhu aunty suggested that they play a round of rummy while, as she euphemistically put it, Vinod uncle got ready for dinner.

It was an evening that Ananya didn't get a very good sense of. It was somewhere lost in the rummy, the Hindi melodies and the food. Sahil had played rummy enthusiastically though he did not have much to say over dinner when Ananya and Deepa tried to make conversation with him. There was one unexpected outcome of the evening, though. Sahil had to get some shopping done in town and Madhu auntywas not confident that she would be able to take him around Flora Fountain and Colaba. Deepa was, of course, too busy so it was arranged that Ananya would take care of helping Sahil with his shopping.

Ananya was pretty excited about meeting Sahil in town and taking him around shopping. He had said he wanted to buy some books and the thought of spending a leisurely afternoon with him browsing through the roadside bookshops on Fountain sounded very inviting. She had lectures in college that morning and had arranged to meet Sahil at the Samovar for lunch.

When Ananya got to Samovar after the lectures she found Sahil there waiting for her. The lunch was a bit of a disappointment because Sahil not only did not like the food but was also upset that there was no air-conditioning. He could not see why Ananya would choose to come to a place like this and pay so much for the food when it had no air-conditioning. Ananya's attempts at showing him the paintings that were on display at the galleries in Jehangir were also met with total disdain. Why would anyone waste one's time looking at this 'modern art', was Sahil's brusque retort.

The idea of spending a relaxing afternoon rummaging through second-hand books also went out of the window. Sahil's friend had advised him on the couple of books he needed to buy to handle the Merchant Navy interviews. He had only enough patience to go through the collections of three vendors and when he found one of these books he decided he had had enough. He was more eager to find out if he could get tickets to see the latest Kung-fu film that was showing at Eros.

Ananya was relieved to find the House-Full signs outside the theatre even though, as a consequence, Sahil subjected her to an hour-long introduction to martial arts movies.

They walked as he talked and by the time he had finished his monologue they found themselves in Nariman Point, outside the Oberoi. Ananya was shocked to find out how excited Sahil was to come to the doorstep of this monument. He insisted that he would stand in the middle of the drive at the entrance of the hotel while Ananya clicked a photograph of him – he absolutely had to save this moment for posterity. Ananya didn't know how to tell him that she was too embarrassed to do anything of the sort and so she quickly clicked the photograph just before the security guard turned up to drive them away.

By the time they were ready to go back home to Mulund in the evening, Ananya had decided she wanted to be left alone. She made the excuse that the general compartment in the train would be too crowded and that she would have to take the ladies'. As Ananya travelled back in the ladies' compartment on her own, Body realised that Mind had somehow managed to get a bit of the upper hand.

Knowledge

It is a week since we first met and though we have met a few times after that it is too early to say I know you well. But I have this feeling that I want to get to know you better. It is with very few people I feel that. I think it has to do with the fact that you struck me as unusual – but strangely when we say that to someone we often mean that that person is very much like us, don't we? You are like me, of course, in your tastes in reading, movies and music – which is all important to even start relating to someone. You are unusual in that you are keen to get beneath the skin of things. Penetrate. Take a deeper look. I miss that in most people I meet. The older ones have a cynicism about knowledge and the younger friends seem to be too caught up with so many other things that they seem to not want to know.

Maybe we will walk this path of knowledge together. I would want to do that. Like we walked from Churchgate to college together the day we met.

It is nice we met that day. I was doing my usual route from Churchgate station but you would not have been there if you didn't have to go to your mum's office. By the way, what does she do, did you tell me? The fact that you forgot to take money from her to pay for the educational tour, the fact that you went to her office and then took the road to college I usually do and found me walking a few steps ahead of you – are these all co-incidences, products of some deep design or just some trivial accidents? Good you came up and talked to me, though. I was wondering if I would have done that. Maybe not. I would have felt a bit too awkward to go up and talk to someone I didn't know.

So I thought to myself as we talked together that this girl Ananya is someone who can go up and introduce herself to a person she doesn't know. That was already a very important part of you I got to know. And we were talking as we took the path across the Oval –towards the Rajabai Tower. When we stood in front of the Tower, you looked up at it and said, 'This is where my dad had an accident.'

'When?' was all I could ask.

'When I was four,' you said and then added, 'He died.'

I haven't still recovered from the impact of that moment. And I said to myself that standing in the middle of the road, Ananya can talk to someone she has just met about her father's death. Ananya is unusual.

I got a music system as a gift for my birthday this year. I have been using it a lot except I had no idea what I should be doing with the mike. I can imagine a musician putting it to some use but what could I do with it? Only recently I figured out that I could read poems aloud and record them and I have been doing these kind of silly exercises with the mike. It is great fun though and also quite freaky, in a way.

I have been reading about these things: how sound gets recorded, how it is converted to electrical pulses by the microphone and that is stored as magnetic information on the cassette. It is freaky to think that a set of words, intonations, inflections lays out a pattern of these magnetic bits on the tape. It would be so amazing if we could see these magnetic bits, to see how our words look. Would they look like words on a page?

Anyway, today I decided I am going to speak into the mike and record it for you. It will be great if you can record yourself speaking and send the tape to me. Will be a great way to communicate, won't it?

I thought it is quite weird to talk into a box like this. At first, I wasn't even sure that I would be able to do the recording. Had no idea whether the small two-in-one I have would let me do it. But it had a built-in mike which actually worked. So here I am.

It is funny you should tell me that I get under the skin of things and penetrate the depths. You could well have been talking about yourself when you said that. Of course, it is not that I am not like that and I agree with you when you say we are similar in many ways. But what impresses me is the way you persist in getting to grips with the thing that has caught your fancy. You do not give up with a superficial understanding of it. I find so many of our college-mates just dabbling in things so as to be able to tell others how many different things they are interested in. In that sense, I find your range of interests somewhat limited. You have just not learnt to float. You are the swimmer who will head straight for the depths. I also like to test the depths but my sense of survival is very strong. If it gets too much for me and I find myself choked and unable to breathe I give up and try to come back to the surface. You would rather sink than give up like that. At least, that's how I have come to understand you.

You are right in seeing me as a person who is able to go and talk to strangers easily. I don't get bogged down by such things. But it was quite unlike me to talk about something like my father's death. I don't know how that happened. It was just that moment of being totally free of any self-consciousness. It just came out naturally.

I have had only my mother with me all my life – and she is all I have. But I can't believe how much of me is shaped by the absence of my father. The absence of near and dear ones when you are growing up can determine to a certain extent, what kind of person you are going to be. I hadn't realised this until recently.

I recorded the earlier bit some time ago. I played it now to see how I sound. I do feel my recorded voice sounds like someone else's. Also, I was quite surprised to hear the last bit about the absence of my father. I had never consciously thought of that before. It is interesting how these "conversations" are bringing out of me things I did not know existed.

I cannot even begin to imagine life without my father. Or my mother. I can only guess what it must mean to you to have lost your father when you were only four years old. But I can understand, to an extent, what you mean when you say that the absence of a person can shape us. I have experienced that in my Daadi's death.

My Daadi died two years ago. The death was traumatic for me in spite of the fact that she had been very ill for a few years. Her death created an absence and a void. The more I dug into that void the bigger it started becoming tying up my life with the lives of my parents and grandparents. I don't dig more into it now but every now and then it opens its mouth, yawning wide, threatening to swallow me and it does so with a force of its own.

After my Daadi's death, it seems almost like I have inherited from her the anxieties and fears that haunted her. And that has made me a different kind of person. My friends find me too intense. I have heard that said to me in school so often and now in college too. Some even think it is put-on. Some have reacted to the way I talk and have described it as being everything from bookish to convoluted and incomprehensible. I only know that it is not an act. The intensity is something that even I have not been able to fully understand – all I know is that it is a force within that seeks to find expression.

But, I don't want to let myself get sucked in by this. Want to get away from it and engage myself with other things. College work, in itself, is too boring. But I have dug out some books on psychology in the college library. I find these very interesting. Am beginning to get interested in Sociology as well. Never realised in school that one could study human beings or society in this manner. And am trying to read as much fiction as I can lay my hands on. That is what is keeping me going, I think.

It's been several months since we started talking to each other through these taped conversations. It has been so good for me. I think I have learnt more through these conversations than what I have in college. It has helped me figure out many things about myself which would not have happened otherwise – not even in real conversations, where the other is talking to you even as you talk and so you are taken along some other path and not allowed to explore the path that you wanted. With these taped conversations, you really get to follow the thread of thought as far as you want, without any interruption but, at the same time, you know that there is a listener who is going to respond or react to what you have said. Why is that not like exchanging letters or written notes? I don't really know. But I think when I write the flow of thoughts is rather different. When I speak it feels more direct, somehow.

I agree with you when you say this form of conversation does not interrupt a line of thought. In that sense, you can really develop an idea to its fullest. The fact that there is a listener, not just a passive listener but an active respondent, at the other end is also important. But I can imagine that we can do the same with writing. If we sustain letter-writing in the way we have sustained these conversations I am sure we can communicate as effectively. As I told you right in the beginning, I feel that this is just another form of writing – on magnetic tape instead of paper. But I am interested in what you say about how this medium allows you to explore yourself. Do tell me more about it.

Well, I meant there are things I vaguely know or have only some clues about which I have been able to understand more clearly. Like my relationship with my mother – her anxieties, my reactions to these. Earlier, I would just react and get irritated. By churning it out on these tapes I am getting a better picture of what is going on in her mind. It gives me the opportunity to look at things from her point of view which is never possible when I am in a purely reactive mode.

There is something else that became very clear in these conversations.

Since I joined college a year before you did – I still can't believe you did your XI in school. I was just waiting to get out of having to wear those ridiculous uniforms – sorry, I was saying since I joined college a year before you did and didn't know anyone at all I decided to go out and make a few friends. Of these, I got to know Shivani and Priyanka quite well. I can almost see you smiling your wicked smile when I mention these names but, you know, they are not a bad sort, at all. They are just different. The problem is that I initially tried to be like them even though I knew that is not what I wanted to be. It seemed like fun because it also allowed me to get a feeling of being able to assert myself – do what I want to do. But I felt sick of all of it very soon because I could not get them to talk about anything except boys, clothes or make-up. So after a while, I distanced myself from them which was all right. But I also started reacting to them in very unreasonable ways, mocking them and making fun of them whenever I got the chance.

It was when I got talking to you about Sahil that I realised how I was wronging Shivani and Priyanka. I felt I was reacting so much to them because there was a bit – quite a bit, in fact – of them in me as well. My infatuation for Sahil, however brief, was not different in any way from what Shivani felt for her boyfriends. It was just that she let herself go headlong into the second infatuation the moment the first was over. It was like a whole line of Sahils she had to go through. But, at the bottom of it all, I wasn't that different. I think I knew this about myself all along but was too damn scared to admit it till I could speak into the tape and get it out of myself.

Yes, I understand what you are saying. It is not that we are not affected by bouts of infatuation like these other girls or that when we see a really handsome boy our hearts don't skip a beat. It is that these girls just stop there. Even their interest in boys is not triggered by anything more than looks. My problem is that even the kind of looks they go for has a superficiality stamped on it. There is a certain character that a face acquires when there is an intelligent engagement of the mind. You can see it in the eyes. I know this sounds like I am getting a bit carried away, but it is true, isn't it?

Thanks for letting me know about the Study Circle. I know very little about Marxism but this will be a good way to get to know more. I am also hoping we get to meet a different crowd at the Study Circle. Have had enough of the kind of people we otherwise meet in college.

Met Vishal the other day just after the Study Circle meeting you didn't attend. He had been talking about some music he wanted me to listen to and had got these tapes. These are his favourite rock bands and he is very excited about them. I am not at all familiar with this music but thought I will give it a shot. Some of it is pretty good, in fact. This band called the Doors, I really liked. I guess you know them since you know this kind of music well.

Yes, I really like the Doors too. Jim Morrison's live performances feel like theatre – it is much more than music, in that sense because it brings poetry and theatre also into it. I have spent quite some time talking to Vishal about music and we exchanged notes about our favourite bands and albums. But I find his passion for rock a bit put-on. It is to the exclusion of everything else. His whole manner changes when he is talking about the music – his voice, his swagger – I find all that very silly. What I found most shocking, however, was his attitude to people in college who don't speak English. Initially, when he started talking about them as "vernies", I didn't quite understand what he was saying. It was only later I figured that he was using the term to refer to people who have had their school education in the vernacular. But, in fact, it is much more than that – as I later realised. It is really a huge cultural divide between "people like us" and "the vernies". The vernies don't wear jeans, or when they do they wear really pathetic imitations, they have oily hair, they eat *vada-pao* and, even worse, admit to watching Hindi movies. Of course, we all watch Hindi movies – I bet Vishal does – but one is not supposed to admit it at all. He found it a huge contradiction that I could discuss rock music with him and then go down to the canteen with three vernie girls for chai. This has really put me off him.

I had come across that attitude to vernies too, in Vishal and a few others but, frankly, hadn't given it that much thought. Maybe their attitudes are a bit diluted in my presence because they think of me as half-vernie, anyway – anyone coming from the suburbs, and that too not from places like Bandra or Juhu, goes down several notches in their ranking, I guess. But I do hear them making vernie jokes very often. Like the other day, I heard them joking about how when a vernie says, 'Balls,' he is actually talking of a girl's boobs. I pretended I hadn't heard them because I was so embarrassed.

I must confess I found that funny though that is always the problem. It is really a thin line that divides humour from prejudice. Sometimes because of this one may even go along with what is being said but when prejudice starts showing up one should make sure to clearly distance oneself from it. This becomes even more tricky for people like us for whom English is, more or less, the only language that is available. I was discussing this with my dad the other day and he was saying that English is firmly entrenched all over in our systems, literature, bureaucracy and everyday transactions. So he was arguing one can't wish it away. He was telling me how even a writer like Premchand kept notes in English for his Hindi and Urdu novels. All that still doesn't say why one should display attitudes steeped in arrogance towards those who don't have the fluency in English. Of course, my dad had no problem accepting that.

Today is our first day in senior college. I am so excited! This is going to be the experience of real college life – quite unlike the last two years. I spoke to Prof. Mistry and he said I have a month's time to decide about my subjects. Like you, I was also very keen on literature but, on the other hand, I felt I could keep up my interests in literature alive on my own. Ma also felt that Economics will be the right thing for me to do. I know you would never do Eco because of the maths involved. But I think I may finally opt for it.

I have decided on Literature, Socio and Psycho. But, frankly, it doesn't matter much unless we have good teachers because what you and I can get out of reading in the library and discussing with each other is going to mean a lot more. I spoke to Prof. Nath from the Philosophy department. He is quite happy to help us with some of our readings in philosophy. That might be a good thing to do.

Though I am quite amused to see how arbitrary this whole process of choosing subjects is. And to think it determines so much of what you will be in later life – at least, in terms of the career it veers you towards. Do we really know what we want to be? I am not even sure I want to be anything. At this stage, I am simply going by some vague interests and instincts in deciding what subjects I should be studying.

Well, I am not sure that our decisions are so uninformed. After all, we like some subjects and we decide to pursue them. Maybe we don't know too much about these subjects but we do get excited about some of them.

In any case, it is about making a commitment to something and having made a commitment to follow it through. That is the sort of thing we may have to do with so many other things in life. Otherwise, one will end up doing nothing at all.

How I wish I had that kind of clarity! I know this is not just about making a choice of subjects in college – this is the kind of thing, as you rightly say, one will have to face all the time. And one does. And that is my problem. I can't understand how others make these choices. I find myself incapable of doing it. If I finally end up making some decision I find that it is arbitrary. To pretend that it is the result of some well-thought out process is something I can't get myself to do. If ever I figure out how we can attribute meaning to our actions . . .

I still don't believe that it is as arbitrary as you make it out to be. There are several levels of meanings and each time we dig further we may uncover more. But the fact that we don't know the ultimate reason behind what we do does not mean that we have no grounds at all to think that our actions have some rationale behind them. I think one tends to get a bit absolutist trying to seek ultimate meanings for everything.

It is funny how you and I spend so much time thinking of the smallest issues. About what we appear as, whom we talk to, what we read, how we understand things. Almost everything. But then there are people like my cousin Indrani – you know the one from Calcutta – well, she fell in love with this boy and my uncle found out and there was a huge row because they didn't approve of the boy but, even more, didn't approve of what she had done. How could she even think of something like love!. They argued that she was only seventeen and that this was no age to get involved with a guy. But I think it was not so much the age but just that they saw it as an act of defiance. They felt threatened by Indrani was saying she was old enough to make her own decisions. Actually, she wasn't and she knew that. She had to be eighteen before she could do anything. And that's what she did.

A few weeks ago, she set out from home to go to college. No one knew that she had packed some clothes in her handbag. Her boyfriend had already made arrangements for them to have a court wedding. So that afternoon my uncle got a call saying they were married. God! You should have seen how the whole extended family, the neighbourhood, the community got worked up about it. Anyway, there wasn't much they could do because the marriage was legal. I wonder what you and I would have done in Indrani's place. Would we have had that kind of belief in our own decision in order to take the plunge she did?

While I can't help admiring your cousin for what she has done and for the courage she has shown, it frightens me to think that someone our age can take such a huge decision. Where does the clarity come from? I can see she is quite unlike you and, certainly not like me at all. It is quite another kind of person who can do something like this.

But there is something else I have to share with you – something that happened last night. You know my cousin, Varsha, is down here from the US with her husband. Varsha is a great fan of Kishori Amonkar who was performing at the IMG in Xavier's College last night – you know they have an Indian Music group there? I like Kishori Amonkar too and it was a great feeling to be allowed to go to a late night concert – Pappa wouldn't have allowed me to go had it not been for Varsha and Vivek. The music was great and I thoroughly enjoyed the whole experience. But I wanted to tell you about what happened on the way back home from the concert. It was an experience that left me shaken.

But I see that there is very little tape left in this cassette. I will have to wait till I meet you to talk about this.

Sacrifice

Mrs. Batliwala had an early business meeting at Juhu that morning. The drive from Haji Ali to Juhu would take about an hour, she thought, and decided to leave home by seven. Her driver was getting the car out of the car-park and to save time she decided to go to there herself. Occupied with thoughts about the meeting, she wasn't paying too much attention as she walked to the car. She was just a few steps away from where her car was parked when she felt her foot land in a squishy mess on the floor. She looked down and found to her absolute horror that her foot had landed in a pile of shit. Shit!?? In the car-park of Sea Palace Apartments?

'Watchman! Watchman!'

The watchman, her driver, the sweeper, a couple of maids who worked in the building all came rushing to Mrs. Batliwala's help.

Mrs. Batliwala was furious. 'What is this? Who has done this? Which of you?'

No one had anything to say in reply.

'I am going to report this to the building secretary. Whoever it is will not stay in this building anymore. I will make sure.'

It was important to find the culprit, no doubt, but what was she to do with her shoe. Her left shoe was a horrible mess and the stink was unbearable. Mrs. Batliwala dared to look down just once and her heart broke to see her favourite brown Gucci covered with the muck. She had been walking, as she always did, with an air of determination. Her unfortunate foot had, consequently, landed quite forcefully in the shit and was splattered liberally till her ankle. Her instinctive reaction was to go back home to shower and change but then a moment's reflection told her that she wouldn't dream of entering her home wearing this shoe. She couldn't even think of entering the lift in this state. Her driver came running with some old newspaper from the car but there was no way she was going to wipe her foot with it. Luckily there was a tap at one end of the car park. She washed her shoe and foot under the tap half-wondering what the water would do to the leather. When she had managed to clean the muck off her shoe and her foot, she decided to go up to her flat and spend the rest of the morning washing herself in the bathtub.

It was not until late evening that she could meet Mr. Motwani, the honorary secretary of the housing society. Motwani listened carefully to her story, summoned the watchmen, enquired with the sweeper, talked to his own driver and did all that was expected of him in his official capacity. The watchmen and the sweeper said that this had been happening regularly in the past few months but they were not sure whether they should talk to any one of the building officials. The watchman had instructed the sweeper to have it cleaned each time but this morning Mrs. Batliwala had walked out into the car-park before it could be cleaned.

Mrs. Batliwala was not happy. She wanted quicker action. The culprit had to be found and punished.

'Let us call all the drivers and maids and ayahs and watchmen and question them. We cannot have them do this to our building,' she screamed.

Motwani tried to calm her down.

'Mrs. Batliwala, please, please. Let us not get so excited. I know what has happened to you is terrible. But if we have to find the culprit we must act calmly. I think it is best to wait till tomorrow morning and ask the watchman to keep a track of who is going to the car-park at that early hour of the morning.'

It was with considerable difficulty that Motwani managed to get Mrs. Batliwala to agree to what he was saying. About an hour after she had left, the watchman returned. He obviously had something to say.

'Saheb, I know who the person is,' he said.

'Why didn't you tell me earlier?' asked Motwani, somewhat irritated.

'Nahi, Saheb. I really didn't know how to say it. Especially in front of Batliwala Memsaheb.'

'Why, what is it?'

'I feel bad to say this but it is Hathiramani Saheb from the eighth floor.'

'What?!!' Motwani was shocked.

'Yes, Saheb, ever since he moved into this building a few months ago this has been happening and I have seen him myself. If it had been one of us I would have put a stop to it long ago. I personally would have taken care of thrashing that person. But when I found out it was a Saheb . . .'

It took a while before Motwani recovered from the shock. He realised this was a situation which needed delicate handling. He decided to meet Mrs. Batliwala in the society office the next morning and discuss the new development with her. When Mrs. Batliwala entered his office the next morning, Prahlad was just behind her. He had been sent down by his grandfather to hand over a cheque to the society office. Seeing Mrs. Batliwala go in, he decided to wait outside the door. Listening to the conversation going on inside the room, it didn't take him too long to figure out what had happened. Motwani was trying very hard to explain to Mrs. Batliwala that there wasn't much they could do now because the culprit turned out to be a resident of the building.

'We will have to ask him to leave,' Mrs. Batliwala thundered. 'How can he make a toilet out of our parking lot? He has two toilets in his own flat – can he not use them?'

Motwani wiped off the beads of perspiration on his forehead.

'Mrs. Batliwala, you have to understand. Hathiramani is as much a resident of this building as you and I are. We can send him a letter or even decide to impose a fine on him. And, of course, we will make sure that he does not do this again. But we can't ask him to leave.'

'We have to. He has no business behaving like this – like a cheap slum-dweller. How did we even let a person like this into our building?' she shouted.

'Well, he had the money to buy a flat here. He has risen from a very humble background, ma'am, so to some extent he is not used to living in a flat.'

'Well, I can see he still belongs there – in the slums, with those cockroaches and rodents. How disgusting!'.

In spite of her apparent expression of disgust, Prahlad could see that Mrs. Batliwala had already begun to show signs of losing steam. She finally agreed to let Hathiramani get away with just having to pay a fine.

The whole conversation kept replaying in Prahlad's mind through that day. He couldn't get over what Hathiramani had done. He couldn't just believe that (as Mrs. Batliwala probably did) that Hathiramani's actions were a result of his being an uncouth parvenu who did not belong to the new exalted society that he had gained entry into just because of his recent acquisition of wealth. Prahlad knew how self-conscious he himself had been when he had been uprooted from Koliwada and placed in Haji Ali overnight. He was careful about how he conducted himself not just with others in the building but even within the confines of his new home. A parvenu, a fully self-aware one that is, takes immense pains to hide the fact that he is one, to erase every vestige of his history. If after all that he still gets shown up for what he is, it is out of ignorance of how to handle the situations that his new status brings him face to face with. But before the situation gets the better of him he will try his best to use his native intelligence to tackle the situation.

On the other hand, Hathiramani seemed intent to announce to the world that here he was, someone from a very humble background who had lived in such miserable conditions that he didn't have a toilet he could use. Rather than trying to hide his history, Hathiramani wanted to connect with it and, in the process, if the world gained access to it he didn't care.

When Prahlad's family had moved from the secure surroundings of their King's Circle home to Koliwada the biggest problem they had faced was coping with the toilet arrangements in their new home. There were two common toilets on every floor to be shared by ten homes which meant that each group of five families had access to one toilet. The toilet locked and each family had a key, so that outsiders would not use it. But to Kamala, Prabha and Prahlad the thought of having to step out of their house in order to use the toilet was almost traumatic. Luckily, they had a small wash area inside the house which, covered with a plastic curtain, functioned as a bath space and a urinal. But the only toilet was the one down the corridor.

Kamala figured that the best thing to do would be to wake up very early and use the toilet when everyone else was asleep. This also suited Prabha because she had to leave home very early for work. But, by the time Prahlad would be up at around seven in the morning, there would be a long queue outside the toilet. For the first few days after moving to Koliwada, Prahlad decided he would use the toilet in school. But even that was not a good enough solution so that he eventually had to get used to the idea of coming to terms with the communal toilet at home. The seven o' clock queue outside the toilet was made up mainly of men; the women had somehow figured out ways of being more discreet in their use of the toilet.

It took Prahlad a much shorter time to get used to this toilet than he had imagined at first. It was a great help, in fact, that the etiquette of the toilet space was that you stood there in the queue without acknowledging anyone else. Of course, Prahlad was new to the place and knew no one but even the others, who knew each other well and would otherwise be seen having a chat, would pretend that they existed in the queue in isolation and no else existed around them. This was a brilliant strategy, Prahlad realised, to ensure one's privacy. A couple of older men would hide themselves behind the morning newspapers while some others would use the time to brush their teeth. This latter custom, though efficient in terms of time utilisation, had its own problems.

On one occasion, the boy who lived two doors away had left the tooth powder in his mouth for the entire time that he was getting done with his ablutions – except that the tooth powder was a home-made variety, in other words, it was charred tobacco – and the boy had gone into a swoon inside the toilet thanks to the effect of the tobacco. The laugh that everyone had when the boy was safely brought out helped Prahlad relax and come to terms with this early morning ritual.

On the other hand, when Prahlad had moved into his grandfather's flat in Sea Palace Apartments he also had trouble with the toilet there. He was not accustomed to using a Western style toilet having grown up using the Indian-style. But it had taken him only a couple of days to sort out his problems and get used to the new setting. He could guess that Hathiramani had similar problems with the toilet in his apartment. But with some effort, Prahlad thought, Hathiramani could easily have worked out these problems. He could have gone further and got the toilet designed to his convenience. He owned the flat and he had decorated the rest of it lavishly. He could easily afford the toilet of his liking. But how was anyone to build the toilet of his liking? No, Hathiramani had not found an architect or an interior designer who could make him a toilet without any walls: where he could sit and contemplate the vastness of the space around him, the blueness of the sky and the greenness of the trees. He did not want a toilet where four walls would imprison him and leave him to suffocate in his own stench.

Unwittingly, Mrs. Batliwala was right. Hathiramani did belong in the slums where he started his life. It was this sense of belonging that made him what he was. His identity was clear; he was a slum-dweller. No matter where life took him, no matter how much wealth came his way, Hathiramani would remain what he always was. Even at his age, Prahlad realised that it was something special to have that sense of belonging. Where did he belong? He didn't belong here in Sea Palace Apartments in spite of the fact that he had made a lot of effort over the last three years of his life here to fit in. And, in fact, he fitted in quite well. In his appearance, his clothes, his bearing, his manner, his tastes in food, books, music and movies and in his knowledge of the world he was very much a person from this part of town. But, yet, something kept telling him how ephemeral all this was. This was not where he belonged.

But, on the other hand, did he belong to the Koliwada that he had left behind? All through his stay in Koliwada he was treated as an outsider. Even after he had made peace with his surroundings, had made friends there, he still stood out somehow. If he had friends it was because the boys who had become his friends were indulgent towards him and they were indulgent because he stood out as different amongst them. But he didn't mesh in; that was clear.

Maybe he was somewhere in between. It was a class issue, after all, and he belonged somewhere in the middle: not in Haji Ali or in Koliwada but in King's Circle's middle class milieu which he had left a long time ago. But did he really belong there? He had sought to find out. He had gone down to meet his old friends in King's Circle, spent a day with them – all his old friends: Rajesh, Sanjay, Ajit, Kamal, Shekhar, Satyen, the whole lot of them. They were all very happy to meet him after such a long time. There was warmth in their manner but somehow Prahlad felt something missing. When he tried to talk to them they felt that he had become probably too much of a townside kid. Or was it that he went to a fancy college? They felt some discomfort relating to him though most of them couldn't quite put their finger on it. Funnily, Prahlad felt that they had grown up in a way where they took their middle-class lives for granted: the security and the comforts it guaranteed. He felt somehow that they would not be able to handle life on the streets which he felt Koliwada had equipped him with. He tried to see if he would fit in with them but Haji Ali and Koliwada kept coming in between: he realised that he belonged nowhere. He realised that he would have to learn the art of living in spaces without belonging to them.

In Wilson College where he studied there was no one Prahlad could talk to about his life, his problems or his confusions. Or rather, he made sure that he did not get so close to anyone, that he would have to reveal the truth about his circumstances. Conversations with friends were about the world out there, never about himself and, consequently, never about his friends' intimate lives. He never visited his friend's homes because he did not want to invite anyone home. It suited him to spend most of his time either in the college library or in his grandfather's library.

In this somewhat stifling world that Prahlad found himself in, Japa was like a breath of fresh air. Prahlad looked forward to spending time with her in the evenings. They would take long walks along the sea-face and she would tell him of herself and her friends, the things they talked about, the stories and the jokes they shared, their passions and their vanities, their loves and their relationships. Prahlad loved listening to these stories. It not only gave him a glimpse of the world he had no direct access to, but it also allowed him to cultivate an air of familiarity with this life when talking to his college friends.

'Why am I boring you with all these stories? You may not even interested,' she would sometimes say but Prahlad would implore her to go on, holding on to every word she said.

He had resisted the changes that life in his new home and in his college were bringing about but it was not possible to insulate himself completely. He was letting himself relax in the company of his college friends by the end of his third year in college and, to his surprise, he found that his friends never asked him awkward questions – they were quite happy to let him be.

The next two years of his college life were exciting for Prahlad. It was a time for making new friends and learning new things. It was also the time when physics suddenly came alive. Till then, Prahlad had not taken to physics – in fact, he had not enjoyed studying anything in college except maths. He was learning more out of reading books on literature and philosophy in the library. His exposure to physics was limited to what was being done in college and that bored him to tears. Things didn't change till he chanced upon some good books on physics at this stage and suddenly a whole new world opened up.

The next couple of years were infused with a heady, dream-like quality. Prahlad almost forgot about what lay beyond college. His grandfather had agreed to take care of his education till he finished his B.Sc. Prahlad would have liked nothing more than to do a Masters in Physics and go ahead to do a Ph.D. But, deep down, he knew that that was not possible. He had to get a job and earn his living – earn not just for himself but also for Kamala.

Japa had finished college by then and spent a year working in an advertising agency. Her grandfather was keen to get her married as soon as he could find the right match. An old friend of his showed up one day. His son, Suresh, who was a doctor, lived in the U.S. He would come down and meet Japa after which the date for the engagement would be finalised.

It was not until he heard that the date of Japa's engagement had been fixed that Prahlad realised how things around him were going to change once more. He would finish college soon and his grandfather would, as promised, find him a job in the printing industry. But nothing else was clear. Would he and Kamala continue to live in Haji Ali? What were his grandfather's plans? Did he want to continue to live in Bombay or settle down in Madras? If they left Haji Ali, where would he and Kamala go? What were Prabha's plans? All these years of staying alone in Surat and the anxiety of being unmarried well into her thirties had made her ill and she wanted to return to Bombay too.

Just around the time Prahlad was beginning to worry about the future, Kamala got a phone call – from Krishnan. He had come back to Bombay, he said. From which it could be inferred that he had left Bombay for some other place – probably, to escape from the clutches of his creditors or, even possibly, the police. He wanted Kamala to come back. Kamala had given him Prabha's number. Prabha was relieved to know her father had returned. She saw this as the best way the family could get back together. Maybe this would even be a new beginning for Krishnan.

She lost no time at all getting in touch with the broker who had helped them find a place in Koliwada the last time around. It was not very long before she called Kamala to tell her that she had found a place in Koliwada and that they should plan to move in there within the next three weeks by which time Prahlad was expected to be done with his final exams in college.

How was he to go back and live in Koliwada after all these years in Haji Ali, Prahlad wondered. No one around him thought that this was of any concern. Neither was he sure how he would cope with living with his father. He had lived all these years without his father and, even worse, with the knowledge that the family had been abandoned by his father. He could not understand how Kamala and Prabha could simply accept him back with no questions asked. It angered him even more to think that Krishnan expected to be so accepted by them as though it was his birthright. He seemed to want to offer no explanation to anyone. In fact, even now he didn't refrain from taunting Kamala at having taken the decision to go and live with his father in Haji Ali, or so Kamala told Prahlad in between the quiet tears she shed. Why do you have to just take everything lying down, he asked his mother. She had nothing to say in reply.

I will just wait till I find myself a job and then I am on my own, Prahlad decided. I have to get a job soon.

Japa's engagement ceremony was a simple affair. Suresh and his parents wanted an early wedding and the two families agreed on the earliest auspicious date. Japa would be married within the month and would leave for the U.S. soon after. Not only was everything around Prahlad changing but it was happening at a dramatic pace.

At the suggestion of the family priest, it was also decided to hold a small puja at home before the wedding. The priest had also obliquely hinted that the puja should not be performed by Prahlad's grandfather – a widower could not be entrusted the job of reviving auspiciousness in the home. Prahlad would perform the puja.

It was the very first time that Prahlad had been entrusted such an important task. He felt quite overawed by the responsibility that was laid on his young shoulders. A fire was lit in the middle of the room and with a folded leaf held delicately between his fingers, Prahlad poured the ghee into the sacrificial fire, chanting the mantras each time he poured the ghee.

Om Prajapataye! Idam na mama,
Prajapataye Svaha.
Om Somay! Idam na mama,
Somaye Svaha.

Om Indraya! Idam na mama,
Indraye Svaha.
Idam na mama.

This is not mine. All this I offer to the elements.

The smoke burned Prahlad's eyes. Tears ran down his cheeks.

Idam na mama. This is not mine. All this I offer to the elements. To the cosmic energies that constitute this world as they constitute me. All this I offer – all this which does not belong to me and which never belonged to me.

As the smoke burned Prahlad's eyes, tears ran down his cheeks.

To what or to whom do I belong?

Death

Prahlad was busy at work in his office when the phone rang. He couldn't identify the voice of the person asking to speak to him.

'Yes, Prahlad here.' It might be one of his clients, he thought.

'Hi, Prahlad. This is Vinay.'

'Vinay..? '

'Yes, Vinay Shah. From Wilson.'

'Yes, yes, Vinay. Sorry I am very bad at identifying voices over the phone.'

'Hell! I was shocked you didn't recognise me. But I must say you sound terribly important.'

'No. Just busy.'

'All right. This won't take long. I am having a party with all our buddies from college on Friday. I would like you to come.'

'But, Vinay. You know I have never liked these parties.'

'Yeah. But, dammit, this is my farewell. I am going back to Rhodesia on Sunday. And don't know when I will ever return. So I want you to be around.'

'Fine, Vinay. I am busy now. But I will call you later.'

Prahlad called Vinay that evening.

'Hi, Vinay. Prahlad.'

Prahlad got to the point quickly. 'Like I was telling you this morning, I don't think I will be able to come for your party. It is not just because I don't enjoy these parties but . . .'

'Hey, No! Man, I am not taking no for an answer. I am surprised you are saying this even though you know you may never meet me again.'

'No, I will meet you. But before Friday. It's just that . . .'

'Just what? Look, I am taking the train tonight to Nadiad. I have to meet my folks there and will return only on Friday morning. And Friday and Saturday I will be busy winding up before I leave. There's a shit load of stuff to be done. Make it Friday evening. You may not be great friends with many of the guys who will be around but they are not bad.'

'No. It's not that. You know I lost my mother recently. It's hardly a month.'

'Oh! I am sorry. I didn't know that. What happened? '

'She was hypertensive and had acute diabetes. She finally had a heart attack.'

'I am so sorry Prahlad. You have often talked to me about her. I know that you were very attached to her. It must be very bad. I understand. All right, if that's the reason you don't want to come I won't force you. But if you feel up to it then land up at my place at eight on Friday. I have to leave to go to the station now.'

By Thursday, Prahlad was beginning to wonder whether it was right to have refused Vinay's invitation. For all those years in college he had avoided going to parties because he was worried that he might be exposed as someone who did not belong there. When he had made the attempt to go to a couple of them he was quite bored with the conversation and just didn't enjoy himself. But it was Vinay's farewell, not just any other party.

He still remembered the day he had met Vinay outside the physics lecture hall. This was in the first year of college and it was only a month after Vinay had come to Bombay from Rhodesia. He had grown up in Salisbury where his family had lived for three generations. His father owned a corner-shop which sold Indian provisions. What Vinay knew of India was what he gleaned during his childhood vacations in his family home in Nadiad and from his limited exposure to Hindi movies.

He was as friendless as Prahlad was in Wilson College and that was the bond between these two. Prahlad also discovered a freedom in relating to Vinay because he felt he owed Vinay no explanation about his family or his circumstances. The other classmates were always more curious about these historical details.

What bound Vinay and Prahlad together was also their contrasting personalities. Vinay had a deep-rooted conviction about the ordinariness of human existence – or, at least, he believed most people are destined to live ordinary lives. It followed as a corollary, he thought, that the best we could do is to enjoy what we can of this life and that enjoyment Vinay sought in simple pleasures like music, cinema or parties. His indulgences, if they could be called that, were tempered by the knowledge that he would return to Salisbury one day to take care of his father's business.

On the other hand, Prahlad had, in spite of all that he had to go through in life, hated the very notion of ordinariness. He believed that those destined for a greater life would be touched by the magic of the extra-ordinary. He always dreamed great things: like wanting to be a theoretical physicist, for example. He worked towards this end not just by immersing himself in the immense tomes on physics he could find in the college library but also by being arrogantly careless about experimental work, which, he was convinced, was for lesser mortals. He would tease Vinay for being so conscientious about his laboratory work but he nevertheless found Vinay's laboratory journals very useful to complete his own work. In return, he would help Vinay solve physics and math problems and, as an added bonus, deliver long lectures on philosophy which Vinay listened to with great patience in spite of the fact that he was not very interested. It was not surprising then that Prahlad and Vinay were both passionate Beatles fans: for Vinay the appeal lay in the simplicity of their compositions, for Prahlad it lay in their profundity.

Should I go to the party tomorrow, Prahlad wondered. It was only a month since Kamala's death. Prahlad had not met his friends since and neither did he feel inclined to do so. He had tried to immerse himself in work but the work seemed more mechanical than ever: there were none of the creative challenges that he had encountered before. Books were his only companions but when he was not reading he felt overcome with intense feelings of loneliness. Sometimes he would go down to Haji Ali and walk along the sea-face but then he would miss talking to Japa. He would go down to the Planetarium to meet his friends, Neela and Nitin, but there was not much he could share with them. He was terrified that he felt a meaningless and purposelessness in everything around him, but it troubled him even more that he was letting himself be overcome by such negative feelings. But the power of these feelings were such that there was not much he could do about them and there was a danger he might even succumb to them, he felt.

I think I need to meet people, thought Prahlad, as he decided finally by Thursday evening that he would go to Vinay's party. When he showed up in Vinay's hostel room on Friday, Vinay was delighted.

'Thanks, Prahlad. You are a real friend. Come sit down. When everyone is here, we will go to New York.'

New York was a small restaurant and bar at the corner of Hughes Road and a regular hang-out for the Wilsonians. Tonight's party is somewhat more formal, Vinay had felt, and he had attempted to reserve tables in New York. The restaurant owner was initially sceptical but reservation somehow sounded like the kind of thing people did in big restaurants, so he was only too happy to accept the request.

The evening turned out to be more interesting than Prahlad imagined it would be. He was meeting his college-mates for the first time since he finished college – Hiten, Anselm, Paras, Rohan, Joolz, Mudz were all there and some others he didn't know. Vandana, Samina and Annie were the only girls in the party. None of the other girls had got permission to stay out so late, Vinay explained.

Prahlad initially remained aloof and quiet. He kept politely refusing the beer that was offered to him, but eventually gave in and decided to have some shandy. The shandy helped him to get into the mood of the party but it was more the attention that he got from his friends that helped Prahlad relax. He was the only one around who had a job – a real job, in a swanky office in the middle of Kala Ghoda. It sounded very glamorous too to think that Prahlad had important advertising agencies as clients. A couple of his friends wanted to see his work-place and when Prahlad pulled out his wallet and handed them his visiting card, his friends looked at him with admiration. That was when Prahlad decided to have his second glass of shandy.

At around eleven, the girls got ready to leave and Prahlad thought that was the right time for him to go home too. But Vinay insisted he should stay back. 'You can spend the night in the hostel, Prahlad. Just relax now and enjoy yourself.'

It was half past midnight when the party finally broke up.

'I haven't eaten much all evening and have had quite a bit to drink,' said Vinay. 'Why don't we go down to Sukh Sagar for *pav bhaji?*'

Prahlad hadn't eaten much either and welcomed the idea.

'This is one thing about Bombay I will miss,' said Vinay, as they sat on the mats spread on the pavement near the stall and watched the *bhaji* being pounded with a ladle. 'It will be more than just this I will miss, of course,' he said, with a touch of sadness creeping into his voice.

'I haven't had the time all evening to ask you about your mother's . . .' Vinay hesitated, because he did not want to use the word death and didn't quite know what to say instead. 'Tell me about it. How've you been coping with it?'

Hesitant at first, Prahlad opened up slowly and started telling Vinay about her illness and her death.

When they finished their meal, almost involuntarily, Prahlad and Vinay started walking in the direction of Opera House, to the bridge which went over the railway tracks. The bridge was a favourite haunt of theirs and they had spent several evenings sitting on the railing facing the railway tracks and watching the trains pass under their feet. Yet, tonight it felt very different. In all these years, they hadn't ever come down to the bridge at such a late hour. Now as they sat on the railing for possibly the very last time together they both felt choked with emotion. Prahlad had just finished talking about Kamala's death and a long silence followed. There wasn't much traffic on the roads, there were very few trains passing under the bridge and an unusual silence gripped the night.

'I don't know what I want to do, Vinay. I really am feeling lost and can't seem to find meaning in anything I am doing. The one reason I wanted to work and earn was because I thought I would be able to rent a flat and live with my mother. Now she is gone and there seems no purpose at all in all this. I just feel like giving up – jumping on to these tracks and ending it all.'

'Hey, don't say that! Our lives are the only precious things that we possess. You can't chuck it away. Don't even talk of suicide. We have to give meaning to the small things we do, Prahlad. If we don't, then our lives have no purpose. Think of the things you can still do. Think of the life ahead of you. You were the one guy I knew who had big dreams – dreams of becoming a scientist, a physicist. What happened to all that, Prahlad?'

'All those were just dreams . . . '

'But you were the one who told me life itself is just a dream. But it is up to us to make something out of it.'

Just as Vinay finished his sentence, a train sped from under the tunnel into the darkness of the night.

*****

As Laila rested her head on the backseat of her car, she felt happy and content. This had been one of those nights. She had not believed that her father would agree to let them go for the Kishori Amonkar concert in Xavier's College and when he had agreed so easily she was both surprised and delighted. Gobind had agreed, of course, because Laila's cousin Varsha and her husband, Vivek, were going with her. He had also given them his car and driver for the evening and Varsha and Vivek had taken the car to the city and met Laila directly after college. It had been a perfect evening – when nothing could go wrong. The weather was great and a cool November breeze kept up their spirits. When they went to the Sea Lounge for coffee they actually had the luxury of choosing the one that offered a splendid view of the sea and the Gateway. They managed to find time for Varsha's shopping, for a quick look at the art exhibition at the Chemould and a meal at Copper Chimney before heading off to the concert. It was one of those evenings when Amonkar was in her element. She scaled the heights of the Himalayas, dug deep into the depths of the ocean and circumambulated the universe several times over, or so it seemed to Laila. The performance had Laila in raptures and she wished that she could freeze this slice of time so that it would never slip out of her grasp.

As the car sped through the city and she felt the cool breeze blow across her face, Laila was supremely happy. And felt that she owed it to herself to feel happy. Owed it to herself to be more positive about things. It seemed that everything had conspired that evening to give her that message. The evening, in all its apparent ordinariness, had held Laila's hand and told her not to give up on existence.

Varsha and Vivek were exhausted and had both nodded off to sleep almost as soon as the car left Xavier's. Laila wanted to take in as much of the night as possible – not often did she get to experience a drive through Bombay at one in the morning and not many nights had this kind of quality about it. She looked out of the window as the car took the road via Metro and New Marine Lines to Charni Road and turned right to go towards Opera House. It was when they turned in at Opera House to go over the bridge that she heard the thundering sound of a train racing under the bridge.

The next moment Laila saw a most horrific sight. A white, ten-storeyed building by the railway tracks suddenly went down like a deck of cards. One moment there was a building ten floors tall and the next moment there was nothing. Laila screamed loudly and the car came to a screeching halt. Vivek and Varsha woke up confused about what was happening. The driver got down from the car and Laila went after him to get a view of the accident. The entire building had collapsed and fallen over the railway tracks. The collapse had occurred just after the last compartment of a train had passed by. Within seconds the bridge was crowded with people who seemed to have appeared from nowhere. There was a great deal of commotion and excitement.

The sight of the building collapse haunted Laila. The positive feeling that the evening had generated completely deserted her when she was confronted with the fact that something as material, as concrete and out-there as a ten-storeyed building could disappear before one could bat an eyelid. The building was reduced to nothing more than rubble. A building is not just the stuff that makes it, the material that constitutes it but it is also the space that is enclosed by this material and it is this space that endows the building with its functionality. The relationship between the walls of the building and the space it encloses is what gives the building its identity. But it takes no more than a moment for it to disappear. And so it is with us human beings – we are not just the stuff that elementally constitutes us but our souls lie in that union of the material, elemental with the non-material, complex. And while we build so much around it over a lifetime it can just disappear in a moment.

Laila was up very early the next morning. She had hardly slept all night. Her mind was full of images of the collapse and she could not sleep thinking of the people who might have died in the tragedy. To her surprise and relief, the newspaper reported no deaths or injuries. It turned out that the building housed offices of diamond merchants. There was only one watchman in the building and he had stepped outside to find a match to light his bidi when the building collapsed. But the trauma of having witnessed the incident was to dog her for weeks.

On instructions from the police, the newspapers did not report an incident that happened a little after the building had collapsed. A fairly large crowd of local residents had gathered and uppermost on everyone's mind was the concern for the people trapped under the rubble, either dead or alive. Then it dawned on someone in the crowd that if it was a building full of diamond merchants' offices then the rubble would contain diamonds. This conjecture spread like wildfire and the crowd started climbing down the sides of the bridge onto the tracks to start their hunt for the diamonds. When the police stopped them, the crowd grew hostile and it led to a riot-like situation. It was only after they fired some teargas shells, that the crowd dispersed.

Prahlad and Vinay sat watching the entire drama that unfolded in front of them. The shock of watching the building collapse had kept them rooted to the balustrade for quite some time. Then they watched the crowds storming the railway tracks and the police driving them away. It was only after most of the crowd had left that they got up to walk back to the hostel. Just too much had happened that evening for them to say even a word to each other.

Prahlad went back to Johnson House the next morning and called up his office saying he would be taking the day off. He was exhausted and wanted to spend the morning in bed. It was only then, lying in bed, that he could take stock of the incidents of the earlier night in a coherent way. The events of the night stood out starkly against the backdrop of the kind of questions about the meaning and purpose of life that were troubling him. It was no co-incidence that he was sitting there on the bridge at the time of the accident. It all happened, he felt, to tell him how precious life was. Almost anything could have happened last night, he thought, and he would not have been alive this morning to think about it. The movement of the train could have caused the collapse of the bridge rather than that of the building. When the building fell, it could have easily fallen towards the bridge rather than falling on the tracks. The riot could have taken an ugly turn and that could have also become life-threatening. It felt like death was lurking around him when he was sitting on the railing with Vinay. But he was still alive, almost magically so. Like the watchman of that ill-fated building. He had to live even if the building fell and that is why at the precise moment he felt like smoking a *bidi*, found he had no matches left and went out into the night looking for a light. There is a magic that we hardly comprehend that sustains life, felt Prahlad, and to that power we owe the fact that we continue to exist.

*****

Laila had planned to meet Prahlad outside the Jehangir Art Gallery at around three that afternoon. She had to go to Charni Road to pick up some homoeopathic medicines for her mother and Prahlad had offered to go with her. After they had picked up the medicines, they decided to go to Dorai's house and started walking down from Charni Road towards Chowpatty. As they reached the bridge near Opera House, Prahlad said: 'Oh! I have to tell you what happened here last night.'

He was surprised to hear Laila say almost the same words to him.

'The building collapse? Oh my God! Were you here too? '

'Very much so. I have spent a good part of my college life sitting on these railings. I was here when the building collapsed, sitting right here with Vinay, my friend from Rhodesia.'

'I can't believe that we were both here that night!'

'It just shows that we are destined for each other.'

'God! You can't stop trying, can you?'

'But what were you doing here at that time of the night?'

'I was driving past after going to a concert in Xaviers'. The vision of seeing that building fall will stay with me for life.'

'Yes. You can imagine what it must have done to Vinay and me getting to see it sitting on the railing. We couldn't have got closer to the building.'

Laila continued as though Prahlad had not said anything.

'I was very disturbed by the sight. It pointed out to how impermanent everything is.'

'Strange you should say that. In fact, it was that night I felt I had learnt an important lesson about the value of life. It was a moment of affirmation.'

'Just shows how different we are. That is why I tell you that I am not the right one for you.'

'Oh no! There you go again! Next you will say Ananya is the right person.'

'Is she? I didn't say it, it came from you.'

'Come on! You are going on about this all the time.'

'It is the truth. So you better face up to it.'

'I thought you didn't believe in anything like truth.'

Laila replied with just a smile.

When they reached Dorai's house, Pandyan told them Dorai was away for a week in Thanjavur.

'Yes, he did tell me that,' said Laila. 'We'll just spend some time in the library.'

Pandyan told them that the library was being cleaned. 'I do that when Aiyya is not in Bombay.'

The library shelves had all been emptied and the books piled up on the floor. Laila and Prahlad had to walk gingerly through the stacks which were four or five feet high. Laila made her way to her favourite divan which stood by the window to the right. She loved the divan because it allowed her to stretch out while reading and simultaneously, through the window, it provided a very good view of the sea. Prahlad chose, as always, the long armed wooden chair to sit on. It allowed him enough room to rest his book comfortably while reading.

But as Prahlad sat down today trying to read a Santayana essay, he found himself distracted. He looked up from his book to find Laila lying on the divan with a book in her hand. Prahlad suddenly realised that he was in a very private world with Laila; a world where only the two of them existed, with the vastness of the Arabian sea behind them and protected by the huge fortress of books in front. It was a fortress whose foundations were laid by Gutenberg several hundred years ago and whose formidable ramparts had been built, stone by stone, over the centuries. It was this mammoth, impregnable structure that protected Laila and him from the world. The realisation made Prahlad want to put down his book and walk up to where Laila was. He got up and sat down on the divan next to her. She looked at him and went back to her reading. Prahlad stretched out and lay down next to her.

'This is getting dangerous,' Laila said.

Prahlad slipped his hand around her waist.

'No, don't.'

Prahlad snuggled closer. Laila's book closed almost of its own volition. Prahlad bent over her to kiss her and his hand moved under her shirt to trace imaginary circles on her belly.

'What are you doing?' said Laila, but she did not push his hand away.

Prahlad could feel the inside of her palm on his back and he shivered. His lips slid down her neck and between her breasts and

Laila gasped for breath. She jerked her right hand involuntarily above her head and it hit a pile of books behind her. The next instant, what seemed like a thousand books came tumbling down on them: they were drowned in a sea of text.

*****

When Prahlad finally got through to Laila it was after seven in the evening.

'Laila, where are you? I have been trying to reach you all these days.'

'I wasn't in town. I went down to Bangalore for a few days.'

'Bangalore? For what? You didn't tell me . . .'

'For what? For nothing. Just like that.'

'I have to meet you Laila. I am calling you from Juhu. Can you meet me now? '

'No, Prahlad. It is getting late now.'

'But I want to meet you. I am coming over to your house, if you don't come down.'

'No, Prahlad. Please.'

'What's wrong with you? Don't you want to meet me? '

'Prahlad, please. I need time. Time to be on my own. I haven't met anyone. I don't feel like it.'

'But I am not anyone! '

'God! Why are you doing this?'

'Laila, please come. I have to see you. I don't know what I will end up doing otherwise.'

'Come off it, Prahlad. What will you do? I really want to know. I don't think it is fair to put that kind of pressure on me just because you want to meet me.'

'Laila, please.'

'Okay, Prahlad. I will meet you at the juice shop in five minutes. But I can't stay very long.'

'It's a whole month. I haven't seen you for a month,' said Prahlad, when they met five minutes later.

'Prahlad, there is just too much that is weighing me down. I need time. Seriously. It does me no good whatsoever to come and meet you like this because each time I end up feeling guilty for what I am doing to you – or whatever I am supposed to be doing to you.'

'It is not about guilt.'

'Do you think so? That is so horribly untrue. I have become the one person to blame in this whole thing. Everyone, whether it is someone as close as Ana or someone who has just been observing us from a distance, sympathises with you. You are the victim and I am the wicked one leading you up the garden path. I gave you no illusions, Prahlad. From day one, I have been telling you that I am not in love with you, not in love. Full stop. With you or anyone else. I am struggling to cope with my own demons and I cannot take on the responsibility of the life of another. It is too much for me. But you persisted and I just didn't want to hurt you. I knew you were going through very difficult times and I didn't want you to be completely shattered. I wanted to see you through those times and, I think, I was right. I have helped you come through. It is only a phase, Prahlad. Things change. You have your world now: your physics and your ambitions, your 'clear, conserved, constructed world', as you would say when you quoted from Savitri. But that was only part of the picture. I was with you for my own reasons as well. I just loved being with you, talking to you, sharing our lives, our intimacies. There is a lot I got from you that kept me going too.'

'So it is good that we can do this for each other, isn't it?'

'To be with each other – to live our lives together, to love one another is a lot more than just that. It means to be totally immersed in one another. But that is not possible. That is what I have always maintained. We are fickle, we are weak and we have no power to transcend our own limitations.'

'I can see that it is Dorai talking now – transcend!'

'Shut up! It's not nice talking like that about someone who has just died. Why are you bringing him into this conversation, anyway?'

'He is the one who came into our lives without an invitation.'

'I am sorry, Prahlad. I don't like this kind of talk. I don't want to talk about this further.'

'Why? Did he mean so much to you?'

'Yes! He bloody well did. Why do you even ask? He meant as much to me as you do or Ana did. There were times I needed to spend time with him when I felt I couldn't talk to you or Ana. So, yes, he meant so much to me and I don't think I owe you any explanations on that count.'

'Every time I try to talk to you, you end up talking about Dorai and Ana. I don't see why.'

'I am sorry. It was you who brought up this talk about Dorai, now.'

'No, I don't mean just now. It is all the time. If I am telling you about us, why do I have to listen to what Dorai felt about it. Or what Ana felt about it?'

'Why not? You are the three dearest friends I have.'

'But I am different. I mean, we are different. We are a couple.'

'A couple? Okay, I have gone some distance in the exploration of my physicality with you. But beyond that what? How have you even attempted talking about our intimate moments? Do you ever feel the need to give voice to what you feel in those moments? Do you even think about it later? There is pleasure in that moment but where does it all go when that moment goes? If it is all that fleeting what value does it have at all? And if our identity as a couple is to come out of those fleeting moments, I can see how much that identity is likely to endure and sustain.'

Prahlad remained silent.

'I guess we need to take some time off and do some thinking, Prahlad. We need to figure out where we want to go from here. I have been disturbed by all these questions for a long time now. But with Ananya going away and now with Dorai's death, I am left rudderless and feel if I don't use this moment to come to terms with the bigger questions facing me, I will do myself and everyone else around me a lot of harm.'

She stopped and looked at her watch. 'I should go home now. And you too. But think of what I have told you.'

Saying this she walked away into the night.

Misery

Sumit was later than usual and Ananya was getting restless. They had to go all the way to Nandan where a Bergman double bill was scheduled. Ananya wondered whether they would make it on time. She was really keen on *Cries and Whispers* which was the first film scheduled to be screened and she hated the thought that she would miss some of it.

'I wish I had gone off to Nandan directly. I should really have done that.'

When Sumit arrived a little while later he was not in the least apologetic. Nor was he looking rushed. He seemed like someone with all the time in the world.

'Why are you so late?' Ananya was not at all pleased.

'Ok, sorry. But it is fine. We will reach on time, don't worry.'

'I have heard that said so often. But we never manage to make it to any place on time.'

'We will. We will. Let me get some chops first. I am starving. We can eat them while we wait for the bus.'

When they had got their chops, Sumit said, 'Ana, just put some *chatney* on this.'

If there was something more than Sumit's disregard for punctuality that Ananya hated then it was this attitude of his which bordered on chauvinism. When eating, he would not serve himself but would expect to be served. It was the same whether they were having a meal at home or out in a restaurant. As it was, Ananya didn't like the way he would stuff his mouth with food and talk but she absolutely loathed it when he would stop in the course of these dual tasks that his mouth was performing and point out to a dish that he wanted served on his plate. When she had brought it up with him a couple of times, he could not understand why she was going on and on about something quite as trivial as this. But this time again she was irritated enough to want to react to his behaviour.

'Why can't you help yourself?'

'You are still upset I am late?'

'No, no. It is not that I can't give you the *chatney*. It is the expectation that I will do it all the time that bothers me. I think it is a very male expectation and that is why I react to it.'

'Orri Baba, your sociology classes have put too much of this gender stuff into your head.'

'What do you mean, gender stuff?' asked Ananya, reacting somewhat sharply.

'Ok. Ok. I am sorry. Sorry for being late and sorry for this. Let's leave it, ok? Chalo, I can see a bus on its way here.'

Through their journey, Sumit talked excitedly about the eighteenth-century and the early nineteenth-century documents he had been studying related to the colonial perceptions about *sati* and how it shaped the history of the legislation against it. When he talked the way he did Ananya would forget every small thing about him that she didn't like. She loved listening to him – he was so well-read and knowledgeable. He was doing a Ph.D. in History from Jadavpur so it was very much his area of work that he was talking about now but his breadth was astonishing. He could talk with consummate ease about the histories and cultures across the world over centuries and he could discuss, at length, their arts, their literatures and their languages. He was an incredible storehouse of information and, in fact, reminded Ananya of Prahlad. But he was so unlike Prahlad in so many ways. His knowledge of the world seemed so much more rooted. He was fiercely political and active in student politics at the University. And, somehow, he seemed so much more of a man – someone so much in control and who knew what he wanted.

Ananya had met Sumit through a friend in Jadavpur where she studied for the second year of her M.A. after moving to Calcutta from Bombay. It was at a time when Ananya, having finished her M.A., was trying to decide whether she should continue in academics and do a Ph.D. A friend suggested she should meet Sumit to seek his advice. In the course of their conversation, she talked to Sumit about her interest in journalism. It turned out that Sumit had a journalist friend who worked for *The Telegraph* and it was not very long before Ananya found herself recruited there as a trainee sub-editor. Now more than a year into the job, Ananya had completed her training period and had a permanent contract with the newspaper.

Ever since she had met him, Ananya felt the need to spend time with Sumit. In spite of all the small differences in the kind of people they were, she felt instantly drawn to him. It was not clear at what stage they came together, there was no statement of a relationship, no declaration of love. It was one of those things that just happened – as silently as Sumit pointing out to a plate of chicken and Ananya, listening to him wide-eyed, doling out generous helpings of the bird on his plate. They never discussed their relationship or where it was going or intended to go. There were no questions, at all.

Whenever Ananya went to Sumit's house in Gol Park, where he lived with his mother and sister, she was treated with the warmth and affection that a family member deserved. She had herself moved to an apartment near Gariahaat that she shared with a friend from work. It was all right to live with her uncle's family as long as she was a student but now that she could afford to live on her own she preferred to do so. But for all the independence her new life offered her, there were days when she missed good home-cooked food: there was only so much of instant noodles and chops she could take. It was great then to be able to go to Sumit's house when she felt like it.

*****

It was now a month since Ananya had last met Sumit. He had been exceptionally busy with the final phase of his thesis writing and submission. He had also been writing applications to secure a fellowship so that he could do his post-doctoral work in England. But he had been turned down by a couple of grant agencies and was, therefore, not in the best of spirits. Thanks to these circumstances, over the last month Ananya could not get to meet him. Sumit was no longer using the student's office in Jadavpur – the Ph.D. room as it was called. Neither was he ever at home when Ananya called. Ananya herself had been too busy at work to even have weekends free and it was only when she realised that a month had passed by without meeting Sumit that she decided to go over to see him at his house.

Sumit was not home but his mother asked Ananya in and offered to make her a cup of tea.

'Why is Sumit so busy? What is he up to?' asked Ananya.

'I don't know, really. He goes early and comes late every day. He says that there is a lot of work related to his going to England,' said Sumit's mother.

'So is he applying for other fellowships, then? '

'No. He says he won't need it now. He is already planning to leave in two or three months.'

'But where will he get his money from? And why didn't he even call me to tell me about this? Is he really going as soon as that?'

Ananya could just not believe what she was being told.

'I really don't know. You should wait and meet him, maybe. Why don't you stay back for dinner?'

Ananya had an appointment with the Mayor early next morning. She had scheduled an interview with him. But she was still intrigued by the plans Sumit had made and was a little hurt that he had done it so secretly. She had to stay back and talk to him.

It was half-past nine when Sumit came back home. Sumit's mother laid out dinner while he went in to the bathe.

'Yes, I will tell you everything. Later,' he said, somewhat abruptly.

After dinner, he offered to drop Ananya home.

'Ok, you were going to tell me something,' said Ananya, as soon as they were out on the street.

'I wanted to tell you this earlier. But have been too busy. I will be going to England in October. I am getting partial aid from the University of Southampton.'

'Is that more than what they were offering you earlier? '

'No.'

'Then? You said that was not enough to live on. Where will you get the rest of the money from?'

'I will be taking care of it from my own resources.'

'Your own resources?'

'Yes. I might as well break this to you now. I got engaged last week. My father-in-law agreed to sponsor my stay in England.'

Ananya felt the dark night swim before her. She stopped in her tracks.

'You must be joking. This can't be true.'

'Yes. It is. I had no choice.'

'Choice? What do you mean? How could you do this?'

She tried hard to keep her composure but the tears came welling up and she broke down. A couple of people stopped on the street to see what was happening.

'Look. Don't create a scene standing here in the middle of the road,' said Sumit, as he tried to hold her arm.

Ananya pulled her arm away and screamed, 'Leave me. Don't even try to touch me. You . . . you . . . horrible…! Just leave me alone.'

She hailed a cab passing by and left Sumit standing where he was.

Later that night, Ananya's room-mate Shompa noticed that all was not well with her. After some cajoling, she managed to get Ananya to tell her what had happened.

'Gosh! Is that what the bastard did? You should have hit him when he told you that,' said Shompa.

'I just broke down and then jumped into the nearest cab and rushed back home. It's so pathetic. It is not even original – more like the plot of one of those third-rate tear-jerkers that one watches on TV.'

'Yes. Life surprises us in the manner in which it can imitate really bad art,' said Shompa, in a rare moment of profundity.

Ananya was herself surprised by the clinical manner in which she could talk about Sumit to Shompa. But that casual air and the brave front she put on deserted her the on her way to work the next day. The realisation that Sumit had left her and that she was alone hit her as surely as the July morning breeze hit her face. It was a very tangible pain that she felt. She had never experienced such a real, physical ache which was due to a condition of the mind. It was as though the traditional rivals, Mind and Body, had decided to bury the hatchet for the time being and were conspiring to make the pain even worse for Ananya.

But Ananya was still not sure what was causing her so much pain. Was it a longing for Sumit and all that he meant to her, was it the fact that he had dumped and hurt her or was it just the fact of her loneliness? It seemed at times that it was a vicious mix of all these that was tormenting her. She could save herself from this condition only by trying to immerse herself in work. But when she took a break, her thoughts would return to Sumit and her loneliness and she'd walk straight into the trap that Mind and Body had set up for her.

There had to be a way out of this trap, she thought. She had to break these conspirators in some way. It was Shompa who showed her the way out, in fact by mixing her a vodka-based cocktail one evening. So far, Ananya had only been a social drinker. Her journalist friends threw parties where it was very difficult and awkward to be a teetotaller and so Ananya had allowed herself to be persuaded to have that occasional glass of wine or beer. Slowly, she had warmed to the idea of relaxing with close friends over a drink after a hard day's work. For the first time now, Ananya was drinking not because she had company, but because she was alone; not because she was happy, but because she was miserable.

Initially, she waited for Shompa to come home before she poured out their drinks. Soon she started drinking alone, for there were nights when dark despair would descend and the tears would flow. She would cry till her insides ached and very often after she had cried she would throw up, leaving her feeling even more miserable. Intermittently, the alcohol would work its pleasurable magic – that was usually when the alcohol levels were between quite-a-bit and just-too-much. The quite-a-bit was a threshold one had to cross to start seeing the world being pulled apart. Solids would melt and go formless as though they were in a Dali painting. Concrete walls would join the wooden furniture in a slow dance. The fixed spatial relations between objects, that gives our everyday world of experience the familiar solidity, would get marvellously violated. Things would start moving slowly into each other as though attempting to erase all distinctions between themselves and merge into a selfless identity. All this would last a moment or two, perhaps, or possibly an eternity. In that state, who cared to ask questions like how long?

*****

'Prahlad! You have done really well. I am so happy for you,' said Laila, as she held him warmly. 'Your mother would have been so happy,' she said.

Prahlad was thrilled and it was written all over his face. He had worked really hard in the second year of his M.Sc. and had got the marks he deserved. Laila looked into his eyes and saw a raw mix of sheer joy, expectation and vulnerability peep through. It was that vulnerable Prahlad whom she had always felt very close to.

'Your results will be out tomorrow,' said Prahlad, not quite knowing what to say.

'I know. But I am not expecting much. I haven't put in much, really, as you well know.'

They settled down in the canteen for a cup of tea. Laila sat at the table she loved the most which gave her a view of the garden and the road outside. She had spent many hours in the last two years sitting here, watching people and imagining the stories of their lives. Or pouring out herself in the pages of the notebook she always carried with her.

'I will miss all this,' she said, her voice choking with uncharacteristic emotion.

'But we will keep coming here. I have already had a chat with Prof. Chitre and he agreed to take me on for a Ph.D. He wants me to appear for an exam that will ensure me a fellowship – and if I am successful in getting the fellowship he is willing to be my guide.'

'A Ph.D.! What you always wanted to do.'

'Yeah, and Prof. Chitre is a particle physicist. Just the kind of stuff I wanted to do.'

'Great, Prahlad. I am really happy for you. Can't help saying it again.'

There was a brief silence.

'So will you continue staying in the hostel here?'

Prahlad had moved into the hostel during the second year of his M.Sc.

'Yes, this University is going to be my home for the next five years. That is why I said you are going to be here in the canteen very often.'

'I don't know, Prahlad.'

'Why? What do you mean?'

'I mean, I don't know. I have to move on. I have no idea what I want to do but I will figure that out. For the next few months, I want to spend time writing.'

'Yes, but you will come and meet me, won't you?'

'It has to change, Prahlad. You are on to new things from here. A Ph.D. and then a post-doc and a life in research. It is a new phase in life for you.'

'Why do you always come back to this?'

'Like a broken record? The image of a record being played over and over again is something I have grown up with. Anyway, I think I will go now.'

'No. Don't go like this. Do tell me you will be coming back to meet me.'

'It has been four months since Dorai's death and we have hardly met in this period and you have done pretty well, Prahlad.'

'Come on, that's so unfair. Every time I called you and asked to meet you, you said no. Moreover, we were both busy with exams and . . .'

'That's right, Prahlad. We will find things to get busy with. This will pass. But I don't want to start this now. Today is your big day and I want you to be happy. I am sure you will want to celebrate with your friends from the hostel. So let me go back now.'

It was more than three weeks before Prahlad met Laila again. There was a lot happening in his life in those three weeks of which the exam he had to take for his Ph.D. fellowship was the most important. The results were expected only three months later but he had done so well in the exam that Prof. Chitre felt he need not wait for the results but could start studying some of the more advanced topics he needed for his Ph.D. After the formality of a departmental interview was completed, Prahlad was admitted as a student and given a desk and a shelf in the students' room. He felt overwhelmed the day he went and occupied the desk. It hardly mattered that it was an old desk with layers of dust on it. It had not been touched for years, it appeared. He wiped the desk clean with a wet mop and proceeded to clean the shelf and the window-sill next to it. It took him some time to clean the drawers. He was told he could just chuck all the old papers that it contained. It had belonged to students who had left the Department a long time ago. There were letters – official and personal, from the University granting extension of the Ph.D. term or accepting a thesis synopsis submission, from conference organisers with impersonal letters of invitation, from journal referees trashing a paper completely saying the calculations presented in the paper had several obvious flaws and the paper was totally unsuitable for publication, from family asking about their son's progress and reminding him that his sister's wedding was not far off, from a fiancé or a lover (it wasn't too clear) talking in the same breath about the impending life-changing decisions that needed to be made and the purchase of two new sarees.

Other than these there were several bills – a fourteen-year old one for the purchase of a table-fan, another nineteen-year old hostel mess bill and many more – some possibly unpaid. There were bank papers, cheque-deposit stubs, post-cards with Ajanta-Ellora frescoes, an empty packet of Navy Cut cigarettes flattened out for so many years that it could not be pulled back into its original shape. What Prahlad was pulling out of the drawers was, in fact, an eloquent narrative of the trials, tribulations, frustrations and the moments of joy that was typical of a Ph.D. student's life. When having cleared the drawers he put in photographs of Kamala and Laila there, he was starting a new chapter of this narrative.

In these three weeks, Prahlad did try to call Laila several times but each time he tried to fix up to meet her it did not work out. But there was just too much happening in his life at the moment for him to be able to do anything about it. It was at the end of three weeks when he had settled down in his Ph.D. programme that Prahlad started thinking of Laila. He had to call her thrice in the span of a few hours before she agreed to meet him.

'What is it, Prahlad? I thought I already told you that I will not be able to meet you when we last met,' Laila said.

'How can you do that to me? You can't just stop meeting me.'

'Why can't I? We have been together for years now and it is not going anywhere. You want to give it the shape of a relationship – whatever that may mean. I can't and I also cannot go on with this. It is come to a point where it is a torture for you and for me.'

'I can't live without you! '

'Stop it, Prahlad! Just stop it! It is pathetic to go on like this for years. I have held your hand for so long and we have come so far. But beyond that, no. I also want time to be on my own otherwise I feel that I will lose my sanity.'

Prahlad was in tears.

'Please! Laila. Don't do this to me. I love you so much.'

'God! Please, can you stop crying? Really, I tell you I have had enough of this. I can't take these emotional scenes anymore.'

Prahlad tried to fight his tears. They sat silently on the park bench for a while.

Then suddenly Prahlad turned to Laila and shouted: 'You can't do this to me. No, you can't! I am in love with you.' He didn't realise he had grabbed her arm as he was saying this.

'Stop! You are hurting me, Prahlad. Prahlad! '

An old man who was sitting nearby turned to look at them and Prahlad let go of Laila's arm.

'Sorry – I am sorry,' he said.

After a few moments, Laila got up to leave. 'I think I should go now.'

As she started walking, Prahlad got up and went behind her. He held her hand, lightly this time, and said, 'Laila, I am sorry. I can't force you to do anything you don't want to do. But remember I love you and I have waited for you for all these years. I will wait for you longer but will meet you again only when you want to do so. One day you will come to me. On your own. Asking for my love. Till then I will let you be. I will wait to hear from you.'

Cruelty

Early one morning, Ananya stirred. She had been to a colleague's party the previous evening and had, as usual, too much to drink. She lay in bed, half-awake but with her eyes closed. She was stirred into a more conscient state by a putrid smell that seemed to pervade the bedroom. She turned on her stomach and hid her face in the pillow hoping the smell would disappear. But even with her nose buried in the pillow she could not get rid of the smell. She turned her face a little to be able to open her right eye when she noticed something on the pillow – a brownish, yellow patch stood prominently against the whiteness of the freshly-washed pillow cover. Startled she lifted her head and discovered, to her absolute horror, that she had vomited in her sleep and had messed up her face, her hair and her bed. Inspite of her throbbing head, she found herself fully awake. The smell and the sight made her already nauseous insides feel even more queasy and she rushed into the bathroom to throw up again.

Ananya spent the next hour or so cleaning up her room and washing herself. No matter how much water and soap she used she did not feel clean. When later she settled down on her sofa with a large cup of tea in her hand, she was overcome with feelings of disgust and self-loathing. How could I let myself do this, she asked herself over and over again. 'I am so horrible. How did I end up like this?'

When her anger subsided, she was overcome with such remorse that she burst into tears. She remembered her mother; she was missing her loving care at this moment. She cried some more, ashamed at the manner in which she had let her mother down. She had not met Deepa for almost a year now and she wanted nothing else, at the moment, but her warm embrace. A couple of hours later, she quickly put on some clothes and headed out into the street. The light, the warmth and the freshness of the air made her feel somewhat better. She went into a phone booth and called up Deepa. Deepa was at work and was surprised to hear her daughter's voice.

'Is everything all right, love?' she asked.

'Yes, ma. I am missing you terribly. Want to be with you.'

'Are you sure you are not unwell? '

'No. I am fine. Just want to spend some time with you. It has been so long.'

Deepa guessed that, inspite of the brave front that her daughter was putting up, there was something wrong.

'Should I talk to Dada?' she said, thinking that a visit to her brother might help Ananya.

'No, ma. It is you I want to meet.'

'Okay, Ana. I think I can take off from work for a few days. I will try to get the morning flight tomorrow. Will you be able to get leave from work? Maybe we can go to Puri – just you and I.'

Ananya thought that Puri sounded like a good idea too. Her editor was not too pleased when she told him of her holiday plans but she hadn't had a break in a long time and he had no way of refusing her.

The holiday in Puri was just what Ananya needed. Deepa had managed to rent a small cottage by the seaside away from the din and chaos of the town. Deepa had, of course, guessed that it must have something to do with Sumit. She knew that they had been more than friends and it didn't take much to figure out that Sumit had left her. Ananya didn't speak a word about it to her though and avoided Deepa's questions. Deepa's maternal instincts soon told her that what her daughter needed was just her presence at the moment. She realised that Ananya did not want to talk about herself but wanted a silent promise of unconditional support from her mother.

Over the next few days, that is what Deepa did. They took long walks by the sea, ate the simple food that the caretaker's wife cooked for them and spent a lot of time relaxing. Deepa felt comfortable enough, for the very first time, to talk to Ananya about her own life, her struggles as a widow, her growing up as a child in Calcutta, the few happy years that she spent with Subir. She also talked to her about Tapan and how they had come together, how she felt anchored with him around and how they had now finally moved apart. Ananya was struck by the candidness with which her mother spoke about her life.

One evening Deepa returned from a visit to the town and among the books that she had picked up from the local bookstore was Barbara Stoler Miller's English translation of Jayadeva's *Gita Govinda*. After dinner, they sat on the patio overlooking the small garden and

Deepa asked Ananya to read out from the book. Deepa did not miss a certain emotion in Ananya's voice when she read:

She raises her sublime lotus face, clouded and streaked with tears,
Like the moon dripping with nectar from cuts of the eclipse's teeth.
Lying dejected by your desertion, fearing Love's arrows,
She clings to you in fantasy, Madhava.

*****

It was a year since Ananya had broken up with Sumit and a sense of normalcy had returned to her life. For almost six months now, she had managed to take a hold of herself and not give in to too much alcohol. She still enjoyed her drink but strictly in the company of friends and in a measured way. There were times when she did feel lonely but when she was not at work she made sure she was with friends or family. Her work was what gave her the most pleasure. Her editor was entrusting her with more challenging assignments and Ananya was enjoying every bit of it and was willing to give it her all.

It was one of those typical June afternoons – hot and humid. Ananya had just returned from a lunch appointment and was happy to be back in the cool comfort of her office. It was a relatively quiet day at work. Ananya had been asked to do a piece for the Sunday supplement and even though the deadline was two weeks away she decided she might do some preparatory reading for it when she had some time on hand. She was engrossed when the telephone rang.

'May I speak to Ananya, please?' said the voice on the other side.

'Prahlad!! What a surprise! Where are you calling from?'

'Hi, Ana. How did you recognise my voice instantly?'

'Why won't I? Are you in Calcutta?'

'Yes. I came here on Friday on a visit to the S.N. Bose Centre. I am collaborating with a Professor from the Centre and will be here for a couple of months.

'A couple of months! That's fab. Tell me, what are your plans for this evening? We could meet up.'

Prahlad was not busy that evening.

'Good. Will you be able to find your way to Park Street, then? Don't sound so confident. Calcutta is not like Bombay. . . . Ok, fine.

I will meet you at seven outside Flurry's. That's a landmark anyone should be able to guide you to.'

When Ananya reached Flurry's, Prahlad was already waiting there. She was happy to see him and it appeared he had changed so much. He had put on weight and his hair was longer.

Ananya embraced him warmly. 'Prahlad! It's so good to see you. How've you been?'

'I am fine. Busy with my Ph.D.'

'Yes. I heard from Laila that you had registered for a Ph.D. But that was some time ago. You must be well into your research now.'

'Well, I have published a couple of papers recently. It's exciting.'

'That's great. You have to tell me more about your work. But before that let's decide what we want to do. I know a good Chinese place just around the corner from here. One of those real Chinese places – not your fraud Bombay-Chinese varieties!'

Prahlad smiled. 'You have changed, Ananya. I called your mother to get your number. She told me you were a journalist with the Telegraph. It shows. You sound so confident now.'

'What do you mean? I didn't sound confident when I was in Bombay?'

'No, not that. But, I guess, we have all matured in these last six years.'

'Six years? Yes, that's how long it has been since we first met, hasn't it? It seems like yesterday. All right, we are already here. This is the restaurant.'

'Shall we order some starters with our drinks? Do you drink, Prahlad? I don't remember,' said Ananya, after they had settled down into their comfortably cushioned sofas.

'I will have some beer.'

'Great.'

Once she had placed the orders, she turned to Prahlad and said, 'Good, now we can talk in peace. There's so much I want you to tell me.'

Prahlad began by talking about his research: his explorations of the sub-atomic world. Ananya watched him like she was watching a performance. She liked the way Prahlad was talking even though she did not fully understand every bit he was saying about particle physics. She found it interesting that his engagement with physics was still innocent – his passion for the subject was untouched by any cynicism.

When he asked her about her job, she was sure that it was nowhere as exciting as particle physics. She even wondered whether he would be interested much in what she had to say. But when she talked about it, she was herself surprised at the enthusiasm and involvement with her work that she displayed. Prahlad seemed to listen to her with rapt attention.

'What about Laila? Are you in touch with her?'

Prahlad's shoulders stiffened a bit.

'I have not been in touch with her at all,' continued Ananya. 'It is over three years now. We exchanged letters around the time that we completed our M.A.'s. That is when she told me about your Ph.D. She told me that she was planning to start teaching in a college but I have not heard from her since.'

'Yes, she is teaching in Jai Hind. But I haven't met her in a long time – it's been two years and nine months.'

'Are you still in love with her?'

Prahlad looked up startled. Ananya had never asked him a question like that before. In the old days, she would never have used a word like 'love' to describe what he felt for Laila.

He remained silent.

'God! You are still in love with her, aren't you? And desperately so. You don't seem to have moved an inch from when we last met. Six years, did you say? Six years, right – that's how long it has been since we became friends and this entire story of your love for Laila started. It's nothing that we made it out to be. It is something very ordinary, Prahlad. When you are just nineteen or twenty, these kind of things happen. We spent so much time together it was inevitable that you would fall in love with one of us. That's so normal. None of us, and I include myself in that count, had the honesty to accept it the way it was. Instead, we cloaked it in pseudo-intellectual discourse. What amazes me is that we kept up that whole act for so long. We should have grown out of it sooner. But, wait, you still seem to be very touchy about all this. Hey! Prahlad, you are not a kid, yaar. Just accept that it was normal what you felt for Laila. You were unlucky that she didn't feel the same for you. That is all.'

'It's not like that.' Prahlad was so choked he could hardly speak.

'Then what is it like? Tell me.'

'I love her very much. And I am waiting for her. To come to me. I told her I don't want to meet her till she decides she wants to meet me and be with me.'

'Prahlad! Are you serious? No you can't be.'

'Yes, I am.'

'Look, Prahlad. I have been very close to Laila and know her too well. She is not interested in 'being with you', as you delicately put it. The entire affair was part of her explorations, her way of coming to terms with her confusions. I am not sure how much she has come to terms with them but I don't see you fitting into the picture at all. You have to move on, Prahlad. You are doing good work – there is a whole world for you to discover. Don't let Laila pull you down.'

'I think I have managed to do all this – like starting my Ph.D. – because of my love for her. It has nurtured me.'

'Well, we have meant a lot to each other in many ways. But that was at a certain stage in our lives. All that churning has helped us reach this point. And we owe it to ourselves to move on.'

She paused for a bit, gulped down the last bit of beer that was in her mug, and said, 'Prahlad. I won't say this again. Because I can see that you are still very raw about this whole Laila thing. You are almost another person when you start talking about her. So what I will say now may hurt you but I will do it just this once. I think you should forget Laila. Laila is history. It's over. What I am sorry about is that she didn't say this to you in these clear terms. It is something about her that infuriates me now, you know, her wallowing in these grand existential confusions. I tried talking her out of it and failed. But she owes you this much, at the least – to set you free. It's as plain as plain can be. She is not interested so she should just tell you so and let you go. But she has not done that. She kept you waiting. But you have waited long enough. It was long enough already a few years ago. I think you have to make the decision now. Tell yourself very clearly that it is all over. That Laila is never going to come back to you..'

*****

It was a few weeks after the Park Street dinner and Ananya had met Prahlad quite often. They would usually meet for dinner or sometimes to watch a movie. Ananya enjoyed Prahlad's company and, in order to keep it that way she made sure that she did not discuss Laila with him.

She had hoped to meet Prahlad this evening too but she had an exceptionally busy day at work and decided to just go back home when she was done. It was past nine when she reached home and as she opened the door to her flat she could hear voices from Shompa's bedroom. It sounded like an argument. Ananya peeped into Shompa's room and found Shompa with her friends.

'Hi, Ananya,' Shompa called out. 'Come in. Meet my friend Charu. You know Nayana, of course.'

'Hi,' said Ananya, somewhat conscious that she had barged into a heated discussion. 'I am sorry if I interrupted something.'

'Just as well. We were just getting to the point of becoming violent and breaking each other's heads,' laughed Shompa. 'No, we were just arguing about planchettes. Charu was telling us about it and Nayana thinks the whole thing is a fraud.'

'But you have seen it happen. I demonstrated it to you,' said Charu to Nayana, continuing from where she left off.

'I did see something happen. I don't doubt that. But whether that is due to spirits or not is the issue. I am convinced that bit is humbug,' said Nayana, with the manner of someone totally convinced about what she was saying.

'Ok, girls. I have had a long day at work and need to go take a shower. I will have to leave you for the moment,' said Ananya, making a quick exit from the room. This kind of hokey-pokey stuff was the last thing she wanted to get involved in.

She spent a longer time in the shower than she usually did and when she had found some comfortable clothes to get into, she went into the kitchen to get her dinner. Shompa had managed to find a lady to cook for them and Ananya was happy to come back home to a good home-cooked meal. She thought she might sit in the living room and watch TV while she ate her dinner. But Shompa's room was very quiet now and Ananya became curious. She walked into Shompa's room to find Charu and Shompa sitting cross-legged on the bed with a wooden board placed in between them. The board had the letters of the English alphabet inscribed along the boundary – black letters inscribed with Shompa's eyebrow pencil, as Ananya could easily guess. Shompa and Charu had placed their fingers on a disc. Ananya recognized it as being the lid of the small box from the kitchen in which they stored *hing*. She looked closely and saw that Charu had her index finger and her middle finger on the lid while Shompa had only her index finger on it. What was strange was that the lid seemed to be moving about the board on its own, visiting the various letters on the edge of the board in the course of its excursions as it slowly spelt out words.

Nayana was reclining on the chair beside the bed with a look of indulgent disbelief on her face. Ananya quietly sat down on the other empty chair in the room and watched the proceedings as she ate as noiselessly as she could. She figured out that Shompa had invoked the spirit of her dead uncle and was asking him questions about herself, her career and, most importantly, about her love life and marriage. Uncle seemed to be in a good mood and did not get irritated with any of the girlie questions or giggles. It was really fascinating for Ananya to see how fast the lid seemed to move at times.

'Wow, I have been told that I will get married and go to the US,' said Shompa when the session got over. 'Charu, this stuff is really good. Thanks for showing me this.'

'It was good, wasn't it? I wish we had a better board though. Somehow this lid seems to get stuck around the joint which runs down the middle of the board,' said Charu.

'Maybe you should use a carrom striker,' suggested Nayana.

'No, but Charu says you need to use a metal disc. Didn't you, Charu?'

'Why? Is metal a better conductor for spirits?' Nayana went on.

'Come on, Nayana. You saw it all happen right in front of you. How can you be such a sceptic?' was Shompa's question.

'So you are also hooked to this now?' asked Nayana, somewhat exasperated.

'But you can feel a force moving the lid. Can't you, Charu?' said Shompa.

'That is called the ideomotor force. It is just your muscles exerting a force unconsciously,' said Nayana.

'Come on, Nayana. Are you saying we were moving that lid ourselves?' Shompa said, her voice getting shriller.

'Yes. You don't realise it. But it is just that,' said Nayana.

'There are so many personal details of Shompa that I had no clue about. Yet, I had my fingers on the lid and the lid was making its way around spelling out the right answers. You need not believe the explanation in terms of spirits but it is silly to say we were just faking, even unconsciously.'

'I was quite surprised to see how fast that lid was moving around. And your arms seemed quite still. At least, I did not see you pushing the lid. I think I would like to try it out myself,' said Ananya, very curious about the planchette now.

'Would you? Let's,' said Charu, smiling. 'Come and sit here. All right, who would you want to invoke? Think of someone close to you who is dead and ask that spirit to come and answer your questions. I will also keep my fingers on the lid because I am the medium through which the spirit communicates.'

Ananya immediately thought of calling her father but she somehow didn't feel it was right. She decided it would be grandmother, who had died a few years ago, whom she would call – Dida was herself a great one for these things, anyway.

'I think I will invoke my grandmother's spirit. But she didn't know much English. Do you think that matters?'

'Not at all! When you are in the spiritual domain you transcend all such limitations and can speak any language. Your grandmother will speak English as well as you do and if you notice that the turn of speech seems somewhat like your own don't be too surprised,' said Nayana, mockingly.

'O, come off it, Nayana,' said Shompa. 'Ananya, just ignore her and carry on.'

Ananya sat down with her finger on the lid and called out to her grandmother in a gentle voice. She was concentrating all her energies in communicating with her spirit. Nothing seemed to happen.

'Ask her again,' said Charu.

'Dida, will you answer my questions, please?'

The lid began to move. Y-E-S A-N-A

'It's a yes,' Charu whispered.

Ananya began by asking her about Deepa. She had been concerned about her mother's health recently. She could feel her grandmother reply with the tenderness of an old woman speaking about her daughter. Ananya went on to ask more questions – about herself, her career. The answers came, somewhat slowly. For some reason the lid was not moving as fast as when Shompa was at it. But there was a definiteness about the movements and no ambiguity in the answers. There were a couple of questions for which Dida started off answering by heading in the direction of some alphabet and then turning around halfway down the board and going in some other direction.

'You should ask her about your love-life,' Shompa was egging her on.

Ananya felt a little silly doing that. Imagine asking your grandmother who the next man in your life will be. But she decided to go along with Shompa's suggestion and ask the question, anyway.

The lid started moving almost immediately after she had posed the question.

'P-R-A . . .' After 'A' the lid moved across the board in the direction of some alphabet. It hit the defect in the middle of the board and got stuck there. It tried moving but kept going along the line of defect rather than in the direction it wanted to. After struggling for a while, the spirit decided to give up and was answering no more questions.

'P-R-A? Who is that now? Don't tell me it is that Prabal from our advertising section,' said Shompa.

'It could be someone she has never met – a Prakash or a Prashant.'

Ananya was quiet. 'PRAHLAD,' she said to herself in the most silent of whispers.

*****

Dear Laila,

I haven't written to you in quite some time and didn't know whether I should write you this letter either. But the more I thought about it I felt more strongly that I should write to you. It is because I feel that you have been caught up in your own world for so long that I need to help you realise that there is a world out there. All this is not just in your head – the world is not just your idea.

I will tell you what I have to say in the most direct manner even if it will sound a bit too cruel. Cruelty, like many other things in a friendship, is not something one should be concerned about. It is like the proverbial kind cruelty of a surgeon's knife.

Ok, to come to the point, it is about me and Prahlad. Prahlad came to Calcutta a few weeks ago for a two-month research project. I have been meeting him quite often and got to know quite a different person from the one I knew in Bombay. He has changed a lot, or maybe I have. Or maybe we have all just remained the same – standing and watching as mere spectators even as time worked its magic. But, all the same, this is a different Prahlad I got to know, someone who seemed to be plumbing the depths. Someone who was not just a memory bank but was actually thinking. And, most importantly, someone who has learned to confidently talk about his inner life. And I discovered something about Prahlad that I think always existed but I was blind to. He is a very good listener. He pays attention to what is being told to him and it is with such concern that one feels that much lighter after sharing one's crises and confusions with him.

The old Prahlad resurfaced, however, whenever we started talking about you. When I first met him, I thought that he was still in love with you. And I thought I should tell him that he should snap out of it because you were not there for him. As I talked to him more, I realised that he was no longer in love with you. But he was somehow tied down notionally to the idea of being in love with you whether you reciprocated it or not. That is when I felt it was important to talk to him and make him realise how wrong he was. I did not know it would work but I felt obliged to help him, somehow.

And I was amazed how fast he managed to make the change. It was almost as though he needed the conversations with someone like me to catalyse the change. These conversations inevitably brought us closer. And before we knew it, it had developed into love. I was happy to tell him that – and he was delighted to know that I was in love with him after having gone through the trauma of years of unrequited love. I could see that a whole new world has opened up for him.

Through all those years that you taunted Prahlad about the possibility of his being in love with me you had probably intuitively seen this eventuality or maybe even willed it into existence. Whatever it is, I know this will hurt you. And when it does, you have to ask yourself who it is that has caused you hurt. Me, Prahlad or you yourself. Do make sure to stare hard at the answer.
Ananya

Control

Stepping out of Dorai's building on to the road facing the sea, Laila was gripped by nausea. She felt a churning in her stomach and her knees felt wobbly. Unable to walk, she sat down on the bench of the nearby bus-stop, pulling her knees up and drawing her body in. She sat in that posture for a while and felt somewhat better. Instead of heading off to Grant Road Station as she would normally have done, Laila decided to cross the road and walk along the beach. The beach was crowded and walking through the crowds, Laila tried hard not to cry. But she couldn't control herself and tears kept flowing down her cheeks. Some passers-by looked at her wondering why she was crying and she looked straight ahead into the horizon to avoid their probing glances. In the last two hours in Dorai's flat, she had managed to fight back her tears because she could see how shaken Pandyan and Padma were by Dorai's death. She knew she had to be there for them till at least a couple of Dorai's friends arrived. But now out on Marine Drive with nothing but the sea on one side of her and a mass of anonymous humanity on the other, she could no longer control herself.

Why did he have to go like this, she asked herself. He was so young. Why did he have to die?

Death is not something you have to be afraid of, Laila, she could hear him say. It is simply a statement of the finitude of our phenomenal existence, he would say.

Just because you say it like that, it doesn't become any easier to deal with.

No, it is not a matter of saying it in any complicated way. I am not using jargon but trying to use language to give me a different perspective to death. Life is a text, and like other texts it is finite in its length. One can probe the infinity of life not in its length but in its depths. You cannot grieve that you will reach the end of the book and that the story will be over. That is the very nature of something that extends from cover to cover. But you can delve deep into any one page of the book, into any one line, for that matter, and it is in that depth that you can discover infinity – the vastness that gives you freedom from grieving over the limited nature of things.

Laila turned to see the sun rapidly trying to reach the horizon as if to dissolve in the vastness of the sea. A cold shudder ran through her as she realised how much she would miss talking to Dorai and how much a source of solace his words had been for her through these years that she knew him. She turned around and crossed the road again to hail a cab to take her to Churchgate. She was not sure she would be able to stand all the way in the train to Andheri today and she had a better chance of getting a seat if she boarded at the starting point.

The train was already crowded at Churchgate and she could only find a 'fourth' seat, squeezed in with three other passengers. Her head was heavy and her mind was filled with thoughts of Dorai. Images flitted behind her closed eyes as she rested her head on her hands. They entered and exited her mind in waves, like the passengers in the train. She dug her face deeper into her palms; she could not sleep but she felt herself moving away from the train and its passengers to a miasmal world where even the images seemed transformed to shadowy, sinister creatures.

When she finally came to, it was less crowded for the train had just moved out of Santa Cruz station. She remembered the brown envelope that Pandyan had thrust in her hand as she was leaving. Wondering what it could be, she opened her bag and pulled it out. When she glanced through the pages of the manuscript she realised it was a story about three characters: Laila, Prahlad and Ananya.

'Why has Dorai done this?' she wondered. 'I am sure it has some deeper meaning. He wouldn't just write a story with the three of us as characters.'

Before she could read it with more attention the train pulled into Andheri station. She quickly picked up her bag and slung it over her shoulders and with the envelope in her hand she fought through the evening crowds at Andheri to see if she could find a rickshaw. She found one with less difficulty than is customary at Andheri station and when she settled down inside she wanted to read Dorai's novel. But the evening was dark already and there was little light inside the rickshaw, so she decided to wait to read it after she reached home.

She was climbing up the stairs leading to her home, when she realised she did not have the envelope with her. God! Where was it?

She quickly checked her bag and then realised that she must have left it in the rickshaw. She went running down and asked the watchman who pointed out the direction in which he had seen it going. That was in the direction of the juice shop which she and Prahlad frequented and it was a junction where rickshaws were parked. But when she reached the junction, she found not a single one. She asked the juice vendor but he was sure he had not seen any rickshaw come from the direction of her building. Either the watchman or the juice vendor was wrong but that did not matter. She had to find the envelope, somehow. She found another empty rickshaw headed her way and she got into it hoping to find the one with her envelope. She did find a few rickshaws, and even a couple with the red seat cover she remembered her rickshaw as having. But she did not find her rickshaw with the envelope anywhere. When she finally gave up and got back home, she sat under the tree in the courtyard behind her building and wept uncontrollably. She had not only lost Dorai but also the one thing that Dorai had left behind for her.

*****

Laila's heart ached. How could he do this? How could he hurt me like this? I am his Laila, his proclaimed love. How could he do this to his love? What happened to all those claims of the eternality of his love, his steadfastness? Is this all it takes? Someone comes up and claims to reciprocate his love and he is willing to accept it and leave me. This hurts. God! How it hurts!

But why should it hurt? I was the one who didn't want his love. I was the one who not only made him wait but finally told him to go away. But didn't really think I wanted him to go. Did he not see how I wanted him? My God! I can't believe that he has really done what he has.

But why should he not? He will say he waited long enough. He waited for me to say I loved him too and to say that I accepted his love as real. Finally he didn't wait. Didn't wait long enough, at least. How long would that be? I don't know.

But what did he want? Those three words – I love you? Or something as soppy as that. Or being together, as he would call it? Did he want me to say that I believed in his love – if at the end of it he was going to prove to me that his love was not worth believing in.

Did he not see what he meant to me at the bottom of it all? Did he not see in all my confusions that I wanted him? To be with him. Just like that. Did it all have to be spelt out for him?

I never doubted I wanted us to be together. Even when I told him to go away. Even when I didn't answer his directed questions. Even when I did not talk to him for weeks on end. I never doubted it because it is something so real inside me. As sharp as this pain is now. The pain, the hurting – where does that come from if I didn't feel anything for him? Will he even suspect that I am suffering now?

Maybe I should say that this is the best thing that happened. He had to move on. He had newer worlds to explore, newer relationships to discover. He has to go ahead and make a career in physics. He needs to be encouraged on that path with the assurance that someone is there to be with him and tell him that she loves him – without any doubts, any confusions. Maybe that is what I should be saying and set him free – of all the traps that I am supposed to have set up for him.

But what about my pain? Why do I hurt?

Who has caused this hurt, she asks me. You, Prahlad or me, she asks. Asks it as though there is an unambiguous answer to it. I willed their relationship into existence, she says. God! The stupidity of this all. Is that how literally they understood what I used to say – as though they were given a script which they felt obliged to enact. Did they not see my questions as just expressions of my fears – my deepest fears? Who else can I talk to about these fears? And who else can become the targets of my fears? They are the ones closest to me – or are they? At least, they were. Ana – doing this? I can't believe it. Ana understood me like no one else did. She didn't even have to understand because understanding is possible only when there is a little distance. We had merged into one identity and it was a different kind of understanding we had of each other – one which was characterised by an immediacy. To think that such a person should now so grossly misunderstand everything that I am, everything that I have always been. Is this how much she understood me?

******

Three years is a long enough time for any pain to lessen but Laila's pain had not eased. There was not much Laila looked forward to these days other than her teaching, her special bond with some students and her reading and music. At other times she would sit alone and write pages of poetry in her secret notebooks. She had become close to a couple of colleagues in college, especially to Fatima. Fatima was the one who had suggested that Laila devote some of her time to teach children from the slums in Bandra. It took some effort to convince Laila and when Laila finally agreed to teach it was not because she was convinced about the value of this kind of 'social work' but was keen to find out what it would mean to her as an experience. Fatima was too polite to tell Laila that she was shocked by her shameless demonstration of selfishness but she did make a note of it in her own mind. It was only when Laila started teaching that Fatima realised how capable she was of developing very special relationships with the children. It was a different brand of altruism which Fatima was seeing for the very first time. In turn, being with the children helped Laila cope with her own pain and come to terms with it.

It was a Saturday afternoon and Laila had been invited to a literary festival at the Max Mueller as a resource person. The meeting went on for longer than Laila had anticipated, and when she walked out, it was well past five. Laila paused to look around Rampart Row, nostalgic about the days she had spent there in the company of Ananya and Prahlad. She turned towards Omega Typesetters remembering the days when she would go to meet Prahlad there. She almost jumped out of her skin when she felt a hand on her shoulder. She found Ashok Bhende standing behind her. He looked exactly like he had done several years ago.

'Laila! I thought it was you but wasn't sure initially.'

'Hi, Ashok! So nice to see you after all these years,' said Laila, embracing him lightly.

'So how're you? And where have you been all this time?'

'Teaching literature in Jai Hind. I don't come to this part of town much these days.'

'You should come here more often. We cannot desert Kala Ghoda when she has nurtured and taken care of us. I am here every day so you should come and meet me here.'

'I will.'

'I am going down to Wayside Inn now. Why don't you join me?'

Laila hesitated then agreed.

'So you are teaching literature, are you?' said Ashok as they settled down in Wayside Inn. 'Tell me more about what texts you are dealing with.'

Laila told him about what she was teaching and what she was reading.

'And your friends – Ananya and Prahlad? Where are they?

'Ananya is in Calcutta. I am not quite sure where Prahlad is. Haven't been in touch with them.'

Ashok gave her a piercing look. He realised that Laila did not want to talk about her friends.

'And have you been writing? I remember you wrote a lot of poetry.'

'I am surprised that you remember – and flattered, in fact.'

'Well, I often saw you sit in a corner and write and I was told it was poetry that engaged you. Though I don't remember reading anything you had written.'

'Well, I didn't show my poems to anyone. Ananya read them and Prahlad read some. But no one else.'

'Why? You didn't think you should publish them?'

'No. I never felt like it. I think it is too private somehow.'

'You know, a poem yearns to be read. The more it is read the more it acquires life. Confined to the pages of a book that no one will set eyes on, a poem simply dies. You should not let that happen to your creation.'

'I don't know. Never felt up to publishing my work.'

'I guess you are like Dorai in that respect. He hated publishing. But even Dorai was happy to read his work out to friends. You should, at least, come and read it to a group of poets.'

'I will think about it. Funnily, Dorai often encouraged me to publish my work. I showed him a few poems and he thought they had potential.'

'Imagine Dorai asking someone to publish. But Dorai had a great sense of what is good literature and good poetry. He could literally sniff out good work. He was such a good writer himself. It is a pity he didn't write much.'

'He felt he lacked the discipline.'

'Though I must say he did show it in the end. When he wrote that novel in a fairly short time. Though it was more a novella than a full-fledged novel.'

'Which novel?' asked Laila, surprised to hear what Ashok was saying.

'The one he wrote before he died. I thought he gave you a copy too. It was called Palimpsest, I remember.'

'He gave you a copy of it?'

'Yes, he did. He left a copy of the manuscript with that waiter who is standing there asking him to give it to me. It is a pity he didn't complete it. There was a last chapter which he couldn't write because he died before that.'

'Did he tell you that?' asked Laila, astonished.

'Yes, he had attached a letter to the manuscript where he told me that he had planned ten chapters. Though it is really bizarre to think that he knew that he was going to die. He was in good health so I don't know how he knew. I guess when death is near you get a sense of it.'

'I am so overcome with all this you are telling me. Frankly, I don't even know what to say.'

'So he didn't attach any explanatory letter to your manuscript, I gather.'

'No, he didn't. He had left a copy of the manuscript for me.'

'In a big, brown envelope.'

'That's right. But no letter. I went to his house half an hour after he died and Pandyan gave me the envelope. You know, Pandyan . . . he worked in Dorai's house.'

'Yes, I remember him vaguely.'

'But the worst thing I ever did was to lose that manuscript.'

'You did?'

'Yes, on the very day I got it. I was returning home and was completely distraught because of Dorai's death and . . .'

'So you didn't read it?'

'No. Do you still have your copy?'

'I guess I will have it stashed away safely somewhere in my shelves. I have kept every little bit of text that has come my way. So with some effort I should be able to find it.'

Laila couldn't believe her luck. She was thrilled that she was actually going to get to read Dorai's novel, after all these years. Ashok asked her over to his flat on Tuesday when he said he would have enough time to search for Dorai's manuscript.

Laila could not wait for Tuesday to arrive. She was distracted through her lectures on Tuesday morning and the students could see that she was somehow not her usual self. At two, she left Jai Hind to go to Ashok's. Ashok lived at the end of Wodehouse Road in Colaba.

'Wodehouse Road has been my address for the last thirty-eight years,' he explained when she reached his flat. 'I came here as a 23-year-old after I got my first job in advertising. I lived as a paying guest in those days and loved telling everyone that I was P.G., Wodehouse Road.'

Laila smiled thinking Ashok always laughed loudest at this own jokes.

He led her into his living room which was his study and his bedroom. He had removed the wall that had once divided the space into a living and a sleeping space, he explained. He could now have one large room where he could sleep, read, write and relax in. Most of the space in this small flat was taken up by books and it produced an overawing effect.

'I am in love with books, Laila. I am a masochist of sorts, you know.'

'Masochist? '

'Yes, this is self-inflicted torture. You know the Chinese who invented printing also invented several ingenious methods of torture. They made the mistake of thinking of printing and book-production as just another form of torture. The Europeans should be truly given the credit for the invention of the printed book because they were the ones to realise its true potential – as a weapon of torture it has no equal. The Europeans could conquer the world with this weapon.'

'There you go, Ashok, with your own creative interventions in history,' said Laila, laughing.

Ashok had got two mugs of coffee ready by then.

'Ok, now to get to work. I will have to look for Dorai's novel. God's Words!'

Laila picked up a book to read while Ashok searched. 'Yes, here it is!' he exclaimed, after a twenty-minute search. 'Finally.'

Laila couldn't contain her excitement. 'I will have to borrow it, Ashok. I need to give it a careful read.'

'Yes, do that. As long as you promise not to lose it in a rickshaw again.'

'No, I won't.'

'That doesn't mean you can lose it in a cab, either.'

'Ashok!'

The moment Laila was in a cab to Churchgate she pulled out the somewhat worn-out pages of the manuscript and started reading it.

'God, Dorai knew what was going to happen. I have to see where he ends.' she told herself and went directly to the last page. She couldn't quite believe what she was reading. It read:

'Masochist? '

'Yes, this is self-inflicted torture. You know the Chinese who invented printing also invented several ingenious methods of torture. They made the mistake of thinking of printing and book-production as just another form of torture. The Europeans should be truly given the credit for the invention of the printed book because they were the ones to realise its true potential – as a weapon of torture it has no equal. The Europeans could conquer the world with this weapon.'

'There you go, Ashok, with your own creative interventions in history,' said Laila, laughing.

Ashok had got two mugs of coffee ready by now.

'Ok, now to get to work. I will have to look for Dorai's novel. God's Words! '

Laila picked up a book to read while Ashok searched.

'Yes, here it is!' he exclaimed, after a twenty-minute search. 'Finally.'

Laila couldn't contain her excitement. 'I will have to borrow it, Ashok. I need to give it a careful read.'

'Yes, do that. As long as you promise not to lose it in a rickshaw again.'

'No, I won't.'

'That doesn't mean you can lose it in a cab, either.'

'Ashok!'

Laila didn't stay much longer at Ashok's place. The moment she was in a cab to Churchgate she pulled out the somewhat worn-out pages of the manuscript and started looking through it.

'God, Dorai knew what was going to happen. I have to see where he ends.' she told herself and went directly to the last page. She couldn't quite believe what she was reading.

10
Well-being

Dear Laila,
Three years. That's how long it has been. That's how long I have been struggling with myself. Actually, it has not been a very equal struggle because, over these three years, the mean one in me always managed to win hands down.

It took me no time whatsoever to write to you when Prahlad and I got together. I enjoyed every moment of it. I felt you had hurt Prahlad all along and that you have also hurt me often. I needed to get even with you. And what better way than to let you know that Prahlad and I had found love together. Found love so easily. Not wasting time like you with all those existential confusions.

When we got to first know Prahlad I did not see him independent of you. When he fell for you and you kept him just hanging I felt pity for him. But it was only pity. I never related to him as a friend. I wish I had done that – it may have helped him, helped the situation. But how could I have become a friend of his? I am sure you would not have let that happen. You had already put both me and Prahlad on our guard – going on and on about the possibility of him falling in love with me. It was embarrassing at first but then it started getting on my nerves. And the more you did it, the more I grew to resent it. I felt sickened by it all.

It was good to go away to Calcutta. To get away from two people – Ma and you. For me the two of you mattered more than anything else but slowly I started feeling the need for my own space where I felt I was not being questioned, watched and told off by either of you. Calcutta was the only place Ma would have allowed me to go to, so that is how I came here. Not because Calcutta meant anything else to me that Bombay didn't. When I came here I found myself groping initially. It was not easy to come from outside and become part of the scene here – it is not even so for a Bengali. But I took my time and found my bearings. First a few friends and then Sumit came into my life. In retrospect, I wonder how that happened. Sumit was so unlike me. His intellect was something to be admired but when I think of him now I think he was a rather uncouth and ill-mannered person. He was also so full of himself that I don't think he had place for anyone else. When I fell in love with him, I remember thinking that he was so unlike Prahlad. I still think so.

Prahlad was different. The Prahlad I got to know in Calcutta over the two months that he was here. The Prahlad who wrote letters to me after he went back to Bombay. The Prahlad who made frequent trips to Calcutta so that we could spend time together. Those eight months seemed wonderful. But that is just about how long it lasted.

I had to set Prahlad free. It was on one of his trips to Calcutta. Prahlad was already seeming distant and distracted, somehow. But it all happened one evening when I had him over for dinner with a couple of other friends. He had a bit too much too drink that evening. The alcohol was doing him good till the point where he was being the good company that he always was. Then, at some point, he withdrew. He pulled out my pile of cassettes trying to figure out what music to listen to. He put on some music, I don't remember what and then he didn't seem to like it. He went back to the cassettes hunting for something in the pile that he would like. He seemed to have found something. I was too busy talking to one of my friends to notice. When he put it on, I was quite taken aback. He had found one of the cassettes with our long dialogues on it. I went up to him and asked him to put it off. But it was your voice on the cassette and he kept insisting that he wanted to listen to you talk. He started making a huge scene and I didn't quite know what to do. It was getting to be really embarrassing. He must have heard you speak for some twenty minutes and at a volume which, in spite of my best efforts to save the evening and distract my friends with some conversation, took over the space completely. After which he started talking about you to my friend telling her what you were like and how he was in love with you and that he never wanted to fall in love with me but somehow had walked into my trap.

When he started crying calling out to you, the guests decided to leave and the evening ended abruptly. I put him in a cab back to his guest house. He came back the next morning with a profuse apology and blamed the evening on the alcohol. He said he loved me and had forgotten you. I looked into his eyes and I could see that he was not speaking the truth. I could see that even he was not convinced. When he went back to Bombay soon after, I wrote him a long letter saying that it was all over between us. He did write back trying to effect a patch-up but I stood my ground.

It hurt me a lot to lose Prahlad like that – but I didn't lose him because I never had him. He was always yours. But I hated to admit that to myself. That hurt more than anything else – even more than having to lose Prahlad. I did not want you to know that Prahlad and I were not together. That would have meant admitting defeat to you. I did not want that. So I thought I won't let you know about it.

Over these three years, there were times when I felt I was wronging you by not letting you know this. But like I said, I am quite a mean person. It amazes me to think that it had to weigh on my conscience for so long before I could admit this to you.

Take care, friend. This may well be the last cassette you are going to receive from me.

*****

Dear Ana,
I thought I won't reply to your message. But felt compelled to, after some thought.

I was very hurt when you sent me the letter telling me about you and Prahlad getting together. I was hurt by what Prahlad had done to me and what you had done to me. But it also hurt that I was so badly misunderstood by you. At the end of it all, someone can turn around and say that I never reciprocated Prahlad's feelings for me so I had no reason to be hurt when he fell in love with you. For the same reason, I could not feel hurt by what you had done. But your misunderstanding of me cannot be defended by any of these arguments. Ana, I thought you understood.

Even in this message of yours I find some bit of that deliberate need to not receive me with any understanding. You talk of my existential confusions as though I were a stranger. Is that how you see me now, Ana? Why is it so important to me that you understand what I am doing? Even now I am trying to reach out to you with my silly monologues.

The fact that you took time to tell me that Prahlad and you have moved apart does not come as a surprise to me. I can't have imagined that you would tell me about it the very next day. And, in any case, it is immaterial to me now. It does not change anything for me. You surely don't think that I am going to make the attempt to get Prahlad back in my life now. You know too well that it doesn't work like that, don't you?

But there is something else that I have to tell you. I could think of sharing this with no one else. I don't know whether even you will believe what I have to say. Dorai had written a novel about you, me and Prahlad. He knew he was going to die and he was hoping to complete, before his death, the ten chapters that he had planned. The day before he died he left a copy of the manuscript with only nine chapters for Ashok Bhende. He died the next day but it appears that he tried to complete the book before that. He tried – we will never know whether he did complete it. He left me a copy of the book too but I was so upset by his death that I lost it on my way home. It was only a few weeks ago that I met Ashok and discovered, by chance, that he had a copy of this novel. I read the nine chapters that Dorai had written – and it was all there, Ana. All that we have gone through. It was all there except for the end.

I still can't understand what it means. How did he write our lives? Were we just playing out some parts that he had written? And why will we never know how it will end? To leave it to us to end it the way we want? Did Dorai want us to accept the responsibility for the finale? Or has that chapter also been written and we will only, out of ignorance, delude ourselves that we are acting of our own free will? Will we ever know?

*****

It was around two in the afternoon when Laila reached Bandra. She was somewhat tired because her Wednesday morning schedule in college was packed with three lectures back to back. She had stepped out of the lecture hall into the staff room with just enough time for a cold samosa and tea before she took the train to Bandra.

The small room in Bandra that she taught in was equipped to be anything but a classroom. These rooms had been rented by a group of women activists who called themselves ACT and other than running the informal classrooms for young children they were also providing the space and the means to women from the nearby slums to work as tailors. The shop, which was a ten-minute walk from the school, was very small and so the school also served as a storehouse for them. When the mothers would come, at the end of the day's work, to pick up their children they would bring in piles of dress material to leave in the classroom. Consequently, the classroom had two old sewing machines on one side and piles of cloth all around. For lack of space, the rest of the stuff was hung on nails driven into walls: everything from scissors, water bottles, tiffin boxes, dupattas that the women wore when they were outside but were just too happy to remove as soon as they stepped into the room, adorned the walls of the room. A small white fan, which had browned with age, hung from the ceiling and provided some relief to the children as they cramped themselves into this room for their classes. The fourteen children would squeeze themselves squat on the floor with their notebooks balanced on their laps. Laila would sit on one of the cloth piles and write on a small blackboard that rested on a stand against the wall. The only window in the room faced an uncovered gutter. The heat and the stench were the first things that Laila reacted to.

'I can't do this,' she told Fatima, after her first session. 'It's so suffocating. I feel like I am locked in a coffin.'

'Please, Laila. Give it some time. Just think of the children.

They need you.'

Laila had failed to connect with any of them. She felt her teaching made no difference to them whatsoever.

'I think they guessed you were uncomfortable. That is why they didn't connect with you. Just relax and give them also some time to relax with you,' Fatima persisted. 'What we are doing in ACT is very important, Laila. Some of the mothers who come to work here have no place to leave their children. Neither can they send them to a regular school. These kids will just hang around doing nothing if we don't use the time to teach them. Just focus on all that for the moment. These smaller issues won't seem so daunting.'

That was over two years ago. And, in the meantime, Laila got more comfortable with the surroundings – so comfortable that it did not seem to matter any more. She looked forward to the time that she got to spend with the children and they had grown to become very fond of her too. It was not that she overcame her pain in their company; being with them just allowed her one more way of coping with the pain. At times, she would look into the eyes of a young student and wonder, 'Is this what is giving me the strength to continue?'

'You don't need anything from the outside to continue,' she could remember Dorai saying. 'If you want to continue with your existence that is because that is the very nature of existence. Anything that destroys it comes from the outside. It is what Spinoza talked of as the conatus – the will to survive.'

'There is also a will to die,' argued Laila.

'I don't think you follow what I am saying.'

'Well, it is simple enough to follow. I don't accept it – just because you are saying it. Or Spinoza, for that matter. It is just contrary to what I feel.'

'You should learn to distinguish your limited experience and your local conditions from general principles of existence.'

'I don't believe that there are any general principles of existence which don't stem out of my experience, however limited or local they may be.'

As she recollected the conversation in every detail, Laila remembered the helplessness with which Dorai then responded to her.

'Conatus?' she wondered aloud. 'Is that what this is? Or is it just an indifference – thanks to which you simply get dragged along from one day to another? Yet, I can't deny that there is something in Shabnam's eyes or Mushtaq's smile that makes me want to look forward to a tomorrow.'

Now, as Shabnam, Mushtaq and the other children sat around her, Laila talked to them about Bombay's water supply, the lakes and the reservoirs. Suddenly someone started banging on the door of the room and Laila could hear people shouting.

It was Razia at the door. She looked pale with fear.

'Where's Imran?' she said, her voice betraying her panic.

'What's happened, Razia?' Laila said, holding her arm.

'I have to take my son from here. Before they come.'

'Who?'

Razia did not reply. Laila looked out and the street was in a state of chaos and agitation. She stepped out and looked into Amjad Chacha's shop which was next door.

'Chacha, what's going on?'

'Beti, you are still here. I thought you must have left.'

'Why? What's happening?'

'The city is burning, Beti. People are being killed. You should go home as soon as you can. It is not safe here.'

'I heard there was some tension in the city – but that was in Dongri.'

'No, it seems to be all over the city. That is what people were saying. Some people are already packing their bags to run away to their villages. You should go now . . .'

'I will have to wait till the mothers come to take these children. They are all still here. Only Razia has come to take Imran away.'

'I will try to see if I can find someone who will take these kids home. But you should leave. I am telling you it is not safe.'

Amjad Chacha went into the room and came out with Laila's handbag. 'Here. Take this and go now. Please.'

There was something in Amjad Chacha's manner when he spoke now that made Laila feel that she should do exactly as he was saying.

The lane Laila walked down was still busy with people who seemed to be running around mindlessly. It was a good ten-minute walk which took her down to the main road leading to the railway station. Laila walked as fast she could hoping to find a rickshaw at the head of the main road. But as she walked ahead towards the main road she noticed that the lane was suddenly emptying. That is when it dawned on Laila that this was not an ordinary situation. She realised that she had not noticed how all the doors of the small houses and shops were shut now.

She looked around and noticed a small lane between two houses. No, it was so narrow it could not be called a lane – it was more like a wedge. In the wedge, Laila could see a small window of a shop was open. Laila dashed in almost at the same time as the shop-keeper was trying to pull the window shut.

'Bhaisaab, please I need to use your phone.'

The shopkeeper looked uncertain. But it was a woman asking for help. Laila got through to her home more easily than she imagined.

'Mamma, I am on my way home.'

Tahira sounded very worried. 'Where are you, Laila? I can send Mohan to come to pick you up.'

Laila was sure that it would not be very easy for Mohan, their driver, to find her. If only she found a way to get to the main road, she would be able to get to Bandra station.

'Can you send Mohan to Andheri station? Asking him to park in the Nadco shopping complex. He will be safe there and I can find him easily.'

Laila got back to the lane she had been walking on and started walking towards the main road. The silence was eerie. She remembered her Bua's stories about the partition days. She remembered her talking about how she had walked through a deserted street holding her father's hand. *'Bhauji was trying to work his way back to the main chowk to look for Maaji and my brothers. We walked through lanes so silent that we could hear our hearts beating.'*

As she walked, she felt she heard a window open behind her. She turned and found a first-floor window just slightly open and got a glimpse of someone behind the frame. Laila's heart started beating faster and she felt her palms wet. She walked faster towards the main road.

'I am almost there,' she kept trying to tell herself.

Laila was almost running as she reached close to the end of the lane. She stopped in her tracks when she saw that there was a police van parked there blocking access to the main road. As she walked closer she saw a Sikh police officer standing outside the van.

'But there were road-blocks everywhere and the police had clamped a curfew on the area by then. We were stopped by a police van. It was a Sikh police officer – I still remember his face so clearly. Bhauji pleaded with him to be allowed to go to the main chowk so that he could look for his wife and for his sons. But the officer refused to let him go because he feared that he would not come out alive.'

When Laila got closer to the van, it was another policeman who came ahead and asked her to stop.

'I have to get to the station,' said Laila, desperately.

'But, madam, there is no way to reach Bandra station. The main road is blocked. Rioters have burnt down houses and rickshaws,' said the policeman in a not unfriendly tone.

'But I have to reach home,' said Laila.

The Sikh, obviously a senior officer, walked up to ask her what was happening. Laila was almost in tears by now.

'Please I have to get to Andheri. My driver will be waiting for me there.'

The Sikh officer turned to one of his havaldars.

'She has to go to Andheri by train. Take her in the jeep along the highway and drop her at Santa Cruz station.'

Turning to Laila, he said, 'Madam, try to get home as soon as you can. It is not safe to be on the roads alone.'

When they drove down the highway, Laila could see huge black clouds of smoke to her left. She shut her eyes.

The train journey was quick and uneventful. She got off at Andheri and walked into Nadco complex and was relieved to find her car there. Mohan was waiting outside the car and his face was creased with anxiety.

'How are things? Will we be able to get home? ' asked Laila.

'We cannot go through Andheri market nor through Juhu galli. There is a lot of trouble in both these places. People are being dragged out of shops and homes. Our best bet is to go via Irla.'

'Ok. Let's go soon.'

The situation on S.V. Road seemed normal though it was deserted. When they reached the junction to turn into Irla, they were stopped by a group of men brandishing hockey sticks and clubs. One of them, with a red tikka smeared on his forehead, held a menacing sword in his hand.

'Where are you going,' asked one of them, peeping into the car to look at Laila.

Before Mohan could say anything, Laila replied, 'Juhu.'

The man ignored her and asked Mohan his name.

'Moh . . ,' he stammered.

'What? Is it Mohsin or something like that?'

'No, no . . . Mohan.'

'Mohan . . . I hope you are not lying. We can find out, you know,' said another of them.

'No, look here is my licence,' said Mohan, panicking and pulling out his driving licence.

'He is showing us his licence,' said one of them, laughing unpleasantly.

Laila saw the man who had addressed Mohan first staring at the small idol of Ganesha on the front panel of the car.

'Ok, go now,' he said to Mohan who raced down Irla and didn't stop till he reached home.

**

It was around four in the morning on 21st January, exactly two weeks after the riots had started. It was the only time Bombay had every day to sit back and look at herself – those fifteen precious minutes. But this morning, she did not have the courage to look at herself. She had never looked so ugly.

**

A few days later, Laila decided to go to Bandra. Fatima had called and asked her to come. She refused to say much on the phone. She just said that Salim was asking for her.

Laila took a rickshaw from the station and as it entered the lane she saw that it had changed beyond recognition. It was lined with burnt houses, broken huts and damaged doors and windows. When she reached her school she was shocked to see that Amjad chacha's shop had been razed to the ground. The school seemed to have miraculously escaped the wrath of the arsonists. The door was broken but the structure seemed safe.

Fatima and the other volunteers of ACT were sitting inside the classroom. Salim was lying with his head on the lap of one of the women there. When he saw Laila, he came running and hugged her tightly. Laila held him close and sat down to listen to the horrific experiences of the people in that neighbourhood. Salim's mother, Sadiya, who also worked in the tailor'sshop had not been able to come early to pick up Salim that day. The other children had left in the meantime. When one of the mothers offered to take Salim with her, he refused to go. Sadiya's fourteen year-old daughter, Zeenat, worked in an embroidery shop and Sadiya's first instinct was to make sure that Zeenat was safe.

She picked up Zeenat from her place of work and left her at her brother's home. Once she had made sure that Zeenat was safe, she rushed to fetch Salim. Salim would be safe with Amjad chacha till she reached him.

At this point in the story, one of the women took Salim out for a walk not wanting him to hear the rest of the story.

Salim was with Amjad chacha in his shop. Chacha had closed his shop but left the door a little ajar so he could see Sadiya coming. He was anxious that she was late and went to take a look outside. A mob of about twenty men were approaching from a distance. He rushed back into the shop and asked Salim to go back and hide in his classroom. He felt that the school would be less of a target for the rioters. Salim went into the classroom and looked around, wondering where to hide. The cloth piles, of course. That is where they hid when they played hide-and-seek. Salim lay down on one pile of cloth and pulled on another pile on top so that only his eyes could be seen. He had a view of the street.

Nothing happened for a while and Salim wondered whether he should move out of his hiding place. Then he heard a lot of screaming. He could hear a voice over the others which he recognised as Amjad chacha's. He could see some of the men come out of chacha's shop onto the street. He could see them hitting someone and kicking him but from where he was he did not get a full view and did not know who was being beaten. Salim simply pulled himself further into the sheets of cloth and blocked out the view of the street.

Amjad chacha was in hospital with a broken leg and a few broken ribs. But he had escaped with his life, Laila was told.

'What happened to Sadiya?' asked Laila.

Sadiya arrived just in time to see the men thrashing Amjad chacha. She tried to jump to the rescue while he kept telling her to go away and save herself. The men dumped him, caught Sadiya by her arms and legs and carried her away.

There was a young woman, in her twenties probably, with a small child of three in their compartment. Four or five men suddenly appeared and tried to drag the mother away.

Sadiya was not found till later, in a ditch. She had been raped and murdered.

Salim was discovered, still hiding between the sheets in the classroom.

'I want to spend some time with Salim. Can I take him out for a while? ' Laila asked Salim's aunt, who agreed.

'Where would you like to go, Salim? ' she asked.

'No. I don't want to go anywhere,',Salim replied.

His aunt managed to persuade him to go.

'Will you come and teach us, like you did before?' Salim asked, as they headed towards Juhu beach.

'Yes, I will. Of course.'

'If you don't come, I will feel bad.'

'No, I promise I will keep coming.'

'I feel bad when I think of Ami. My Ami died.'

Laila held him close to her and could feel his tears.

When they sat on the beach, with the late afternoon sun casting its light on his face, Laila saw a glimmer of hope in his eyes. He beamed from ear to ear, like any child would, when she bought him a *gola*. He watched, with fascination, the *gola* being made and pleaded with the *golawala* to add more of the green syrup. As he put his lips to the ice-ball and sucked the syrup, Laila could see life re-asserting itself.

*****

Prahlad had been invited by the experimentalists from University College, London for a morning's discussion over coffee and muffins. In the year and a half that he had been in London as a post-doc in Birkbeck College, Prahlad had visited UCL several times. But each time he went past the wooden cabinet in the main building of the college which housed Jeremy Bentham's body he could not help experiencing an eerie sensation. It amazed him to think that as rational a man like Bentham would have sought to make himself available for posterity in this manner.

Prahlad's professor, John Ross, was also present at the meeting.

'I need to have a chat with you, Prahlad. Soon after this meeting,' he said.

The meeting went on till almost lunchtime so Prahlad had to hurry to John's office to find out why he wanted to meet him.

'Yes, Prahlad. My friend in Bombay, Amit Bhattacharya, has sent me this letter. He is organising a conference in Goa in three weeks' time and they have some room to accommodate young researchers. I thought you could give a talk on our work on R-parity violation. And, I am sure, you will want to go home too.'

'Well, the travel is expensive.'

'No, I am sure we have money left in our project to take care of that. I will ask Debbie to check that out this afternoon.'

'No, John. To be frank, I am not too keen on going to India. There is a conference in Trieste at around the same time and I rather fancy going to Trieste.'

'Are you sure? All right then. I will write to Amit saying you can't make it.'

Prahlad decided to go down to the SOAS cafetaria for lunch. There was a chance he would meet one of his Indian friends there. But today none of his friends seemed to be around so he settled down to his vegetarian curry rice all on his own. Of course, he missed home. He missed the life in Bombay, he missed his friends. London was good but he didn't have too many friends here, at least not like the ones he had in Bombay. But then Bombay had changed too. It wasn't anymore like what it had been for him ten years ago. If he did go back whom would he meet? He would get to meet Prabha but even she had settled down in Surat. But there was no one else. He no longer had friends in the

University: most of them had moved on and not stayed in touch. He didn't care too much for some of them either. But, most importantly, both Laila and Ananya had moved out of his life. And Bombay would never be the same without them.

It was about an hour after lunch, when he was in the middle of some long calculation that Debbie walked into his office with a letter.

'You have a letter from home,' she said.

His heart missed a beat when he saw the writing on the envelope. It was Laila's handwriting. He opened it eagerly and read:

Hi Prahlad,

It was strange when I decided to write to you, because I didn't know where you were. It was from the Physics Department at the University that I got your address. I was surprised, and impressed, to know that you were in London. It is great to know you are doing well in your work.

I really don't know what to write to you except to say that when you left me you said you would wait to hear from me. You wanted me to ask you to come back. So here I am. Asking you to come back. Waiting where you had left me.

Love,
Laila.

Prahlad stared at the letter and read it again. He almost couldn't believe what he was reading.

A little later he went into John's office.

'John, this conference in Goa. I think I want to go.'

'Great! I am happy you changed your mind. I will send Amit an e-mail right away.'

'And, I want to leave by the end of this week. I plan a two-week holiday in Bombay before I go to Goa.'

A week later, Laila and Prahlad were sitting on Juhu beach watching, as they always did, the setting sun. They had been talking for more than two hours and now there was a brief lull in the conversation.

Laila broke the silence.'Prahlad, do you love me?'

'Yes, I do.'

'As much as you always did?'

'Yes.'

'And if I say I want to be with you?'

'That is what I want.'

Laila held Prahlad's hand. 'I don't love you, Prahlad. But I care deeply for you. Do you want to be with me, even then?'

'Yes. I do.'